Alexandra Sokoloff is a California native and a graduate of U.C. Berkeley, where she majored in theatre and minored in everything that Berkeley has a reputation for. After college she moved to Los Angeles, where she has made an interesting living doing novel adaptations and selling original suspense and horror scripts to various Hollywood studios, with one film made so far: an adaptation of novelist Sabine Deitmer's thriller, *Cold Kisses*.

Alex is a former Director of the Writers Guild of America, West; she's also the founder of WriterAction.com, a large and unruly cyber-community of professional screenwriters. Next to writing she loves dance more than breathing: jazz, ballet, salsa, Lindy, swing – she does it all, every chance she gets.

The Harrowing is Alex's first novel and the story is based on incidents from her high school and college years and grew out of her fascination with the correlation between mental/emotional illness and paranormal events. *The Harrowing* was nominated for Bram Stoker and Anthony awards for Best First Novel.

Visit her website at www.alexandrasokoloff.com

THE HARROWING

ALEXANDRA SOKOLOFF

piatkus

PIATKUS

First published in the US in 2006 by St. Martin's Press, New York
First published in Great Britain as a paperback original in 2009 by Piatkus
Reprinted 2009

The epitaph on page 90 is from John Donne's 'Holy Sonnet VII', from *The Complete Poetry and Selected Prose of John Donne*. New York: The Modern Library, 2001. Page 219 contains a line from *The Hollow Men*, by T. S. Eliot, from *T. S. Eliot, Selected Poems*. San Diego, Calif.: Harcourt Brace Jovanovich, Publishers, 1936.

A CIP catalogue record for this book
is available from the British Library

ISBN 978-0-7499-4158-1

Typeset in Baskerville by Action Publishing Technology Ltd, Gloucester
Printed and bound in Great Britain by CPI Mackays, Chatham, ME5 8TD

Papers used by Piatkus are natural, renewable and recyclable products sourced from well-managed forests and certified in accordance with the rules of the Forest Stewardship Council.

Mixed Sources
Product group from well-managed forests and other controlled sources
www.fsc.org   Cert no. SGS-COC-004081
© 1996 Forest Stewardship Council

FSC

Piatkus
An imprint of
Little, Brown Book Group
100 Victoria Embankment
London EC4Y 0DY

An Hachette UK Company
www.hachette.co.uk

www.piatkus.co.uk

For Dad, who told me ghost stories

ACKNOWLEDGMENTS

This book would not have been possible without the creative contributions and encyclopedic knowledge of Kimball Greenough.

Eternal love and gratitude are also due:

My family, Alexander, Barbara, Elaine, and Michael, for their constant support and inspiration.

Michael S. Bradshaw, my partner in crime, for everything, daily.

My awesome editor, Ben Sevier at St. Martin's, for making this happen and for general magnificence, and Jenness Crawford, for all her help.

Frank Wuliger, Scott Miller, Brian Lutz, and Sarah Self, for their expert representation, and Frank, again, for his limitless patience and support.

Brad Anderson, Channing Dungey, and Jorge Saralegui, for their creative input and good company.

The Westside Writers Group, under the direction of the most excellent Sid Stebel, for getting me here.

The whole WriterAction.com community, for being there, 24/7.

Katherine Fugate, for reading, love, and support.

The Book Club, Diana, Karl, Rebecca, Tom, Elaine, Dana, Obb, and Frantz, for making it be about books.

The Coven, for the magic.

And all my Berkeley posse – you know who you are – just because.

Chapter 1

It had been raining since possibly the beginning of time.

In the top tier of the cavernous psychology hall, Robin Stone had long since given up on the lecture. She sat hunched in her seat, staring out arched windows at the downpour, feeling dreamily disconnected from the elemental violence outside, despite the fact that every few minutes the wind shook the building hard enough to rattle the glass of the windowpanes.

In milder weather, Baird College was the very definition of pastoral. Wooded paths meandered between ivy-swathed stone buildings. Grassy hills rolled into the distance, dotted by trees ... all unmarred by the slightest sight of civilization.

But now the old oaks lashed in the wind under roiling dark clouds that spilled icy rain on the deserted quad. In the bleak light of the storm, the isolation seemed ominous, the campus hunkered down under the pelting rain like a medieval town waiting for the siege.

The cold of the day had sunk into Robin's bones. The wind outside was a droning in her ears, like the hollow rush of the sea. Inside, Professor Lister's soft German

1

accent was soporific, strangely hypnotic, as he quoted Freud from the wood-planked dais far below.

"'The state of sleep involves a turning away from the real, external world, and there we have the necessary condition for the development of a psychosis. The harmless dream psychosis is the result of that withdrawal from the external world which is consciously willed and only temporary ...'"

Robin's moody reflection stared back at her from the window: dark-eyed, somewhat untidy, elfin features framed by a tumble of nearly black hair. All in all, a chance of prettiness if she weren't so withdrawn, guarded.

She pulled herself away from the glassy ghost of herself, blinked around her at a sea of students moored behind tiers of wooden desks.

People were shifting restlessly, looking up at the clock above the blackboard. A little before three, Wednesday. Tomorrow was Thanksgiving, and everyone was impatient, eager to escape for the holiday. Everyone except Robin. The four-day weekend loomed before her like an abyss.

Thanksgiving, right. Thanks for what?

At least there would be no roommate.

She sat with the thought of no Waverly for four days, and felt a spark of something – not pleasure, nothing so life-affirming as that, but a slight relief, a loosening of the concrete band that lately seemed to permanently encircle her chest.

No mindless, venal chatter. No judging cornflower blue eyes.

And no one else, either, Robin reminded herself. *No one at all.*

The anxiety settled in again, a chill of unnamed worry.

Four days in creepy old Mendenhall ... completely alone ...

The professor's soft voice whispered in the back of her head. "'In psychosis, the turning away from reality is brought about either by the unconscious repressed becoming excessively strong, so that it overwhelms the conscious, or because reality has become so intolerably distressing that the threatened ego throws itself into the arms of the unconscious instinctual forces in a desperate revolt ...'"

Robin glanced down at the professor, startled at the confluence of thought. She wrote slowly, "Reality has become so intolerably distressing ..."

She stopped and quickly scribbled over the words, blackening them out.

Somewhere close, another pen scratched furiously across paper. Robin glanced toward the sound.

Across the aisle from her, a slight, intense, bespectacled young man was hunched in his seat, scribbling notes as if his life depended on it. A mini-tape recorder on the desk in front of him recorded the lecture as well, in the unlikely event that he missed something.

Robin had seen him a few times around the dorm: pale skin and hollow circles under his eyes behind his glasses, shoulders hunched under the weight of an over-stuffed backpack, always scurrying to or from class, as scattered and distracted as the White Rabbit.

He looked younger than the other students, and older, too. Probably skipped a grade or two and rushed into college early, full throttle, driven by parents or some inner demon of his own. Robin knew something about that.

She studied him, feeling relief in concentrating her attention on something outside herself.

There was a coldness about him, an ancient guarded-ness that she recognized as unhappiness. His face always set and unsmiling, if possible, more tense and miserable than Robin herself. Yet there was something luminous about him, as well – almost holy, something like a monk in his ascetic intensity.

She thought these things with detachment, as if from a great distance, merely observing. It did not occur to her to speak to him, or smile, or communicate in any way. It did not seem to her that they were on the same dimensional plane; she watched him through glass, as she watched the storm.

So she was caught completely off guard when the young man turned and looked her straight in her eyes.

She stared back, startled.

The young man immediately blushed behind his glasses and quickly dropped his gaze to his yellow pad.

Robin sat, flustered. The bells in the clock tower above the main plaza outside struck once, sounding the three-quarter hour. A hollow sound, reverberating over the campus.

On the podium below, the white-haired professor paused, listening to the bell. The chime died, and he turned back to the class.

"But while Freud contended that the forces that drive us come from within us, our own unconscious, his disciple and colleague Jung believed there was a *universal* unconscious around us, populated by ancient forces that exist apart from us, yet interact with and act upon us." He paused, looked around at the class.

"So who was right? Do our demons come from without, or within us?"

He half-smiled, then closed his binder. "And on that cheery note, we'll end early, since I know you're all eager to get away."

The class collectively surged to its feet, reaching for coats and notebooks and backpacks in an orgy of release. The professor raised his voice over the tide. "I'll need all of you to discuss your term paper topics with me next week, so please make appointments by E-mail. Have a good Thanksgiving."

Robin closed her notebook and stood, feeling as if she were rising through water, but only partway.

The surface seemed far above her.

She came through the double wooden doors of the psych building on a moving sea of students. The cold slapped her out of her sleepy daze and she halted on the wide marble steps of the building, blinking out over the quad. Raindrops splashed on her face, ran down into the collar of her shapeless wool coat.

In the distance, the clock tower chimed the hour, three reverberating bongs. A sound of release – and doom.

So now it begins, Robin thought ... and had no idea what she meant.

Students jostled her from behind, pushing her along down the steps. She fumbled in her backpack for her umbrella, forced it up above her head, and joined the streams of students surging through the uneven stone plaza. She looked at no one, spoke to no one. No one looked at her. She could have been a ghost.

In the two months she'd been at Baird, she'd made

5

exactly zero friends. It wasn't that she was a monster. With her fine pale features and thick dark hair, she had a darkling, changeling quality, intriguing, almost elemental.

No, she wasn't hideous; it was just that she was invisible. She'd been in a fog of darkness for so long, it seemed to have dissolved her corporeal being.

She walked on, blankly. Rain wept down the Gothic arches and neoclassic columns of the buildings around her, whispered through the canopies of oak. Someone else, someone normal, would have felt a moody pleasure in the agelessness of it. Any kind of adventure could be waiting over a stone bridge, under an ancient archway ...

By all rights, she should have been wild with joy just to be there. With a – let's face it – lunatic mother who in her best, properly medicated periods was barely able to hold on to temp work, Robin would never have been able to afford a school like Baird. Even with her grades, the AP classes she'd loaded up on, hoping against hope that the extra credits would get her a scholarship and *out* ...

The scholarship hadn't come, but the miracle had. Her father, known to her only as a signature on a monthly child-support check, had come through with a college fund – full tuition at his alma mater. A few strings pulled, a favor called in from a college pal on the board, and Robin was in, free, saved.

It had nothing to do with love, of course. Robin knew the money was guilty penance for abandoning his defective daughter to her defective mother. *Who* wouldn't *have fled long ago ... only I couldn't,* Daddy, *could I?*

He had a new family now – perfect golden wife, two perfect golden children.

A voice in her head rose up, taunting her. *He threw you away. Cast off. Cast out. You're nothing.* Nothing—

She gasped in, for a moment almost choking on her own volcanic anger. Then she pushed it back down into the dark.

When his letter came, her mother had raged and cried for days. Robin ignored the hysterics, coldly cashed the check, and packed her bags. *Take his guilt money and get the hell out, fuck you very much.*

But get out to where? The school was fine – *she* was the one who was all wrong. There was some fatal heaviness about her, a yawning black hole in the center of her that repelled people. They could see her darkness, her bitter, bitter envy of the light.

She'd escaped Mom but was still surrounded by herself.

Nothing *but* herself for the next four days.

And if she started hearing voices, alone in the dark, gloomy Hall?

Well.

There was always the full bottle of Valium in Waverly's bottom drawer.

More than enough to end it.

The thought was cold comfort as she walked through the wind.

Chapter 2

The exodus had already begun. Students with bulging luggage poured out the front door of Mendenhall and down the steps in a steady stream.

Robin came up the rain-drenched walk, blankly side-stepping residents climbing into cars and airport-shuttle vans idling in the circular drive that set Mendenhall apart from the other Victorians lining the west edge of campus.

Mendenhall Residence Hall, known to all as "the Hall" (sometimes "M-Hall," sometimes even "home"), was a converted mansion, a sprawling hodgepodge of turrets, balconies, fire escapes, and gabled roofs, all under a spreading canopy of oaks. Once a fraternity house, until the campus had started admitting women in 1932, it looked like some mad designer had added a wing in every direction from every architectural style and period ever since. Under the dark skies, it was as gloomily Gothic as anything Hawthorne or Poe had ever conjured from the fevered depths of their imaginations.

Robin moved up the steps, past students hoisting duffels and carry-on bags, hugging and shoving good-byes. Their raucous put-downs and farewells seemed to come from a great distance, barely audible. It was so easy for Them, the Normals. Vacation, friends, love ... they bubbled over with life and enthusiasm, fairly scorching her with their light.

She pushed down the black surge of envy and stepped through the triple-arched front door into a murky entry hall lined with rows of locked mailboxes. She hesitated by the boxes. Her hand slid automatically into her coat pocket for keys, even as a voice in her head mocked her.

Why bother? You know it's empty. Spare yourself and go upstairs.

She pulled the keys out of her pocket, quickly jabbed the smallest into the keyhole of her box, and pulled open the door.

Empty.

See? Nothing. Nothing. *You're nothing—*

Robin shoved the mailbox door closed to shut out the voice. She twisted the key, turned away blindly.

The entry opened into a decrepitly grand but effectively useless hall. Benches with high backs like church pews hugged the paneled walls. Across the hardwood floor, veneer long worn away, a sweeping staircase led up to three floors of big old rooms with diamond-cut bay windows and recessed window seats.

On this dark day, the two-story hall felt more cavernous than usual, ominous, even. Robin paused in the doorway, looking up. She'd never noticed how the high windows near the top of the balcony looked like watching eyes.

Just stop it, Robin ordered herself. *You're staying, and the last thing you need to do is to start freaking yourself out about this.*

She crossed the bare floor to the staircase and made her way up, her legs still stiff with cold. The wide steps, of shiny old wood with carpet runners for safety, felt slightly spongy under her feet, beginning to give under the constant tramping traffic of sixty-some residents per year. Robin's nostrils flared with the familiar smell of Mendenhall – an old smell, sickly sweet, a little musty: accumulated layers of dusty carpet and wet wood, vying with laundry detergent, pot, stale beer, sweat, lingering perfume. And sex, of course, always sex.

On the second floor, she turned to the right and walked the length of the landing into an enclosed staircase leading up to the third floor. In the dark, she pulled up short at a sudden movement right above her ...

A guy with straggly hair and Lennon glasses brushed past her on his way out, duffel slung over his shoulder. He mumbled, "Sorry," not looking at her.

Robin started up the last flight of stairs without bothering to respond.

Her own floor was the third on the girls' wing. Not that anyone enforced the segregation; students went back and forth between all the wings at all hours of the night. And everyone but the Housing Office knew the Hall supervisor was living with his girlfriend in a flat three blocks away.

She stepped through the open door to the third floor and was assaulted by prevacation music blasting from various rooms in a mind-boggling cacophony: Eminem, Green Day, the Sex Pistols, *The Marriage of Figaro* from some high-toned rebel.

Robin walked down the carpeted hall, the open doors on both sides of the corridor revealing girls throwing clothes and books into duffels and backpacks, rushing in

and out of one another's rooms with college-age disregard for personal space, shouting cheerful good-byes.

As she passed a doorway, the group inside burst into
laughter. Robin stiffened. Were they laughing at her?
The shapeless Goodwill coat with holes in its pockets,
her worn shoes?

No, no one was looking. They didn't see.

Her steps slowed as she neared her room. The door
was closed, but she could tell Waverly was there from
the twist in her gut.

Should I go somewhere ... wait till she's gone?

She hesitated, deliberating.

Oh well – she'll be out soon enough.

She reached reluctantly for the doorknob and went
in.

Robin's roommate was packing half her closet into a
Luis Vuitton bag on her perfectly made bed, and, thankfully, was too busy dictating her travel plans and
retrieval instructions into a cell phone to do more than
glance huffily at Robin.

Robin crossed to the far corner of her side of the
room, stripped off her wet clothes, found a long sweater
on the floor to pull on over her leggings. She kept her
back to her roommate, who traveled peevishly from her
closet to the suitcase on the bed as if she were alone in
the room.

Waverly Todd was beautiful. Apart from that, she
had no redeeming qualities. Certainly, she must have
been punishment for some terrible transgression in one
of Robin's past lives. A preening, prissy, size-two
Southern belle, she could take up the whole room and
all the oxygen in it no matter what she was doing.

She had followed her football-scholarship boyfriend out of Charleston to the hinterlands. A fish out of water in the cold East, she hated everyone around her with a black passion.

The girl clearly belonged in a sorority and had, in fact, been firmly interred in the Tri-Delt house, most prestigious on campus, until this year. Robin gathered that during rush week there had been some incident with the boyfriend that got Waverly kicked out of the house, and the boyfriend ousted from his frat, as well. Waverly was fighting mad about her expulsion from the Greek golden circle into the outer darkness of general housing. She raged against her banishment and took her fall from grace out on Robin, the lowly civilian, by being generally insufferable in every way she could invent.

Robin's only consolation was that her very existence was as annoying to Waverly as Waverly's was to her.

Robin hung her detested coat to dry above the radiator, dug her *Ancient Worlds* textbook out of her backpack, and curled in the window seat with her back to the other girl.

The room itself was fantastic, really: diamond-beveled windows, a cozy, creaking recessed window seat, delicious dark mahogany paneling up half of the wall. But the decor was a battlefield, lines strictly drawn. Waverly's half of the room was fussily, oppressively feminine: Laura Ashley linens and cut-crystal knicknacks perkily punctuated with various plush stuffed animals, a framed photo of the boyfriend on the dresser.

Robin's half was dark and cryptic and arty: black sheets and worn Surrealist prints on the wall, the melted

Dalí watches a defiant blot in Waverly's Martha Stewart universe.

Waverly finally hung up on whatever relative she was torturing and turned her full attention back to her suitcase. Robin bent over her book. She had no intention of actually studying, but she kept up the pretense of reading to annoy Waverly. It was working. Waverly watched Robin suspiciously, irritated to paranoia by Robin's stoic refusal to acknowledge her presence. The silence fairly crackled between them. Finally, Waverly had to speak.

"You're not going home?"

Robin turned a page, not looking up. "No."

"You're just going to *stay* here? By yourself?"

Robin's eyes never moved from the book. "Looks like it."

Waverly's gaze narrowed; her drawl lengthened. "You never *go* anywhere, you know."

Robin's voice was flat. "I must be weird or something."

"Or *something*," Waverly sniffed.

The door crashed open and a tall, broad jock filled the door frame.

The boyfriend.

In the window seat, Robin stiffened, every molecule of her being instantly aware of him. If Waverly was a black hole, Patrick O'Connor was the sun, big and blond and full of life. Robin could feel her heart lifting, hope returning.

He swaggered into the room, duffel hanging from his shoulder. "Taxi's here," he complained in Waverly's direction, Southern accent rich as butter. "Ready to roll?"

Waverly continued rearranging her suitcase, adding outfits she had no chance in hell of wearing over the four-day break. "He'll wait," she knifed back.

Robin kept her eyes glued to her book, raging inwardly. *Why* Waverly? It was always the golden, stupid ones who were chosen.

It was pathetic, really, a typical Southern disaster in the making. High school quarterback fucking what brains there were out of the prom queen. Prom queen bent on marriage, quarterback overflowing with hormones, scamming on every other girl in sight.

As if to illustrate the point, Patrick ran his hand along the curve of Waverly's ass as she bent over her suitcase. She pushed him away. Unfazed, Patrick twisted his hand in her hair and pulled her head back to kiss her, full mouth grazing on her lips, dropping lower to nuzzle on her throat.

Robin's jaw tightened; she pretended not to watch. *Pathetic.*

Even more pathetic was that against all logic and better judgment, Robin was hopelessly in lust with him. It was a stupid cliché, doomed, she knew – but Patrick was the only person at the school who'd paid any attention to her at all, who smiled when he saw her, as if she weren't broken or damaged beyond repair. Granted, he lighted up for everyone, especially when he wanted something. But at least Robin felt *there* when he was around. At least he saw her. He *saw* her.

She'd listened to them make love in the dark, not knowing or caring that she was awake, and imagined herself under him, his mouth on her throat, his hands holding her down, his heat filling her—

She started back to the present as Patrick turned Waverly loose and flashed his grin at Robin, warm and

14

brilliant. "Hey, Rob. Could *not* motivate myself out of bed this morning. I miss anything in Ancient Civ?" A direct blue gaze, irresistible.

Robin closed her book on her finger, kept her voice casual. "Besides that next Friday's the midterm?"

Patrick's look was comically dismayed. "Fuck a duck. I'll choke." His voice dropped, low and caressing. "'Less I can get your notes." The Carolina drawl that was like fingernails on a blackboard from Waverly was a lingering tease in Patrick's voice, full of warmth and promise.

Robin felt her knees go weak, but she put her book aside and stood, moving past him to her desk. She could feel Patrick's eyes on her. He stepped to her side (*so close!*) as she flipped through a spiral notebook. The heat of his body beside hers made her stomach twist with longing.

She ripped four classes' worth of notes on creation myths from the notebook and turned quickly, pages in hand, so he couldn't see she was trembling. "That's the last two weeks. You haven't been for a while."

He looked down into her eyes and she felt her breath catch. "Saved my ass. I owe ya—"

Waverly's voice came from behind, a shrill note of warning. "Are you finished coming all over my roommate?"

Patrick winked at Robin, turned and hoisted Waverly's suitcase, then his duffel bag, and then hooked an arm around Waverly's waist and slung her up over his shoulder in a fireman's carry. Waverly pounded on his back, her voice rising to a banshee shriek. "Put me down, you *asshole*!"

Patrick ignored her and carried her out, calling cheer-

15

fully back over his shoulder. "See ya, Rob. Happy Turkey Day."

Robin could hear Waverly starting to swear a blue streak, her voice fading down the hall.

She kicked the door closed behind them and stood still in the fading light.

Chapter 3

By five, the dorm was completely, eerily empty, halls dark and silent as the grave.

Robin had expected to feel at least some relief at Waverly's departure. Instead, she felt a dread closing in on panic.

She had never experienced the dorm without dozens of people in it. Deserted, it was much bigger than she'd realized, three stories and two and a half wings of crooked corridors, confusing to navigate without the landmarks of familiar faces. All the floors looked disconcertingly the same when the doors were shut.

And Robin hadn't really imagined how different it would feel – that there was a life force in the presence of others that pervaded the building. Even when she was in her own room, consciously unaware, her subconscious must have registered all the others.

Now the Hall was as empty and dead as a shell.

Without people, too, the dorm seemed to lose its very insulation. The wind reached icy fingers through minute cracks in the walls, snaked its way up through the floorboards. The rain had started again, slanting and relentless, and with it a fresh assault of wind. The windows rattled like bones; the whole structure shifted and groaned on its foundation.

And it had finally occurred to Robin that the communal bathroom was all the way down the hall. She'd have to leave her room in the middle of the night, when anyone could be lurking around, lying in wait for lone college girls stupid enough not to go home for vacation. No one could possibly hear her if she screamed and screamed.

Stop it, she ordered herself. *Go out there right now instead of being an idiot about it.*

She opened her door to a dark hall of closed doors, all locked to silent rooms. She took a breath and made her way down the corridor to the bathroom.

She stepped through the doorway – and pulled up short, stifling a gasp. There was someone else in the bathroom.

A slim girl with a wild mane of questionably blond hair was leaning over one of the sinks lined up under the long horizontal mirror. Her mouth was pursed in concentration as she outlined her already-blackened eyes with kohl. Her torn lace blouse and short skirt revealed an elaborate navel piercing and several provocatively placed tattoos. A piece of red yarn was tied around one wrist, knotted in several places and frayed at the ends. Some L.A. thing, no doubt; she positively reeked of California.

The girl – Lisa, Robin thought her name was – had a room on the opposite side of Robin's floor. She had the paleness and perpetual yawn of a druggie, but there was an interesting fuck-you fire in her eyes. In the two months of the short term, Robin had seen numerous boys leaving and entering her room at all hours of the night and day, almost never the same one for even two days in a row.

Lisa glanced at Robin sideways in the mirror, drawled, "Love these *holidays* ..."

Robin felt again the blistering envy of the fierce, crackling life in the other girl. But this time, along with the envy was something more – a yearning, an uncharacteristic impulse to reach out. She hovered by the lockers, gathering the courage to ask the girl if she was staying – then jumped as a voice spoke right behind her.

"You comin', or what?"

Robin twisted around. A sullen leather-jacketed young man with dyed black hair slouched in the doorway.

Lisa half-smiled ambiguously, stuck the kohl pencil behind her ear, and sauntered out past Robin, a hip-shot walk, oozing an indolent and perhaps slightly stoned sensuality. She disappeared in the direction of the stairwell with the boy.

Robin stood looking at her own reflection in the mirror for a long time. Dark hair, dark eyes, dark clothes ... dark, dark, dark. The harsh fluorescents hummed above her head. Beyond the tiled divider wall, a shower dripped.

She reached out and put her hand on the mirror, blocking out her own face.

Chapter 4

The wind felt along the building outside ... scratching for entry, whispering to get in.

Robin was walking along the dark hall ... past closed doors ... moving inexorably toward a door at the end with brilliant light along the cracks of it. The whispering was all around her, growing as she approached ... louder ... louder

The door crashed open, tearing from its hinges, unleashing a storm of formless swirling energies, howling with rage ... rushing forth—

Robin woke to dim gray light, with her heart pounding crazily in her chest.

The shutters banged steadily against the window. The wind moaned as rain pelted down, icy, miserable.

She lay still, burrowed in bed, unnerved by her dream, the images of inchoate swirling things.

She'd fallen asleep while trying to read Jung's explanation of archetypes; she could feel the heavy lump of book beside her in the bed. That's where the swirling things had come from.

She reached for the book and looked down at the page.

The archetype is an irrepresentable, unconscious, pre-exis-
tent form that seems to be part of the inherited structure of
the psyche and can therefore manifest itself spontaneously
anywhere, at any time ...

Robin wasn't sure she understood the concept, but there was something disturbing about it. A preexistent form that could spontaneously manifest itself anywhere, at any time? Not exactly something she wanted to hear this weekend.

In fact, everything about Jung so far was unnerving ... a man who'd begun his psychological studies back in the 1920s by going to séances – which, although cool, was somehow not what she'd expected to be studying in college.

She looked out the window at wind churning the trees, and shivered.

Then her stomach growled almost comically and she realized she was starving. She stared out at the storm in dismay.

She hadn't thought about food, or that there would be too much of a gale outside for her to try for a convenience store or for the Lair on campus – which, she suddenly remembered, would be closed over the holiday anyway. She made a quick mental inventory of the stock on her closet shelf. It was as bleak as the day: a box of Triscuits, some packages of instant cocoa, and a stack of the student's friend, Top Ramen – none of which was even remotely appealing. Waverly never ate, of course, though Robin knew there was an emergency bottle of Jack Daniel's hidden behind her spare comforter on the top shelf of her closet, kept around to wash down the designer pain medication Waverly no doubt lifted from a mother as blond and petite and shrill as she was.

Robin's only hope of food was a trip to the second floor, where a communal laundry room housed a Coke and candy machine, and there would surely be coffee and perhaps someone's leftovers in the kitchenette.

But that meant going out into the hall.

She lay under the pile of comforters as long as she could, clinging to the warmth, until caffeine withdrawal forced her up. She dressed randomly, a skirt over wool leggings, a bulky sweater over a turtleneck, black on black, while rain pelted against the window behind her.

Her door creaked open into the corridor as she stepped carefully outside her room.

With all the doors closed, the hall was dim, spooky, far too reminiscent of her dream. She glanced toward the end of the hall ... but of course there was only a wall, no door edged with brilliant light.

She stood uneasily in the doorway, listening for any sound.

Nothing but the wind scraping along the building outside.

A fragment from Lister's lecture hovered in the back of her head: "... *Jung believed there was a universal unconscious around us – populated by ancient forces that exist apart from us, yet interact with and act upon us.*"

She eased the door closed behind her, irrationally not wanting to disturb the silence, or draw attention to herself.

What are you afraid of, archetypes? she mocked herself. *That's mature.*

She hurried down the carpeted hall, descended a flight of pitch-black stairs as quickly and silently as she could manage.

The second floor was as deserted as her own, a dark tube of locked doors. Blue light spilled from the open doorway of the laundry room. Robin swallowed and crossed the hall.

Inside, she reached along the wall and flicked on the light, grateful for the spluttering glare of the fluorescents. The washing machines were silent cubes, the dryers black, watching windows against the wall.

Robin walked past the line of washers to the lighted Coke machine, a cheery red in the monochromatic room. She reached into her skirt pocket, slid in quarters until a Coke can dropped into the tray with a sharp clunk.

Robin flinched, raw-nerved, at the sound.

Behind her there was a huge inhalation, like the rush of breath. Robin gasped, whirled – and stared at the generator, which had whooshed on behind her.

She ran all the way back to her room and slammed the door behind her, leaned against it, shaking, berating herself.

And wondered how she could possibly make it through three days.

The phone call came right after noon, just as she'd known it would.

When she picked up, her mother was drunk, of course. Robin could almost smell it through the wires, sweet, stale whiskey. 'Tis the season, though for Mom, any old season would do.

Robin had carefully explained, the last time she'd

23

called and found her mother not too out of it, that she'd be staying at school over Thanksgiving. Her mother had seemed to absorb it at the time.

But somewhere along the line, something must have been lost, and her mother had missed the fact that Robin wasn't going to be coming home. Now her voice was edged with hysteria.

Robin tried for calm. "I told you, Mom. I can't leave. I have a huge exam next week. Practically everyone's staying. We've having a big dinner here ..."

She flinched and held the phone away from her face. Drunken rambling came from the earpiece.

She sank down on the window seat, looked down at a lone student, head bent against the rain as he crossed the deserted street. The wheedling and cajoling segued into recrimination, and then the crying jag. Robin rested her forehead against the cold glass. The words didn't matter — she'd heard it before. It was all some dark, unfathomable mass, a vortex of chaos and confusion.

Her mother was screaming now — her father again, always her father. "You're just like him. Lying, selfish bitch ..."

Robin choked out, "I gotta go, Mom. Waverly needs the phone. I gotta go." She punched off the phone and backed away from it, swaying, sick.

Instantly, it began to ring again. She threw herself down on the floor, groped under her desk, found the phone outlet in the wallboard. She pulled out the cord and the phone was still.

She sat back on her knees, hugging herself, feeling her mother's energy like a bottomless whirlpool, taking her down, down.

It wasn't *him* she was afraid of being like.

That was what she came from. *That* was what she was. Broken, defective, fatally abnormal. No wonder no one wanted to come near her.

It was all black, all nothingness.

The abyss.

Pure dark now. The rain gusted outside, the trees shivered in the wind. The Hall shuddered in its own kind of agony, impervious to the one human sound deep within it. But something in the dark corridors leaned forward ... listening.

Robin was tightly curled in the window seat of her room, arms wrapped around her knees, sobs tearing through her. The blackness had descended again, leaving no room for anything else.

After a long while, she looked up, drew a shaky breath. Her chest hurt from crying, but now, suddenly, she was calm. Exhausted, but deeply calm.

She stood, swiped at her eyes with an overlong sleeve, and crossed unsteadily to Waverly's bureau. She knelt on the brown carpet and opened the bottom drawer, pushing aside sweatshirts and petite tees in pastel colors – to find the bottle of Valium.

She shook it. More than enough.

And suddenly, she was clear.

25

Chapter 5

The wide main staircase descended into the murky gloom of the bottom floor, lighted only by red neon EXIT signs.

Robin stood at the top of the stairs with Waverly's bottle of Jack Daniel's in one hand, the bottle of pills in the other, looking down into the abyss.

She'd cracked the bottle in her room, even swallowed the first pill, washed down with whiskey – and immediately realized that not under any circumstances was she going to have Waverly be the one to find her.

She could just hear the shrill screaming, the exaggerated hysteria. In the lounge, she could abandon herself to the infinitely more acceptable kindness of the first returning stranger.

She swayed slightly, brushing against the banister, but she didn't feel drunk at all. A dreaminess had come over her. Now that she'd decided, everything seemed so easy, and simple. Not that she hadn't thought of it before, but thinking wasn't the same as deciding. Deciding was freedom.

She started down the stairs.

The shining floor below reflected the dark red lights, creating the strange impression that she was descending into a lake. In fact, she felt as if she were moving through water, a trancelike, not unpleasant feeling, a bit like having no body at all. There was a distant roaring in her ears, like a vacuum, like the sea.

Down she went, and down.

The roaring became more distinct, whispering, like a million formless voices overlapping. She wasn't alone, she realized with crystal clarity. But the thought wasn't frightening, not at all. They wanted her, the voices ... They were welcoming, beckoning ...

She stepped off the last stair – was jolted back to reality as her foot hit the floor. It was solid after all. And the voices were gone. She stood for a moment, then moved across the red streaks of light into the dark main hall, toward the high arched doorway of the lounge.

It was empty, a long, deep room with faded Victorian elegance; once a grand parlor, it was now used as a common living area. Robin paused in the archway and felt the heaviness of time emanating from the room. It was like a stage set waiting for the players: dark walnut paneling and tall arched windows; on one end a cluster of heavy scarred tables etched with decades of graffiti, in front of a wall of built-in bookshelves, on the other end a separate cluster of battered, sagging couches in front of an ornate fireplace, creating distinct lounging areas for studying and for TV. A dusty chandelier hung from the molded ceiling; a cloudy mirror cast rippled reflections over the hearth. A few lamps at the periphery of the room were on very low, lamps with hideous gold-painted plaster bases. They always seemed to be on, like night-lights, perhaps an attempt to keep drunk students from falling over themselves when they stumbled in late at night.

Robin walked unsteadily the length of the lounge, her shoes sinking deeply into the worn plum-colored carpet with cabbage roses. The room seemed immense to her, the walls distant shadows. She finally reached the other side and lowered herself into an overstuffed chair near the fireplace. The chair swallowed her, a comfortable paralysis.

The rain pounded outside; the wet night shone blue through the arched windows.

Robin stared into the gloomy depths of the unlighted hearth, uncapped the bottle of Jack, and took a deep slug. The whiskey raced through her like amber fire, a fierce, tingling burn. She blinked back tears and drank again.

She sank deeper into the chair, her body heavy and loose. She turned over her palm dreamily to look at the bottle of pills. They rattled dryly inside the orange plastic, a good few dozen. Freedom.

Robin took another slug of whiskey. The room swam, and through the pleasant spinning she noticed hazily a quality of anticipation in the room itself, a curiosity. The room seemed to be waiting for her, almost holding its breath.

The distant roaring was back in her ears ... like the sound inside a seashell ...

Robin set the whiskey down beside the chair and pushed down on the childproof cap of the medicine bottle. It felt like a great effort to twist it open. She poured the entire bottle of pills into her palm.

She took a breath, then sat up, leaned over the pills in her hand. A line floated into her head, a fragment of

Sappho from the margins of her *Ancient Worlds* text-book: "I love, I burn, and only love require, and nothing less can quench the raging fire …"

She swallowed through the ache in her throat, lifted her hand.

In the back of the room, someone coughed.

Robin jumped from the chair, twisted around.

In the darkness at the back of the long room, a slight, pale young man in glasses sat hunched over several piles of books spread out on one of the heavy tables.

The pure shock of it sobered her instantly. Through her confusion, she recognized the face: the White Rabbit, from her psych class. A name popped into her head that she hadn't known she knew: Martin.

Her hand curled around the pills in her palm, hiding them. She eased that hand behind her back. "I thought … I was the only one here."

Martin looked at her without speaking. Robin was flustered. Had he seen what she was about to do? Had he – the thought turned her crimson – coughed on purpose? To alert her, or stop her?

Ambient light from a streetlamp outside glimmered off his glasses. She couldn't see his eyes to know for sure. Desperate to break the silence, she cast around for something to say. Her eyes fell on the books stacked in front of him and she recognized the titles. *Totem and Taboo. Psychoanalysis and the Occult. Dreams and Telepathy.* All Freud. Not required reading for class, either. *He must really be into it.*

She groped for words to make the situation seem more normal, spoke carefully so as not to slur her words. "Is that for Psych 128? I've seen you in class."

He stared at her, pale-eyed behind glasses.

"Behavioral or developmental?"

She blinked, then realized what he was asking. "Oh, I'm not a major. I'm just ... there."

Martin looked at her blankly, returned to his book without comment.

Robin stood for a moment, feeling dismissed. She turned her back to him, carefully opened her fist, and poured the pills, warm from her clenched hand, back into the bottle. She capped it and slid it into her skirt pocket with a feeling of relief at accomplishing the maneuver.

She glanced back at Martin. He was bent over the shadowed table, completely absorbed in his book. She wanted to flee, but the arch of the doorway seemed too far away to negotiate; she didn't trust her legs.

At a loss, she looked around the room and focused on the dark fireplace. *Well, a fire, maybe. I could do that.*

She put a hand on the arm of the chair and lowered herself to kneel on the smoke-stained stone base of the hearth. Carefully, she pulled logs from the wood box and piled them onto the andirons.

She stole a glance back at Martin. He seemed to have forgotten her entirely.

Invisible again, she thought bleakly. *The Forgotten.*

The dreamlike languor had returned, but the motions of building the fire, wadding and packing newspaper between the logs, kept her awake. She sat back on her heels, looked around on the flagstone hearth and in the wood box for matches.

A voice spoke right behind her, at ear level. "Try this."

Robin twisted on her knees in startled disbelief.

A slim, edgy young man lay stretched out on his back

30

on a sagging faux-leather couch the size of a small barge. A *Rolling Stone* magazine lay open on his chest. He looked at her, a cool gray gaze, extended a lighter without sitting up.

Robin breathed out. "God. I didn't see you."

His face was expressionless. "You weren't looking."

Robin forced herself to reach and take the lighter from him. She flicked it and held it to several edges of the newspaper with a trembling hand. To her relief, flames blazed up obligingly, catching and spreading.

Willing herself to act normal, she turned to the young man and handed the lighter back. He kept it in his hand, pulled a crumpled pack of cigarettes from his shirt pocket, and offered it to Robin with a slight, silent gesture. She shook her head. He lighted up and smoked, all interest in her abruptly withdrawn, like a door being shut.

Robin turned back to the fire, watching the rolling flames. The pleasant, drowsy lull she had been experiencing, the presence, almost support, of the house was gone, and she felt anxious and wary of these strangers, vaguely ashamed. Her silent, womblike room had turned out to be crawling with people, and now she was stuck pretending she had not been here to—

Her mind flinched away from the thought, though she could feel the pill bottle digging into her thigh. She glanced carefully at the whiskey bottle, mercifully concealed by the side of the couch. She didn't *think* either of the boys had seen. Not that they'd care.

She sneaked a look at the one on the couch.

He was staring ahead of him with an abstracted look, off in his own world. *Looks like a musician*, she thought, and decided it was his hands that made her think so,

31

even more than the long limbs, scruffy hair, and *Rolling Stone* on his chest. His hands were alive, deliberate – precise and graceful with the cigarette he held, even though they seemed huge, almost the wrong size for the litheness of his body.

As she looked up from his hands, she realized he was watching her watch him. She blushed deeply, instantly, and he looked at her, unsmiling.

But before either could speak, if either was going to, a voice called from the doorway of the lounge, big and hearty and familiar. "Hello, orphans. Happy Turkey Day."

Robin turned, caught her breath as she saw Patrick roll through the archway into the lounge, dressed in a Green Bay jersey and sweats, pulling a massive beer cooler on creaking wheels behind him.

Her heart leapt with sudden life, hope knocking against her chest. The young man on the couch shook his head slightly and returned to his magazine. In the back, Martin stiffened, hunched lower over his Freud.

Patrick navigated a little unsteadily toward the big old TV. "Let the games begin."

He stopped, finally noticing Robin kneeling on the floor. A strange look crossed his face; he looked almost as surprised to see her as she was to see him. "Hey, Robin. You stayed, too, huh?"

The look on his face was almost guilty. Robin thought of the duffel he'd been carrying yesterday, the show he'd made of leaving with Waverly. *He doesn't want her to know he stayed*, she realized.

Patrick flipped open the cooler and dipped into the ice for a beer, handed a dripping long-necked bottle to

Robin with a gallant flourish. "Drink up," he ordered. "I'm way ahead of ya."

Robin gingerly shook icy water from the bottle and used the edge of her sweater to twist off the cap. Self-conscious, she drank too quickly, but the beer was instantly warming.

She sat back against the armchair and found, to her surprise, that her dark thoughts of before had retreated. The fire was a hot blaze; the room felt full of maleness and possibility.

Patrick found the remote on the top of the TV and clicked it on. The sound blasted in the room, preshow for the college game.

Martin looked up from his table, irritated.

Patrick instantly turned toward Martin. *Eyes in the back of his head,* Robin thought – not the first time she'd noticed.

"Not bothering you, are we, chief?" he asked Martin pleasantly enough, though everyone in the room knew that football was going to be the order of the day. Martin ignored him, hunched farther over his book in the yellow light of the gooseneck lamp. *Ancient enmity, brains and jocks,* Robin thought from her seat on the floor. She took another swallow of beer, grimaced at the yeasty bite of it.

Patrick raised his voice, apparently to include the young man on the couch. "Nebraska versus 'Bama. Any bets?" He winked at Robin and she colored.

The young man on the couch barely looked up from his magazine.

"Pass." Robin noticed his hands again.

Patrick looked at him more closely, seemed to recognize him. "You're in McConlan's band, right?"

The young man looked over the top of his magazine. His voice was dry, flat. "No. He's in mine."

Patrick grinned easily. "Whatever, dude." He pulled another bottle from the ice, tossed it toward the couch. The young man caught it expertly, one-handed. Robin was aware that the exchange was a test, some masculine jockeying, animal prowess, and found herself glad that the slim young man had passed.

Patrick glanced back toward Martin, waved a beer. "How 'bout you back there, bud? Join the living?"

Martin sighed pointedly without looking up from his book.

Patrick lowered himself into a big armchair with a clear view of the TV. He looked at Robin on the floor by the fire and suddenly leaned down close to her for a moment. She caught a scent of beer and aftershave, was dizzy with the nearness of him. "Waverly doesn't need to know about this, know what I'm sayin'? I just – didn't feel like going home." He looked at her, blue eyes serious and pleading.

Robin felt a rush of understanding and fierce protectiveness. Of course she understood. He didn't want to get any nearer home than she did. She looked back at him and saw that he knew. A warm feeling of intimacy surged between them, secret and safe. She felt lightheaded with the sudden bond.

And then the moment was broken by a feminine drawl from the doorway behind. "Well, well, what have we here? Island of lost souls?"

Robin turned reluctantly. The girl from the bathroom – Lisa – stood slouched against the frame of the entry, an exaggeratedly sensual pose, cutoff sweater revealing miles of bare skin above a short skirt. Robin realized through a haze of Valium and beer that she was not surprised to see her. From the moment in the bathroom, she had somehow known that Lisa would be here.

Lisa pushed off the doorjamb and strolled into the room, yawning, raccoon-eyed. She leaned over Patrick's chair and pointed to a beer. "Pop me?"

Patrick twisted the cap off a bottle, extended it, grinning lazily, as if he were in on some joke. Lisa touched his hand, let her fingers linger on his as she took the bottle from him.

Watching, Robin's eyes clouded, her chest tight with the knowing that she had no chance at holding anyone's attention with this girl in the room. She felt canceled out, banished again to oblivion.

She watched in despair as Lisa turned from Patrick to the young man on the brown couch, pointedly looking him over. He looked back, expressionless.

"Got a smoke?" she deadpanned.

The young man tossed the pack to her.

Patrick spoke up, sounding amused. "Anything else we can get you?"

Lisa smiled cryptically around the cigarette in her mouth. Her silver bracelets clinked against one another as she cupped her hands around the lighter; the red string dangled on her other wrist. She exhaled and theatrically removed a bit of tobacco from her lip, met Patrick's eyes. "I'll be sure to let you know."

She tossed the pack back to the young man on the couch, then strolled around the room with a languor Robin was sure was drug-related.

First, she looked Martin over at his table in the corner, eyes gliding over him, then the titles of his books. Robin saw Martin tense under her scrutiny, bracing for some comment, but Lisa passed without a word.

She circled back around to Robin and stopped, looking her over for a long time, just smoking, taking her in. Robin blanched under the bluntness of her gaze.

"You're on my floor. They stuck you in with that Southern cunt—"

Patrick instantly flared up from the easy chair. "Hey, hey, who're you calling a cunt?"

Robin caught the glint of delight in Lisa's eyes at the rise she was getting, suddenly understood it was a game. *Like passing your hand over a lighted match.*

The blond girl looked back at him with wide-eyed innocence. "Settle down, cowboy. I'm sure she's a fine piece – of *humanity.*"

Patrick stood, facing Lisa belligerently. The young man on the couch reached for the TV remote, turned up the sound, an automatic coping gesture that seemed almost familial, hinting at long experience in drowning out fights.

Patrick was bristling, truculent. "Shouldn't you be down at the Mainline makin' your tuition?"

Robin flinched at the implication. The Mainline was a no-tell motel on the outskirts of town, heavily patronized by students who wanted privacy; the very name was a frisson of sexuality. Robin's cheeks burned, but Lisa was unfazed by the reference. If anything, her slouch became more provocative; her eyes widened, and her voice dripped with a honey drawl.

"I just came from there. Saw your Miss Muffett dragging her tuffet past the football team."

Robin saw Patrick's neck tense, back muscles rippling under his Green Bay jersey. *Too far,* she thought, alarmed. She'd seen his temper before. He started toward Lisa. Robin stood, quickly stepped in between them, looked up into Patrick's angry face. "She doesn't *know* Waverly. She's just amusing herself."

The slim young man on the sofa glanced up from his magazine, looking at Robin with a hint of interest.

Lisa turned on Robin with exaggerated surprise. "The mouse roars. Didn't think you and Wave were so tight."

She stared at Robin, then at Patrick, calculating. Suddenly, she smiled broadly at Robin, as if to say she'd figured it out. She sidled closer to Patrick, drawled, "Ah'm just playin', darlin'." She reached a heavily braceleted hand to stroke his cheek, then ducked away before he could react.

At a safe distance, she pulled a small enamel box from her bodice, lifted it, querying brightly, "Vicodin, anyone?"

Patrick turned from her, disgusted but no longer ruffled. He flopped back down in front of the TV, reached for another beer, and drained it. Robin breathed slowly out in relief.

Lisa popped a pill in her mouth and dry-swallowed, then glanced around the room, in search of new prey. Her eyes fell on Martin, small and silent in the back, the light of the gooseneck lamp casting dark shadows under his eyes.

She circled back to him, eyes shining with anticipation. Robin stiffened, watching, feeling strangely protective.

Lisa stood over Martin, bare midriff at eye level. "Don't want to join the party?" she asked brightly. Martin's jaw clenched, but he continued reading. Robin

37

felt a tug of something almost like affection.

Lisa leaned over him suggestively, pretending interest in what he was studying as she brushed her breasts against his ears. "Plenty of psychology going on over here, you know."

Martin looked up at her, expressionless. She smiled down at him sweetly. "Might be time for some hands-on experience."

The sky outside rolled with thunder. A crack of lightning illuminated the room in blue-white light. Another downpour.

"Oh fucking Christ," Lisa muttered, with an agitation that was not feigned. She walked sharply, straight at the tall windows, staring out – and suddenly lunged. Robin flinched back, startled, as Lisa pounded her hands flat on the glass, shouting, "If this doesn't stop, I'll go out of my mind!"

From the couch behind her, Robin heard the slim young man say under his breath, "Go?"

But she felt a stab of sympathy for the girl, herself.

Another crack of thunder made them all jump, then the room was plunged into blackness as the lights and television went dead.

Lisa screamed shrilly. There was a heart-stopping beat – and then everyone broke up laughing. Even the young man on the couch and Martin were chuckling.

Robin looked around at the faces, shadowed by firelight. There was a new, warm intimacy in the room, a palpable relaxing of guard. The tight knot that had been in Robin's chest for as long as she could remember miraculously loosened.

The laughter died down, and the five of them looked around at one another. The young man on the couch spoke. "See if the generator kicks in."

Firelight played on their faces as they waited. The room remained dark, the TV silent. Patrick groaned suddenly. "Oh *man* – Alabama third and goal ..."

"Out of luck, dude," the slim young man informed him.

Lisa turned, smiled wickedly. "Here we all are, ladies and gentlemen. What *shall* we do in the dark?"

Patrick reached into a back pocket and pulled out a Baggie stuffed with pot. "Endure." He removed a packet of Zig-Zag papers from the Baggie and got to work rolling.

Chapter 6

The fire blazed in the old stone fireplace.

Lisa, Patrick, and Robin lounged on the floor in front of the hearth, backs propped against the couch and armchair. They passed Robin's bottle of Jack Daniel's and a fat joint, all now quite comfortably stoned.

Robin sat in a dreamy haze, melted against the back of an armchair. Flames from the fire burned warm on her face; her body was loose and pleasantly numb. It seemed almost impossible to believe that barely an hour ago she had been in the blackest despair – a step, a swallow away from darkness and oblivion.

She looked around at her companions and felt a powerful affection for all of them. Lisa, with her amazing hair, oceans of curls, the archness now gone from her face. Patrick, sprawled on the floor beside a line of empty beer bottles, his muscular body as relaxed as a big cat's. Robin felt warm all over from the heat that seemed to roll off him in waves.

Her eyes drifted to the faux-leather couch. The slim young man, who had the interesting and vaguely titillating name of Cain, had not moved since the beginning of the evening, except to reach for the joint.

Aesthetic, she thought. *Such a fine face, regal, almost.* And sensual, too, the way he was playing with the nap of the carpet with those hands, those hands ...

He looked up and met her eyes for a moment. She looked quickly away.

In the back of the room, Martin continued to study, resolutely alone. Somewhere along the line, he'd left the room to find candles, and they flickered now on the table in front of him, washing his face in soft light. Robin was reminded again of a monk in his solitary cell. *If he'd just loosen up ... just come over and sit down with us ...*

And then there was ...

She turned her head to look, then sat up slightly, frowning around the room. No, of course there were only five of them. Why had she thought there was a sixth?

Across from her, Patrick casually leaned over and picked up Lisa's wrist, held it provocatively as he examined the red knotted yarn. His husky voice sounded far away, barely awake.

"What's the string for, Marlowe? One knot for every guy you fucked last night?"

Lisa snatched her hand away. "Kabbalah," she said loftily. She caressed the string on her wrist.

To Robin's surprise, Martin snorted from the back table. "The Kabbalah of Madonna," she heard him mutter.

Lisa didn't hear, or ignored him. "It's protection from the evil eye," she informed Patrick. "And horndog jocks."

"Damage's been done, babe." Patrick leaned back,

41

grinned at her lazily. "Might as well take it off."

His tone was so suggestive, Robin was almost sick with jealousy.

Lisa stretched languidly. Her raveled sweater rose to just below her breasts. "Keep dreaming, cowboy."

Patrick took a deep toke of the roach he held, then suddenly turned and put his hand on the back of Robin's neck and drew her head to his.

He put his lips over hers and slowly blew smoke into her mouth. The rush was unbelievably sexy. Robin dissolved, rode waves of dizziness and desire as the smoky kiss went on and on.

Patrick turned her loose and stretched back down on the floor. Robin sat back against the armchair, sinking into the rose carpet again, floating into a daze. The floor beneath her seemed to rock like a boat. Lisa's eyes gleamed in the dark.

The six of them were silent again.

Robin sat up in confusion, as if jolting awake.

Six.

There were only five of them. Why did she keep thinking six?

She looked around the room, just to be sure.

Five of them, and it seemed almost inevitable that they were here.

As if reading her mind, Patrick suddenly spoke to the ceiling.

"You know why we all are here? 'Cause we all've figured it out. What's Thanksgiving anyway? You kill a big bird and you stuff it and you eat it and you fight with the fam, and when the blood's cleaned up and no one's talkin' to anyone anymore, you sit around and get wasted and watch the game. So I say, fuck the turkey,

42

stuff the family, and cut to the game."

Robin gazed at him, riveted, and thought she had never felt so close to anyone in her life.

Cain laughed from the couch. "You are so full of shit." He took a toke of the joint Lisa had just passed him, gazed around at the rest of them. "We're all here because it *sucks* at home."

A silence fell, thick and hot. All of them dropped their eyes, avoiding one another's gaze. The fire seemed to roar behind them, flames crackling. Robin felt flushed all over with heat − and shame.

And then Patrick laughed shortly, extended his bottle, and clinked with Cain's. As their eyes held this time, there was no testing between them, only acknowledgment.

Robin surprised herself by reaching in and touching her own bottle against theirs.

And behind them, Lisa spoke softly. "Hear! Hear!"

Hunched over the table in the back, Martin was still.

Robin felt a sudden wild elation − at the knowing that for the first time in her life she was not alone. Patrick locked eyes with her, a raw, hungry look, almost purely sexual.

Lisa reached across the carpet and grabbed the bottle of Jack Daniel's, lifted it. "Pop quiz. 'Why It Sucks At Home' − in twenty-five words or less." She extended the bottle to Patrick with a dangerous smile.

He handed it back to her, mockingly gallant. "*Ladies* first."

Lisa sat back on her heels, counted her words off on her fingers. "Bad girl from bad family does bad things with bad people ... feels really ... bad. Will try *anything* to feel good."

43

There was bright sarcasm in her voice, facetious and facile. But Robin understood she'd spoken the exact truth, and admired her for it.

Lisa drank deeply from the bottle, wiped her mouth suggestively, and thrust the bottle toward Robin, bright manic eyes daring her.

Robin slowly reached and took the bottle, felt the smooth square glass under her hand. Lisa watched her, waiting. Robin half-shrugged, tried to match Lisa's light tone. "Mom is crazy … Home is crazy …"

She stopped, looked down at the stained rose on the carpet. Then she spoke softly, hating the quaver in her voice. "So Dad threw us away and started over."

She forced her eyes up, looked at the others. "I feel like I'm broken. And I hate everyone who's whole."

There was a silence, then Cain suddenly reached from the couch, touched her arm. "Who doesn't?"

She looked at him, felt tears push at her eyes and throat. She raised the bottle and drank, grateful for the sting of whiskey. Then she looked again at Cain and extended the bottle, meeting his eyes in the darkness.

She could almost feel him pull back, though he didn't move. Then he took the bottle, spoke flatly. "Mother – dead. Father – unknown." His lips twisted. "In case you're wondering, foster care in this country is truly for shit."

He drank without looking at anyone, then turned to Patrick, holding the bottle out.

Patrick looked at the bottle, slumped deliberately back against the armchair. "Ha. No way, losers."

Cain and Lisa exploded at him simultaneously.

"You pussy." Lisa shoved his leg hard.

"Cough it up, wuss."

44

Patrick's eyes darted around, defensive. Robin looked at him with silent reproach.

Patrick grabbed the bottle from Cain. He took a deep toke from his joint, spoke through held breath. "Prominent surgeon Dad commits Mom to mental hospital to get custody of son. Pumps son full of steroids to create ultimate football machine."

He exhaled smoke, stared at the three of them truculently. There was a stunned silence as the words sunk in.

Cain spoke softly into the void. "And you hate football."

Patrick smiled thinly. "Got that right, Coach. But it's all I know." He chugged whiskey. Behind him, logs snapped and popped in the fireplace.

Martin coughed in the back. They all turned, surprised, as he began to speak, the flickering light from the candles playing over his face. "Orthodox rabbi father's only wish is for only son to take over rabbinate. Only – son doesn't believe in God."

He started to laugh, then stopped abruptly. A silence fell again, a speechless intimacy. Smoke from the joint drifted in the air, burned harsh in Robin's throat.

Lisa spoke dryly. "Well, that was fun. What the hell do we do next?" She pushed herself up and stood, stretching languidly as she meandered toward the built-in walnut cabinets.

Robin looked at Cain and Patrick, then leaned over for the bottle of whiskey and stood. She walked over to Martin's table and stopped beside him, extended the bottle.

He looked up at her, startled, blushing. Robin pushed the bottle closer, insistent. Martin reached hesitantly to take it.

45

In the room behind them, Lisa screamed.

Everyone jumped, twisting toward her. She was half inside the built-in game cupboard by the fireplace, tugging at something.

She pulled back, freeing a long box from beneath a stack of old board games, and turned into the room to display her find.

"Looky looky."

The rectangular box was brown with age and frayed at the edges, but Robin recognized the graphic on the front instantly. A Ouija board.

Lisa's face was glowing, energized. She carried the box over to a round table and dragged the table across the carpet, positioned it in front of the fire. "I bet there're plenty of spirits in this old place."

Robin got a brief glance of faded handwriting on the inside cover of the box as Lisa took the board out and set it up on the table's surface.

Robin watched her with a dreamlike sense of unreality. A séance? It was too weird. She'd just been reading about Jung and séances the night before.

On the floor in front of the hearth, Patrick pulled out the Zig-Zag papers and started to roll another joint. "Then we can play Spin the Bottle, and sing 'Kumbaya' around the fire."

Lisa flipped him off and darted back to the study tables in the dark end of the room. She sidestepped Robin and smiled sweetly down at Martin as she snagged one of his candles. She crossed back to the round table, shielding the flame with a cupped hand, and set the candle down, then sat in front of the board and looked around expectantly. "Who's going to do it with me?"

46

None of the guys moved.

Lisa looked back at Robin. "Come on, you look sensitive to me." Her eyes held Robin's across the long room. There was a challenge in the air, and a charge that was almost erotic. Robin was very aware of all three guys watching them with heightened interest, and she envied Lisa her brash narcissism. She knew how to play a room; it was impossible to ignore her.

Lisa half-smiled, as if reading Robin's mind. Her eyes flicked to Patrick knowingly. "They really want us to, you know. Guys *love* to watch." Her gaze locked back on Robin's.

All right, then, Robin thought suddenly. *I can play, too.*

She walked across the room to the table, pulled out a chair, and sat down opposite Lisa.

Lisa's smile broadened. "I'll be gentle." She reached to put her fingers, tipped in polish the color of dried blood, on the heart-shaped wooden planchette. After a moment, Robin did, too. It was a familiar feeling, an instant sense memory of childhood. *I guess just about everyone's done it, on a rainy night like this ...*

Sprawled on the floor, Patrick laughed to himself as he licked the edges of the joint. "'Double, double, toil and trouble ...'"

"Shut up," Lisa ordered. She looked across the table at Robin in the firelight, daring her. "Let's get someone good." Robin had to admit she made a convincing Gypsy, with her wild hair, lace camisole peeking out of a torn sweater, rings glinting on her slender fingers.

Robin stared down at the board. It was old – yellowed with age, not the faux finish of a modern mass-production. Antiquated letters at the bottom spelled out

47

BALTIMORE TALKING BOARD. The wood was blackened around the edges, almost as if it had been—

Burned.

The realization gave her a shiver of unease.

Lisa raised her voice, addressed the darkness beyond the glowing circle of the fire. "Is there anyone there?" Her eyes shone across the table, knowing as a cat's.

"Did Alabama score?" Patrick said through an exhalation of green-smelling smoke.

Lisa kicked at him from beneath the table. She spoke to the board and the ceiling at the same time. "Does anyone want to speak to us?"

Robin kept her gaze on the black letters on the board, the wooden indicator beneath her hands. Rain gusted outside, pounding into the pavement. There was no movement at all.

Lisa winked at Robin. "We'd like someone dark ... and mysterious ... and sexy as hell."

Cain's head was tipped back against the armrest of the couch. Smoke drifted toward the ceiling from his cigarette. "There are 900 numbers you can call for this."

Lisa spoke over him, ignoring him. "Is anyone there?"

They listened to the silence. The logs crackled. The planchette was motionless under their fingers.

Robin felt drowsy from the pot and from the comfortable darkness.

The heat from the fire shimmered in the room. She gazed into the shimmering, and again felt the presence that she had noticed before from the house, a sense of curious waiting, of leaning forward ...

Violent longing stabbed through her – a wish that something would happen, that someone would hear,

48

move, respond, that a door would open and everything, everything, would change.

There was a sort of electric tingling under her fingers ...

The planchette suddenly moved to

Y E S

Robin jumped.

Across the table, Lisa gasped slightly, then looked sharply at Robin.

Her green gaze narrowed. "Way to go."

Robin stared back at her. *So that's the way it's going to be*, she thought. *The Lisa show.*

Patrick rolled over on the floor, raised himself up on an elbow to make a circular motion with his hand. "Ladies, ladies – momentum."

Robin jumped again – and saw Lisa flinch, too – as the planchette began to move under their hands, slow, sweeping circles. Robin looked at Lisa. Lisa's eyes sparkled back at her.

The pointer suddenly took off, racing across the board.

Robin watched the letters appear under the cutout circle in the middle of the planchette. The pointer spelled quickly, continuously, with slight stops in the neutral center between each word.

I   A M

Lisa read aloud for the others with exaggerated import. "I ... am ..."

Patrick made spooky sounds on the floor. Martin glanced over in spite of himself. On the couch, Cain shook his head, flicked his Zippo to light another cigarette. But Robin saw he was smiling.

Lisa's good, she thought. The movement of the planchette was smooth, credible – no obvious pushing. The pointer felt like it had a life of its own.

Lisa smiled into the darkness flirtatiously. "Well, hello." She swept her hair back from her face with a ringed hand before she put her fingers back on the planchette.

The pointer instantly moved to

HELLO

And then it spelled quickly

LISA

Lisa read out with the moving indicator and turned away from the table with childlike delight. "Guys, he knows my name."

Patrick put his hands to his mouth, mock-shuddered. "It *must* be real."

He was grinning, clearly enjoying himself. He'd stripped down to a tank and now basked bare-armed in the heat of the fire, leaning back on a sofa cushion, watching the girls as if they were his private show. Robin's eyes traveled up his thighs to the juncture of his legs, remembering the soft thrill of his lips on hers, his breath hot in her mouth ...

50

Her face flushed, and she was glad for the darkness.

Lisa shook her hair out of her face and raised her voice, addressing the board. "Do you have a name?"

The pointer jerked to life. Lisa read out with it.

CALL   ME

The wooden piece hesitated. Robin and Lisa watched it circle aimlessly over the board, as if unsure how to answer.

Patrick chuckled from the floor. "Make it good, Marlowe."

Then, as if inspired, the pointer spelled out quickly

ZACHARY

Robin felt a tingle up her neck, like fingers brushing her hairline. The candlelight flickered, making the black letters seem to pulse.

Lisa's eyes jumped to Robin's, a quick, probing look. Then she shrugged, spoke lightly. "Nice to meet you, Zachary."

"Charmed," Patrick drawled over the top of another beer, then belched for emphasis.

The pointer responded instantly, smooth circles and a slight pull between letters. Robin found herself both lulled and impatient at the slow-motion conversation; waiting for the letters was like trying to run in a dream.

THE   PLEASURE   IS   MINE

Lisa finished the sentence triumphantly and looked up

from the board. Her eyes were sparkling. "A *gentle-man*." She glanced sideways at Patrick.

"Those are the ones you wanna watch, honey," he retorted.

Lisa turned back to the table and beamed at Robin. Robin smiled back, warming to her enthusiasm. So what if it was a game? The fire was blazing, making shadows dance in the corners of the room. The circular swaying of trees through the window, the ebb and flow of the wind, the popping of the fire – all were dreamlike, seductively hypnotic, and Robin decided to play along. What could it hurt?

Lisa was addressing the board again. "Have you come to tell us anything, Zachary?" The two girls watched the board as it spelled out the letters.

ANYTHING   YOU   WISH

Lisa smiled secretively in the flickering candlelight. She turned and informed the rest of the room. "He says, 'Anything you wish.'"

On the floor, Patrick snorted through a swallow of beer. "Ask him who wins the game."

Lisa seemed about to retort, but the indicator moved instantly, obliging.

ALABAMA

Robin read it out, and Lisa finished the sentence with her.

BY   14

Patrick sat straight up, pleased. "Can I bet on that, dude?" His voice was warm, hazy from pot.

The pointer moved again. Robin and Lisa watched the letters in a little island of concentration, reading out together.

BETTING IS CLOSED

The girls leaned over the board to watch the last word forming. As Robin realized Lisa's joke, she smiled, and they called it out together in perfectly matched, stoned accents.

DUDE

Robin and Lisa broke out in delighted giggling. On the couch, Cain muttered, "Pretty hip ghost."

Patrick sat up from the floor, laughing heartily. "You should be charging for this, Marlowe." He nodded to Lisa.

Lisa shook her head, cascading curls caught by the firelight. "*I'm* not doing it, I swear." She smiled across the table at Robin.

Robin found herself wondering. Nothing that Lisa said could be trusted, obviously. It *was* a game, and it was working. Lisa was the center of attention, which apparently she needed to be at all times, and the boys were mildly amused, enough to keep watching. Robin was aware that even Martin was following the action at the board, not with his whole attention, maybe, but as background noise, like having music or the television on.

At the same time, Robin found a strange thing happening.

She'd played Ouija with slightly older cousins as a nine-or ten-year-old, and even though the candlelit bedroom setting and thrill of inclusion by the older girls had given the game an edge of newness and excitement, she'd also known *she* was the one being played, that Cousin Jeannie had been moving the pointer to spell out slightly racy hints of boys who were madly in love with whoever.

And at first, she'd been quite sure that Lisa was moving the pointer, just as her cousins had. But somewhere along the line, it really felt that Lisa had stopped and something ... else ... had taken over.

She shivered, and realized that Cain was sitting up on the couch, watching her, a question in his eyes.

Lisa spoke into the darkness with a strange intensity, something more than just playful curiosity. "Who are you, Zachary?"

The question hovered in the air. The planchette was still.

Lisa glanced at Robin, frowned into the silence. "Did you live here in the Hall?"

The planchette abruptly moved under their fingers, and Robin realized she'd been holding her breath. The wooden pointer slid simply to

Y E S

Robin was startled by a sudden image, very clear in her mind: a young man, pale and dark-eyed, with slightly longish dark hair, slim and tall and, yes, a bit haunted. Hovering at the corners of her imagination, but for a moment quite clear and real.

And then gone. Robin snapped back to the present.

The fire beside the table was crackling, almost too hot on her back. Across the table, Lisa was looking at her oddly. Robin realized, mortified, that everyone else was silent, staring at her. Outside, the wind crooned through the trees, a hollow sound between buildings.

Robin leaned forward and addressed the board. "When? When did you live here?"

The planchette jerked and then circled under their hands, as if pondering, a mesmerizing movement.

And then the letters came again, and this time so slowly, almost teasing, that both Lisa and Robin leaned forward and read urgently under their breaths, pushing the letters and guessing each word a little before it was actually completed.

THERE   IS

Robin was aware of all three guys leaning forward, too: Cain on the couch, Patrick on the floor, Martin at his table in the back, all riveted, completely captive.

NO   TIME

Robin's breath caught in her throat, and Lisa finished.

HERE

The sentence hung in firelit orange and dark.

Robin and Lisa looked at each other, chilled. Scattered around the room, the guys were still.

Lisa cleared her throat slightly and leaned forward, bracing her elbows on the table.

"What do you mean, 'here'?" Her eyes met Robin's, glanced away. "Where is 'here'?"

The planchette jerked and then circled, with no response. The moment seemed suspended; the red yarn on Lisa's wrist trailed across the letters like blood. Robin could feel the others waiting, leaning forward slightly, perhaps not quite breathing. Her entire attention was on the smooth age-yellowed surface of the board, the formal black letters, the scorch marks.

And then, as if some decision had been made, the word came. Strange and unfamiliar, so that both she and Lisa spoke the letters out individually.

Q L I P P O T H

Chapter 7

Robin was the first to put the letters together, the word alien in her mouth.

"Qlippoth?"

Martin looked up from his back table with sudden interest.

In the hearth, the logs crackled and popped, sending showers of sparks up the chimney flue. The shadows of flames rippled on the walls.

Lisa nodded hesitantly at the pronunciation, guessing rather than knowing Robin was right. The others stared around at one another in the flickering light, mystified.

"Take me to your leader," Patrick intoned, zombielike. The joke fell somewhat flat, everyone still unnerved.

Lisa pressed her ringed fingers into the planchette, spoke into the darkness, her tone falsely bright. "How about in English, Zach?"

The silence was too thick as the planchette circled. Robin could actually feel everyone in the room leaning forward as she and Lisa spoke the words.

Robin was peripherally aware of Martin being very still in the back, staring at Lisa.

Lisa looked at Robin. "The shells? Do you mean the shelves?"

"The beach?" Patrick guessed.

Cain spoke dryly from the couch. "There was a doo-wop group in the fifties – Clam Chowder and the Shells."

Patrick snickered, partly in relief at the break in tension, Robin thought. Lisa glared toward both boys. Then the girls jumped as the indicator moved again, unbidden.

Again, Robin could feel the guys leaning forward in the silence to hear. Lisa read the words aloud, somewhat short of breath.

NO   MATTER
I   AM   WITH   YOU   NOW

Robin stared down at the board, felt another prickle of foreboding. The pointer moved again, almost jaunti-ly.

AT   YOUR   SERVICE

The unexpected joke relaxed them all. Robin and Lisa smiled across at each other.

Patrick groaned from the floor. "Ahh, don't encour-age her."

Lisa laughed, reassured, and flirted back at Zachary. "In that case, at least tell us what you look like."

Robin could feel a change in the quality of the movement under her hands ... a playful sensuality.

THE MAN OF YOUR DREAMS

Lisa laughed again, harder than was really called for. She vamped, à la Mae West. "Well then, come up and see me sometime."

Always the tease, aren't you? Robin thought. *Just can't help yourself.*

Lisa caught Robin's gaze in the yellow light, and there was an edge in her voice, a challenge. "*You* ask something."

Robin hesitated, torn between desire and distrust.

Lisa gave her no quarter. "Okay, then I will." She reached for the pointer, raised her voice. "Zachary, tell us. Is Robin a virgin?"

Robin froze. She saw Patrick choke on his beer ... and, behind him, Cain rolling his eyes.

She flushed. "All right, just stop." She started to withdraw her hands from the pointer, but Lisa put her hands firmly on top of Robin's, holding her there, smiling wickedly.

The planchette began to move. Robin's face was hot, but somehow she couldn't make herself let go. She stared at the letters as they materialized.

I LOVE I BURN AND ONLY LOVE REQUIRE

She jolted, recognizing the bit of poem she had been thinking of as she held the pills in her hand.

59

Am I doing this? she wondered, disoriented.

Lisa read the sentence out, quirking her eyebrows – whether in mockery or pleased surprise, it was hard to tell.

Patrick murmured from the floor, "Oh, baby." Robin turned crimson, but through the rush of blood in her ears, she recognized a note in his voice she hadn't quite heard before: appreciation. Her heart fluttered. *Maybe ... maybe there* is *hope.*

Lisa widened her eyes at Robin. She raised her voice brightly. "How romantic of you, Zachary. The rest of you clowns should be taking notes."

Robin was surprised to detect an undertone of grudging jealousy. *Jealous of what?* Robin stared across at her, her mind racing. *Is she spelling things out? Am I?*

Lisa caught her eyes, leaned forward slightly. "See, he likes you. Come on." She held Robin's eyes, seductive, appeasing.

After a moment, Robin put her hands back on the planchette, by now far too intrigued to stop.

Lisa looked around the room, reenergized. "Anyone? Questions?"

A moment of silence, then Patrick volunteered, without moving from the floor. "Okay, Zach, old man." He paused portentously. "Will I pass history?"

On the couch, Cain audibly snorted. Robin heard Martin in the back muttering under his breath, "In your dreams."

They were listening then, just as present as she was.

The indicator jerked slightly under her hands, and she blinked back to the board, staring at the letters as they formed.

Robin was no longer surprised how quickly and smoothly the board was spelling out the messages, it seemed natural, inevitable.

Lisa read out the words, and Cain half-laughed. "The cosmic fortune cookie."

But Robin noticed that he had been intent on Lisa's words. His magazine lay forgotten on the floor beside the couch. *You're into it. Not a complete cynic after all.*

Patrick was speaking, and she was instantly attentive again as he called out, "How, Zach? You gonna take it for me?"

And Robin realized that something had changed. The tone of Patrick's voice was easy, companionable; he was talking to the board the way he would talk to a person.

And there was something else, as well. She could feel the *house* listening. As completely absorbed in and amused by the conversation as the rest of them were.

You're stoned, she told herself.

The planchette was moving under her hands, and Lisa read with it.

A S   Y O U   W I S H

Patrick pointed a little hazily at the board, his words slurred. "You're on, dude. Eleven o'clock next Friday, right, Rob?"

The pointer jerked simply to

Y E S

And Robin felt a stab of apprehension.

Across the table, Lisa's eyes were bright, almost feverish. She saw Robin looking at her, and looked away quickly, as if caught. She turned in her chair to speak to the room. "Someone ask something none of us would know," she demanded. There was a dark sense of urgency under her words.

Patrick lolled his head back against the edge of the couch, swigged his beer. "What's my mother's maiden name?" he offered.

Behind him on the couch, Cain rolled his eyes. "It's not an ATM machine."

The board was already spelling out a name.

C O L E

Lisa spoke it. "Cole."

Patrick sat up. "*Hey*. That's right."

The others looked around at one another.

Now Patrick actually stood, struggling to his feet, swaying a little as he crossed to the table. He looked down at the board, then at Lisa.

"You've been checking up on me, Marlowe." But his voice didn't have its usual tone of light banter.

Lisa tipped back in her chair and looked up at him, defiant. "I don't know your *first* name, cowboy."

Patrick looked at Robin now. His smile was broad, but there was uncertainty in it, too. "Okay, Robin – you wormed it out of Waverly."

Robin shook her head. Her eyes met his, and for a moment she saw something. Fear?

Patrick laughed a little weakly.

Lisa turned in her chair, looked over at Cain, challenging. "Your turn. Ask."

Robin had expected a protest. Instead, it was rather dizzying how immediately Cain spoke. His voice was flat, but there was an urgency beneath.

"How did my mother die?"

Robin's eyes jumped to his, startled, and she saw his set gray gaze for an instant.

It's started. It's got us. Quick, wild, thoughts ...

Then the pointer jerked to life. Across the board, Lisa sounded the words out.

W A N T   M E   T O   S A Y ?

Robin drew in a sharp breath. On the couch, Cain was very still. The shadows from the fire leapt wildly on the walls.

Then Cain spoke softly, and the fury of his words dug into Robin's chest. "That's fucking clever, Marlowe."

Lisa shoved back her chair. "Hey *I* don't know what that means."

Cain looked angry and lost all at once, and Robin knew. *It's true, then. Something really bad happened. How did Lisa know?*

And if Lisa didn't *know?*

Robin looked at the board. The indicator was still, poised above

?

She shivered, chilled. Something had changed. There had been a sudden turn of corner. *What's happening?*

Her eyes drifted to the edge of the board, the burn marks there, as if somewhere, sometime, the board had burst into flame.

Lisa pushed her hair back, her bracelets clinking faintly. "Somebody ask something else." She stared around at all of them.

Patrick stood in front of the fireplace, legs braced. "Okay, Zach. What am I thinking right now?"

Even before the planchette started to move, Robin felt a pull of something – fathomless.

No ... she thought – but too late.

Lisa was leaning forward, edgy and tense, breathing out the letters as they came.

A B O U T   K I L L I N G

Robin gasped as she realized the message.

Y O U R   F A T H E R

The logs popped in the hearth, showering sparks. Patrick towered over them, swaying with alcohol. He spoke quietly, dazed. "Who's moving that?"

Rage swept through him like wildfire. "I said, Who the fuck is moving that?"

It was so not a game anymore. Patrick was beyond drunk, and so angry, a tidal current of fury. Lisa and Robin both sat frozen at the board. *He's so big*, Robin thought, unfocused, as if seeing it for the first time. *Steroids. Football.* She felt suffocated, unable to breathe.

Cain spoke carefully from the couch, not moving. "Take it easy, man." His voice was so balanced, Robin leaned into the sound with relief, immediately surrendered the situation to him.

Patrick didn't seem to hear. His face was ruddy, his accent lower, like an older man's, thick and snarled, almost incomprehensible. "Marlowe, I swear to Christ I'll make you eat that board."

Robin jumped as he started toward the table, tossing a chair out of his way.

Cain was instantly on his feet, faster than Robin would have thought possible, blocking Patrick. She felt a wild rush of fear.

And then Martin's voice came calmly from the back of the room.

"Actually, that was obvious."

Patrick wheeled around.

Martin sat very still in his chair. Candles flickered over the books in front of him.

Patrick's eyes narrowed. "What kind of shit are you talking—"

"Oedipal conflicts run high in the South. Competitive sports are a classic battleground." Martin tipped back in his chair, nonchalant, almost lofty. Robin's pulse spiked with alarm. *Oh, careful.*

But then Martin shrugged, and spoke softly. "And who hasn't thought about it?"

Patrick stiffened. He looked at the smaller boy with laser eyes, but everyone knew Martin had given him the courtesy of the truth.

The fire simmered in the hearth. The room was very quiet, everyone looking at Martin. When he spoke, his voice was hypnotic in the moving firelight. "You've got two intelligent women there. Astute enough to pick up on emotional clues."

Now that the danger was past, Lisa came to life again, shoved back in her chair, agitated. "Except that I'm not moving that piece of wood."

Martin half-smiled, tolerantly, gestured with his pen.

"Your subconscious is. That's the whole point, isn't it? Induce a high state of concentration, and seemingly uncanny thoughts come out."

Is it? Robin wondered. *Is that all there is? Could one of us have known – somehow, intuitively – that Patrick wanted to kill his father, that Cain's mother died badly?*

She looked at Lisa. Lisa caught her eyes, looked quickly away.

Lisa is smart. Under all that posturing, she doesn't miss a thing.

Cain moved forward, his face tense in the half-light. He looked at Robin, then Lisa. "Ask, then. Ask what's doing it."

Lisa scooted her chair back to the table, put her hands on the indicator. After a moment, Robin did, too. Lisa spoke into the dark. "Zachary, are you ... reading our minds?"

Robin tensed as the pointer jerked under their fingers. It circled dreamily, not stopping on anything.

Teasing, she thought.

And then at once, decisively, it began to spell. Lisa leaned over the board to read, her hair falling around her face. The pointer scraped through the silence.

N O   O N E   W H O   C O N J U R E S
U P   T H E   M O S T   E V I L

Martin's sharp voice interrupted Lisa's reading. "I want everybody to come back here."

Patrick turned on him, growling. "What the hell—"

Martin spoke over him. "Just do it." His face was flushed, excited.

Patrick stared back at him in mild disbelief, bristling.

66

Cain stood still; even Robin was surprised at the authority in Martin's voice. But after a moment, everyone stood and walked across the long room to the table beside the bookshelves.

Martin pointed to the psych text lying open on the tabletop. "Go on, look at the book. And someone read the passage at the top of the page that it's open to."

They all looked at one another; then Robin stepped to the edge of the table and read the small print. "'No one who, like me, conjures up the most evil—'" She stopped, startled.

The others crowded in closer behind her to see.

Robin glanced at Martin, who nodded. She looked back down at the page and read the whole passage out, more slowly.

"'No one who, like me, conjures up the most evil of those half-tamed demons that inhabit the human breast, and seeks to wrestle with them, can expect to come through the struggle unscathed.'"

The silence was heavy in the shadowed room. Robin saw Patrick's eyes dart from Martin to Lisa, wary and appraising.

Martin turned and faced them. "Freud. I was just reading that passage before I came over."

The fire crackled behind them.

Martin looked at the girls. "Pure thought transference. It was in my mind ... and you – one of you – picked it out."

Or Zachary did, Robin wanted to say, but she didn't. The room was spinning, a vertiginous excitement. She could see Martin's eyes were shining, the detached academic stance gone.

Cain looked at her across the candlelight. "I heard

you say you were in his psych class. You've read the same book."

His face was cold. Robin felt a rush of indignation. "No, I haven't."

She stared at him.

Martin reached across the table for his legal pad. "We'll test it. We each write something secret about ourselves and leave it back here. Then we ask the board – and see what happens."

Cain laughed shortly. "Forget it. I'm out of here." He started for the door, a long, lithe stride.

Robin faced him, calling out, "I didn't set this up."

Cain turned under the arch of the doorway, looked back at her. Robin stared back at him, and she could feel his hesitation, the question in his gaze.

But then his face closed and he walked out. Robin stood, her face as hot as if she'd been slapped. *Be a prick, then*, she thought. She was barely aware of Martin speaking impatiently from behind her.

"Doesn't anyone else want to know what's going on here?"

Robin turned slowly. Martin was tearing strips of paper off his yellow legal pad. He looked at Lisa, extended a slip of paper and a pen.

Lisa frowned but took the pen and paper.

Patrick strode over to the table. "What the fuck." He reached for a strip.

Martin turned to Robin. She took the yellow strip, stood for a moment, then reached into her skirt pocket and scribbled quickly with her own purple pen.

Martin was writing, too. He folded up his paper so no one would be able to see what he had written. The others folded theirs, as well.

68

"Everyone put their papers down on the table," he directed.

Patrick rolled his eyes in obligatory protest, but they all added their squares of paper to Martin's.

Now Martin crossed the carpet to the table in front of the fire. The others followed.

How funny – he's taken total charge, Robin thought. *And we've let him. Even Patrick. Not such a White Rabbit after all.*

Martin stopped in front of the board and looked expectantly at Lisa and Robin. Almost obediently, the girls sat across from each other again. Lisa put her hands on the planchette and Robin followed, with some reluctance.

Martin cleared his throat and then spoke rather formally. "We'd like to ask some questions."

Patrick and Martin hovered beside the table. Robin could feel everyone holding their breath, but the pointer didn't move.

Lisa bit her lip. "Zachary?"

The planchette didn't move at all. Robin's hands felt heavy and awkward on the wood. Lisa looked across at Robin in the flickering light, and Robin knew she felt it, too.

"Zachary?"

Another long beat, then Lisa shook her head. She took her hands from the pointer, looked at the boys. "He's gone."

"What do you mean?" Martin frowned at her.

"There was something there before. An ... energy. You could feel it. It's gone." She looked at Robin. Robin met her green gaze, nodded.

"Maybe it's playing hard to get," Patrick half-joked.

"Let me try," Martin said abruptly.

He's really into this, Robin thought uneasily. But she stood, moved back from her chair so he could sit.

Martin sat down across from Lisa, put his fingers on the indicator. He spoke stiffly into the air. "Is ... something there?"

Darkness ... silence ...

Nothing.

Lisa tried again. "Zachary?"

They sat for a long moment, fingers quivering on the wooden pointer.

The wind rushed the building, rattling the windows, whistling through the cracks of the wood, worrying the old bones of the house.

The pointer was completely lifeless.

Lisa looked at Robin again. "Nada. He's gone."

Chapter 8

There was something anticlimactic about trooping upstairs, carrying candles from Martin's table to light their way. The moving candlelight was disorienting, they had to feel their way up along the banisters in the darkness. The stairs creaked more than Robin had ever noticed in the daylight world.

No one spoke. After all their intimacy it was as if they were strangers again. *Almost as if we're ashamed ...*

Robin was dying to ask, to compare notes, to see if anyone would even acknowledge what had happened. *Did it only happen to me?* Her face flushed with a sudden paranoia. *Are the rest of them all in on it together, setting me up?*

With a flash of unease, she remembered the books on the table in front of Martin: *Psychoanalysis and the Occult. Dreams and Telepathy.*

Was it all going to turn out to be some horrible, humiliating trick?

Robin caught a glimpse of Patrick's face, startlingly coarse and crude in the candlelight, and she turned away quickly, disturbed.

As they reached the third-floor landing, Martin stopped and turned, about to speak, but Patrick broke the silence first, stretching suggestively. "Well, ladies, I hate to sleep alone on a holiday. What do you say, Marlowe?"

Lisa deftly avoided the arm he tried to drape around her, shot back at him, "You wouldn't be able to handle me after Miss Tri Delt."

Patrick leered toward her. "I bet Martin could use a good mauling."

Martin ducked his head and skittered off into the dark of the boys' wing.

Lisa exploded. "God, you're an asshole."

"You want him back? I can arrange it – for a cut—"

Lisa slapped Patrick viciously across the face. There was a stunned, frozen beat, then in a split second Patrick had grabbed her arm and pinned her against the wall, pressing his body into hers. Both were breathing hard; Lisa's eyes flamed with fury. The sex between them was palpable.

Robin was frozen against the opposite wall, invisible.

Patrick smiled slowly, pushed back off the wall, releasing Lisa.

"Not worth the sperm."

"You'll never know," Lisa snarled after him as he sauntered off into his own wing. She whirled and slammed through the door of the girls' wing without a word to Robin.

Robin stood in the juncture of halls, feeling abandoned, bereft. After a moment, she stepped after Lisa into the pitch-black of the girls' wing – and froze, her heart pounding.

A taper floated before her in the darkness of the hall.

Robin caught her breath, then realized the candle was her own, reflected in a mirror down the hall.

She turned and saw Lisa standing against the wall, watching her obliquely, the light from her own candle flickering on her face. "Want to sleep in my room?" she asked suddenly.

Robin was caught off guard – flooded with paranoia again. Was this part of the game? Get Robin to her room and scare the shit out of her later, when she was asleep?

Then Robin flashed back to the electric feeling of the planchette under her fingers, the ominous quotation the board had spelled out in the end – "The most evil of those half-tamed demons" – and realized that no matter what prank Lisa could dream up, it couldn't be worse than going back to her room alone.

She nodded briefly. "Okay."

Lisa started down the long hall, and Robin trailed her in the dark to a door with—

A window? Robin thought for a moment, startled. She looked closer at the door and realized it was a painting of a window frame, looking out on a desert landscape at night, sand dunes stretched out under a huge moon.

Interesting. We're all so much more interesting than anyone would have guessed.

Lisa handed Robin her candle so she could unlock the door. She pushed it open and let Robin by – into a room like a Moroccan harem.

For a moment, Robin forgot her suspicions and looked around her in wonder at twin beds pushed together to form one big lush bed, draped veils, tin-framed mirrors on the wall, a carved wood screen, big pillows on the floor. Books lay open everywhere, over-flowing ashtrays beside them. Robin noticed a Madonna CD case open on top of the dresser. *So Martin was right,* she thought, startled. *Or did he know Lisa before tonight?* She felt another sickening wave of paranoia.

Robin turned and caught Lisa watching her narrowly.

"You have a private?" Robin asked, flustered.

Lisa widened her eyes in mock innocence. "Can't seem to keep a roommate. Oh well." She grinned at Robin, tossed her a T-shirt to sleep in. She pulled her own torn sweater over her head, then peeled off her camisole with deliberate languor, exposing a Celtic tattoo on her left breast.

She turned to examine herself in the dresser mirror, stroking her stomach, trailing her hands down her waist. She held Robin's eyes in the reflection.

God, everything's an act with you, isn't it? Robin thought. But there was a charge in the room, electric and titillating.

Irritated, Robin moved to the bed, set her candle on the bed table, and unzipped her skirt.

So we're not going to talk about tonight at all, then?

As she slid off her skirt, Waverly's prescription bottle fell from the pocket and rolled on the floor, rattling. Robin reached for it, her face hot with shame, but Lisa was too quick for her. She scooped it up and looked at the pills with an expert eye, then turned her gaze to Robin, speculatively.

"How many were you going to take? All of them, or just enough to get you some attention?"

Lisa gasped as Robin grabbed her wrist, held it hard. "I won't tell. You were moving it, weren't you?"

74

Lisa's eyebrows quirked. She smiled thinly. "Sweetie pie, I swear I thought *you* were."

They looked at each other for a long moment. Robin felt chilled. Then Lisa shrugged, her eyes sparkling. "Well, well, well. This could get interesting."

She climbed into bed, flashing long bare legs, and snuggled under the covers.

Robin sat slowly on the other side, confused – and strangely exhilarated.

Lisa twisted down on the cap of Waverly's prescription bottle and popped a pill, then offered it to Robin. "Valium?"

Robin shook her head.

Lisa leaned to her bed table to blow out the nearest candles, then paused, her face wreathed with the flickering glow. She called out brightly into the shadows, "Night night, Zachary. Sweet dreams." She huffed the candles out.

Chapter 9

The last candle flickered out, drowned in its own wax. In the pitch-black of Lisa's room, the girls slept, crashed out on opposite sides of the wide bed. But there was something else there, not asleep. The darkness of the room seemed to breathe ...

Robin stirred, frowning ... She opened her eyes ...

A pale young man stood in the shadows at the foot of the bed, looking down at her, his sunken eyes dark and fathomless ...

Robin jolted awake, her heart hammering madly. Her eyes jumped to the end of the bed.

No one.

She breathed out slowly, realized she had been dreaming.

She sat up, looked around her. Though her arms were still covered in gooseflesh, there was no one else in the room. *Obviously*, she chided herself. *What did you really think?*

The light was sluggishly gray, but bright enough to register as afternoon.

She glanced down to her left. Lisa was sprawled on

her side of the bed, dead to the world.

Robin looked past her, out the window, at yet another miserably rainy day.

Suddenly, the rest of the evening came back to her, a flurry of weird, disturbing images and emotions: the electric tingling under her fingers; the heart-stopping feeling of someone, or something, really in the room and moving the wooden pointer; fear and fierce exhilaration – the promise of something wildly mysterious just out of reach.

She felt confused and excited and *alive*. For the first time in ages, she couldn't wait to see what happened next.

She sat up with a wild desire to laugh, then forced herself to stop, breathe, and get out of bed as carefully as she could. Lisa didn't move.

Dressed now and reasonably combed, Robin slipped out of Lisa's room and quietly closed the door behind her, clutching a Sartre coffee mug she'd grabbed from Lisa's bookshelf.

She peered down the hall. With the overhead lights still on the fritz and all the doors closed along both sides, the corridor was as dank as if it were midnight. She stood for a moment, letting her eyes adjust to the dark, then moved through the murky hall, descended through the hollow stairwell to the second floor.

The tiny kitchenette was dark, the lights still not functioning. Robin stepped into the room – and pulled up short. Someone was at the counter. She recognized the lithe frame even before Cain turned, holding a Pyrex pot of coffee. His black T-shirt had a graphic of an eyeball dressed in top hat and tails, no doubt from a band Robin would have recognized if she'd been sufficiently hip.

His face brightened slightly, seeing her. "Oh, hey." He extended the pot, offering her some.

"How'd you get it hot?" Robin asked, puzzled.

Cain shrugged, flicked his Zippo lighter with his free hand. "Don't even try to keep me from my coffee."

Robin stepped forward, holding out the Sartre mug for him to pour. When the cup was full, he lifted his eyes, meeting hers. "Any more spooks last night?" he asked, his voice heavy with irony.

She said carelessly, "It stopped after you left. We figure you were doing it all along."

She felt a rush of pleasure that he laughed, startled. "You got me."

Their eyes met again, a moment of surprising heat. Robin looked away quickly, confused, and gulped coffee, scalding the roof of her mouth.

The frisson of attraction was still there as they walked down the main staircase, a little flustered with each other. Unsure of how to talk to Mr. Skeptic about the previous night, Robin kept silent. But then she caught Cain looking at her. They swayed against each other and it felt like electricity crackling between them.

Robin pulled away and spoke abruptly, caffeine and nervousness making her brusque.

"So what's your major, anyway?"

He actually flashed her a smile. "Pre-law – can't you tell?" She found herself relaxing, smiling back. "What's yours?"

"Undeclared." And then she fired back impulsively, "Can't you tell?"

Cain didn't laugh this time, but looked at her so intensely, she had to look away.

They'd reached the bottom of the stairway, and

although Robin had been completely unaware of where they were going, it seemed inevitable that they moved across the hall to the lounge.

They stepped into the arched doorway and both halted, staring. Robin felt her breath knocked out of her.

The room was a shambles, furniture overturned, the couch pushed across the room and tipped on end against the wall, books dumped from the shelves as if a cyclone had spiraled through the room. Robin looked around her, speechless.

In the gray light from the windows, Cain's face was tight. "Someone's playing games."

Robin turned to him, startled. "Who?"

His eyes narrowed. "Smells like frat boy to me."

Robin stiffened, protective of Patrick, but said nothing as she moved slowly into the room. The round table she and Lisa had used last night was still in front of the fireplace, seemingly the only thing in the room that hadn't been tossed. She walked up to look.

The board was centered neatly on the table, with the pointer poised over

Z

Robin gasped, staring down. Cain stepped quickly to her side. She looked at him, stricken. Cain started to shake his head, then something thudded behind them and they both spun.

Patrick stood in the doorway, holding a beer. He stared around at the mess. "Whoa ... "

Cain ground out, "Park it. We know you did it."

Before Robin could protest that she thought no such

79

thing, Patrick was speaking, staring at Cain. "Get out. You didn't?"

Cain laughed humorlessly. "I don't believe this shit."

Patrick spread his arms, the picture of innocence. "Hey, it wasn't me, man. Maybe Marlowe."

"Right. Little Lisa moved all this stuff."

Behind Patrick, Lisa and Martin walked in together. They both stopped still in the doorway, with an almost comic double take as they registered the chaos of the room.

"Oh my God," Lisa breathed.

Patrick turned to her. "Zach left us a present."

Martin looked around, taking in the damage, eyes blinking behind round glasses. Then he looked straight to Patrick.

The implication wasn't lost on Cain. "Yeah, that's what I think, too."

Patrick turned on Cain, pointing at Martin. "It coulda been *him*, you know. Or the two of them together." He waved his hand to include Lisa.

Martin looked to Robin. "You guys didn't do this? It isn't a joke?"

Robin looked at him, then at the others, slowly. "I don't know." They were silent in the dim hush of the room.

Lisa pushed her hair back. "Well, I know. Show them." She nudged Martin – a surprisingly proprietary gesture. Martin took the newspaper from under his arm and unfolded it to the sports section to reveal a headline. He displayed it like an attorney with Exhibit A:

C O R N H U S K E R   R O U T – 2 8 – 1 4

Patrick gaped. "Alabama by fourteen. Fuck me backwards." He grabbed the paper, scanned the article.

Robin was reeling. *We couldn't have known that. Not any of us.*

"Now tell me how we just happened to call that, dude." Lisa gloated.

Cain's face had gone very still. He glanced at Robin sharply, and she looked back, bewildered.

Lisa was already pulling out a chair, seating herself at the table in front of the board. "Okay, Zach. Time to wake up." She looked up at Robin expectantly. Her eyes gleamed in the muddy light.

Patrick looked up from the newspaper, glancing around at the rest of them. "How the hell did someone know that?" His eyes came to rest on Lisa.

Lisa smiled at him, catlike. "*We* didn't. Zachary did."

Cain spoke, his voice hard. "Bullshit."

"Interesting, though, isn't it?" Martin said. "I for one can't think of any logical explanation for any of us knowing those game scores. Which leaves us with two alternatives: Coincidence ..." He paused importantly.

For effect, Robin thought.

"Or ... we actually achieved some kind of precognition. Perhaps through our mutual concentration on the board."

Lisa sat back in her chair and laughed. "We could keep blatantly ignoring the obvious. Or we could just *ask* him. Zachary."

Cain laughed shortly, shaking his head. "It's your game. Go on and play." His glance grazed Robin, and for a moment she thought he would say something more, but he merely walked out through the arched doorway, leaving the four of them in the dim paneled room.

81

"*Robin*," Lisa urged from the table. Robin took a step forward.

"I'll do it," Martin said abruptly, and brushed past Robin to sit across from Lisa. The two reached simultaneously over the board to put their hands on the planchette, and Robin noticed again that they seemed strangely comfortable with each other.

Patrick moved in closer. He caught Robin's eyes for a moment, then looked away.

Lisa pressed her fingertips into the wooden pointer. "Zachary, are you there? We want to talk to you."

The room was silent. Robin found herself holding her breath. The trees outside the tall windows swished in the wind.

But the planchette was motionless under Lisa's and Martin's hands.

"Zachary, did you move the furniture?" Lisa demanded.

The planchette was still over the black letters. Lisa shifted in her chair, wheedled suggestively. "Please won't you come talk to us?"

Nothing.

Robin moved closer to the table, impatient. *It won't work with Martin. He knows that – we saw it last night.*

Lisa looked up at Robin, as if reading her thoughts. Martin looked at the two girls, then stood reluctantly, ceding his seat to Robin.

Robin sat, extended her hands to the pointer.

Lisa met her eyes, pressed her fingers into the wooden piece. "Zachary … "

Beside the table, Martin and Patrick watched, everyone holding their breath.

82

Robin leaned forward slightly, trying to feel ... something. "Zachary ..."

The planchette was still and dead under her fingers. Lisa looked at Robin.

Robin shook her head slightly, spoke to the others. "He's not here."

Martin nodded, looked at the girls, at the board, thoughtfully. "The conditions aren't right. Why?"

Robin took in the other three against the shapes of tumbled furniture. She didn't know how, but suddenly she knew. "Cain. We need everyone."

Chapter 10

The rain poured down monotonously outside. Lakes formed in the lawns of the faded mansions; muddy rivers churned in the footpaths under the drenched and drooping trees.

In the window seat of her room, Robin had a book open on her lap, as if to fool herself that she was studying. But her gaze was fixed on her spiral notebook, where she was doodling a rather romantic sketch of the pale young man from her dream.

She wrote, "Zachary."

She paused for a moment, then wrote the letter Q.

She stared down at it, traced it, trying to remember the rest of the strange word that the board had spelled last night. Qloth? Qiloth?

But the word evaded her. She frowned, then wrote:

The shells?

The shelves?

????

She could feel the icy wind through the glass of the window, scratching at the building to get in. She pulled the comforter closer around her, looked up, brooding.

The wind swirled the trees outside, shaking the branches, bending the old trunks. Robin shivered, disturbed by the violence of it. There was an anger there, an anger at exclusion.

Something interrupted her thoughts, and she turned her head back into the room, suddenly listening.

There was someone in the corridor outside.

She could feel rather than hear at first. Footsteps, muffled by carpet, barely audible ... approaching ... stopping at her door ...

Robin looked at the door, waiting for a knock.

Silence.

Robin tensed. After a moment, she pushed the comforter off her and stood. She moved to the door, reached out—

Something prickled on the back of her neck and she stopped, her fingers inches from the knob. She spoke aloud, wary. "Hello?"

There was no response. She was listening. But it *felt* like someone was there.

Panic tightened her chest. She stood paralyzed, her heart pounding.

She grabbed the knob, twisted it, pulled the door open.

The corridor was empty.

She looked both ways down the dank hall, then slammed the door. Simultaneously, there was a rattling behind her.

She turned with a gasp – to see something slide very fast down the wall on the opposite side and crash to the floor behind Waverly's desk.

Robin stood frozen, her pulse racing, her throat tight with fear.

Dead silence. Nothing moved.

Stop it, she ordered herself. *Something fell off the wall. Just go look.*

She pulled herself together, walked over to the desk. She leaned gingerly on the edge to peer behind, and frowned. She crouched, reaching, and withdrew a small decorative shelf. Above her on the wall, the nail hole gaped in the plaster, the nail lost.

Stupid. Nothing ... You slammed the door, remember? The vibration.

Then she looked at what she held in her hand and her breath stopped. A shelf?

A *shelf.*

"The shelves," she whispered, triumphant.

The lounge was cold and empty and dim. None of them had moved the furniture back into place, and Robin hesitated in the doorway, weirded out by the jumble of upended pieces, silhouettes in the dismal light from the windows.

Who *had* done it? Patrick was the obvious suspect, she had to admit. He was strong enough, and yes, it seemed like him to do it. But Cain was plenty strong, and he'd been so opposed to the whole séance to begin with. He could easily be hazing them – teaching them a lesson.

Lisa you couldn't trust as far as you could throw her, and it was clear she'd do anything at all for attention, but she'd been in bed with Robin the entire night. And Martin was just ... unlikely. Somehow, Robin doubted he could be loose enough to prank them like that.

But even as she thought it, something in the back of her mind countered: *As an experiment, maybe? Some ... psychological test?*

She felt a wave of unease, remembering the books Martin had been studying: *Psychoanalysis and the Occult. Dreams and Telepathy.*

She looked around the wrecked room.

Whoever had done it, it hadn't seemed so sinister when they were all together.

And what if none of *them* had done it?

She shivered, hugging herself. *But that's what you want, isn't it? You want it to be Zachary. You want him to be real.*

A draft stirred her hair, warm, like breath.

She turned sharply, eyes searching the room.

Of course, there was no one.

And then her eyes fell on the built-in bookshelves against the wall.

Several large volumes had been ripped from the bottom shelves and lay scattered on the floor, some face-down and open, pages crushed.

Robin frowned, forced herself to move forward into the room, past the overturned table where Martin had been studying, the scattered candles on the floor, the knocked-over chairs.

She stood above the pile of books and looked up at the shelves they'd fallen from.

Two long shelves of tall, slim leather-bound volumes.

Robin's eyes widened as she realized what they were.

Yearbooks.

There were books tumbled on the floor, open to pages of photos, serious-eyed students in black and white, who looked both younger and older than Robin felt.

But it was one volume on the rug that drew her.

Without even hesitating, Robin stooped for the book

that had fallen facedown and now lay in the middle of a patterned rose. The cover had the date 1920 in cracked gold.

She touched it and felt the same electric charge she'd felt from the planchette.

She opened the cover and in a flash, before she looked down at the page, she knew what she would see.

Chapter 11

Robin stood outside Lisa's room, knocking hard on the door with the moonlit desert scene.

After an eternity, the door swung open. Lisa stood in a camisole and bikini underwear. Her black-rimmed eyes were barely open; she looked half-dead.

Robin held up a yearbook bound with cracked leather, BAIRD LAW SCHOOL 1920 stamped on the cover in gold. "Look." Her face glowed with excitement.

Lisa blinked and squinted at the book, which was open to a full-page black-and-white photo with a dedication: "In Memoriam: ZACHARY PRINCE 1901–1920."

The photo showed a pale young man, startlingly like the one from Robin's dream: broodingly handsome; dark hair and haunting eyes.

Lisa drew an admiring breath. "Oh, Daddy."

Robin's eyes were shining. "He was here. In the law school. He died here – in 1920."

The girls looked at each other, electrified.

Kneeling beside Lisa's bed, the yearbook between them on the coverlet, they looked through the book page by page, scouring for any hint of who Zachary had been. The epitaph below the photo was maddeningly discreet, and vaguely disturbing: "Arise, arise from death, you numberless infinities of souls."

There was no detail of the death, no other photos of Zachary, save a smaller version of the same photo among the other third-year law students. Beneath that photo of Zachary it read "Law Review and Sigma Chi."

"That's what Mendenhall used to be, the Sigma house," Lisa murmured. "So I bet you anything he lived here. He probably died right here in the Hall."

Though it was a long shot, they went to Lisa's laptop and tried Googling him. There were 212,000 matches for Zachary Prince, but none with any connection to Mendenhall or Baird, no 1920 obituaries.

"Damn, damn, damn." Lisa shut down the computer in frustration. "We *have* to find out what happened."

"There'll be old newspapers in the library," Robin offered.

Lisa grimaced. "Which is closed until Monday, of course." She smiled rather wickedly at Robin. "Oh well – we'll just have to ask him."

Now dressed in a raveled sweater that showed purple lace through fraying black cashmere, Lisa pounded on a door in the boys' wing. Robin hovered behind.

Lisa pounded again. Patrick's voice groaned from inside. "Go to hell."

Lisa tried the knob; it turned. She pushed the door open and marched in. Robin followed.

Inside, the walls and shelves were covered with rock posters and concert paraphernalia. Otherwise, the room was surprisingly neat ... almost rigidly so.

Patrick was sprawled in bed, bare-chested, hair mussed. Robin flushed, seeing him. Lisa was unimpressed. "We need you, cowboy," she informed him, and jumped into the bed, bouncing slightly.

"That's what they all say." Patrick pulled her comfortably against him, as if they'd known each other for years. It was an easy intimacy, with none of the charged antagonism of the night before.

Robin stood awkwardly in the door, mortified.

Patrick glanced over at her and lifted the plaid comforter on the other side of him with a lazy smile. "Room for one more ..."

Robin blushed deeper, if that was possible. Lisa flopped the yearbook on Patrick's chest, open to Zachary's picture. "Robin found Zachary."

Patrick stared down at the photo. Robin could see he was unnerved.

"Fuck me ..."

Lisa rolled away from him and stood, kicked the bed imperiously. "Get your ass up and let's play."

She grabbed the yearbook off Patrick, threw a sweatshirt at his head, and pulled Robin out the door.

As the girls headed down the dark corridor outside, Lisa smiled at Robin knowingly. "He likes you, too."

Robin colored. "He's with my roommate."

Lisa shook her head, rippling her mane of hair. "And how high school is that? He's out of the South, away from Daddy ... Miss Nascar is holding on like hell, but he's better than she is and he knows it. Baby doll, that cowboy's looking for the real thing."

She ran ahead down the hall, glanced back with a teasing smile before she ducked around the corner.

Her mood suddenly lifted, Robin ran, too. She caught up to Lisa at another door, where she stood knocking authoritatively.

There was a standard drug-store-issue plastic sign posted on it:

NO MINORS

How Cain, Robin thought, amused. And then she glanced at Lisa, wondering, *How does she know where everyone lives?*

Lisa was already pushing the door open, striding inside. Robin followed, more hesitantly.

Cain lay back on the bed in the dim light from the window, playing an acoustic guitar, an intricate melody. He barely looked up as Lisa strode to the bed.

Robin hovered inside the open door, looked around the room. On the floor-to-ceiling shelves, law books competed with a staggering collection of vinyl and CDs. An electric keyboard and guitar were shoved in one corner. Posters of Malcolm X, Che Guevara, and Johnny Rotten glowered from the walls.

On the bed, Cain was pointedly ignoring the year-book Lisa held open in front of him.

"You found this open on the floor, huh? Right to this picture. Isn't that convenient."

Robin bristled, defensive. "It wasn't open." *But it was set off from the other books. Almost ... positioned*, a voice in her head reminded her. *It could be a setup – someone playing a game ...*

Lisa was speaking impatiently. "Oh, come play with us. You *know* you want to." Lisa leaned over Cain seductively, one knee on the mattress.

Cain didn't budge. He looked up at her with that level gray gaze. "Don't you ever get tired of yourself, Marlowe?"

Lisa's eyes blazed, but she didn't flinch. "Every minute of every day, Jackson."

The two locked eyes for a long moment, a hot, contentious look. Robin felt herself bristling, something twisting in her chest.

Cain shook his head. "Pass." Then he looked directly at Robin. "And I think you should, too."

Robin looked back at him, startled. Before she could respond, or even process, Lisa flared up at him. "Crap out if you want, but don't spoil everyone else's fun."

Cain dropped his eyes to the guitar. "Whatever." He bent over the strings and didn't look at Robin again.

Robin felt her face burning, but Lisa grabbed her arm and pulled her out of the room, slamming the door behind them so hard that the NO MINORS sign fell to the carpet.

But as she dragged Robin toward the stairwell, Lisa was smiling, cheerful − that constant, mercurial shift. "He'll be down," she informed Robin lightly. "Trust me."

They found Martin's room at the very dark end of a third-floor hall. Unlike most of the other student rooms, his door was unadorned by any message boards, posters, or signs.

Then Robin caught sight of a small rectangular metal piece nailed into the door frame just below eye level, almost unnoticeable against the dark wood: a little scroll with Hebrew lettering. The word *mezuzah* flashed through her mind, though she wasn't sure that was right.

Lisa was knocking and knocking. "Martin, we need

93

you. Pretty please? I'll breathe on your glasses ..."

There was no answer. Lisa pressed her ear to the door, listening, then stepped back, shaking her head. She pushed back her hair, defiant. "Come on."

Robin followed Lisa down the main stairs to the lounge. Lisa's face was grimly determined; she hugged the yearbook to her chest like a shield. But some of the energy had gone out of the mission. Privately, Robin had serious doubts about what they could do without the others. There had been something between them the night before. Maybe the sudden, unexpected intimacy, maybe just the drinking and smoking. *But whatever it was, it was all of us.* She was quite sure.

She followed Lisa through the archway of the lounge and almost ran into her as Lisa abruptly halted.

Martin was there, standing over the round table with a legal pad and a pen, looking down at the board, a small figure amid the weirdly tumbled furniture.

Lisa said, "Hey!" loudly, and he jolted, clearly startled to see them, almost flustered at being discovered.

Lisa crossed the carpet to join him in front of the fireplace, blithely unaware of his consternation. "We were just looking for you," she informed him, with that exasperating imperiousness that Robin was beginning to warm to. "We want to do another sitting. You're game, aren't you?"

Martin blinked at her. "Quite. I've been reading up on Ouija boards. There's a good bit of legitimate research on the subject on the Internet." He took off his glasses, gestured at the board like a small professor. "Our experience wasn't unique, you know. It's amazing how many cases of supernormal effects have been reported by reputable people."

Lisa winked at Robin. "*Reputable* people."

Martin put his glasses back on and looked to Robin, a diffident glance. "Something happened between us last night ... the collective focus on the board, possibly the combination of personalities, some link between all of us ..."

Robin was startled to hear what she had just been thinking coming out of Martin's mouth. Behind them, the wind blew a spattering of rain against the windows, like a handful of tiny rocks.

"We achieved some kind of mental communication at least. Possibly precognition, as evidenced by the game scores in the newspaper." Martin glanced at Robin again. "Taken from a psychological perspective, it would make a good subject for a term paper."

"Hate to burst your Freudian bubble," Lisa said loftily. She slapped the yearbook open on the table in front of him.

Martin stared down at the photo of Zachary, clearly taken aback.

"Zachary was as real as you and me. He lived here. He probably died here."

"A ghost?" Martin looked up, not at Lisa, but at Robin. "Surely *you* don't believe that."

Lisa looked offended. "What's your supernormal explanation for the furniture?" She waved around at the shambled contents of the room.

Martin blinked at her in the grayish light. "It's highly likely the furniture was a prank. We can't discount the human element."

It was a perfect deadpan delivery. Robin and Lisa burst into spontaneous laughter. Lisa reached out, tousled Martin's hair with something like affection.

"God, no – not the human element."

As if on cue, Patrick sauntered in, marginally dressed in sweats and a jersey. He yawned, surveyed the room and the others lazily. "What, no food?"

Robin and Lisa looked at each other and collapsed into giggles again. Martin smiled shyly, enjoying the joke. Robin felt a rush of warmth and camaraderie, and found, surprised, that she was on the verge of tears.

Patrick looked around at all of them, then pulled a new bottle of Jack Daniel's from the waistband of his sweats. "Lucky I came prepared."

Lisa stooped to pick up the candles from the floor in the back. She arranged them on the table beside the board and fished in a pocket for a lighter.

Almost automatically, Robin turned and knelt beside the fireplace, reached for logs to make a fire. Patrick hefted the yearbook, flipped through it. "So that's Zach, huh? My man don't talk much like a 1920s ghost, though, does he?"

Lisa rolled her eyes. "What does a 1920s ghost talk like?"

Patrick layered a British accent over his Southern one. "I say, old sport. Ripping good."

Lisa scoffed, "He didn't say he was English."

But as they bickered, Robin thought fleetingly that Patrick was right. There was something off about Zachary's speech patterns. Inconsistent.

Martin spoke impatiently, as if reading her mind. "The point is, it's *not* a ghost. The messages are coming from *us*."

He glanced down at his legal pad, which, Robin could see, was covered in notes.

"The history of the Ouija board is fascinating, really.

The game became quite the rage in the 1920s. The occult movement, with its various forms of mysticism – séances, tarot, ceremonial magic, Kabbalah" – he glanced at Lisa briefly – "had taken off in Europe, and then America, due to the unprecedented number of deaths in World War One: And it was a dark time in general – World War Two already on the horizon, and of course ..." He trailed off, took his glasses off and wiped them.

Robin realized instantly what Martin wasn't saying. *Hitler. The Nazis.* She remembered Martin's reference to his rabbi father. *We all have our ghosts, don't we?*

Martin replaced his glasses on his nose and continued. "Suddenly, a whole generation was desperate to contact deceased loved ones. In fact, this very board dates from 1920."

He pointed to a cluster of Roman numerals beside the BALTIMORE TALKING BOARD imprint.

Robin thought, *1920 again. I wonder—*

But the thought evaporated as Martin continued.

"The spirit board was a rather sophisticated technological innovation for the time. Before the advent of the board, participants in séances attempted to communicate with the 'beyond' through table tipping or tapping." Robin could almost see the quotation marks in the air as he spoke.

"'Spirits' would supposedly rap through the tabletop" – he demonstrated by tapping his knuckles sharply on the table – "which restricted questions to those requiring yes or no answers, or forced querents to count knocks corresponding to numbers of the letters of the alphabet – A was one knock; Z was twenty-six." He rapped a few times – four, five, six – then lifted his hands. "Well, one

97

can only imagine how tedious it must have been, waiting."

Lisa murmured, "Insufferable," but everyone was riveted.

Martin passed his hands over the board like a magician. "But then one Georges Planchette invented the alphabet board and this little piece." He picked up the wooden indicator. "The planchette eliminated the need to count knocks numerically − the board could simply spell out words, or indicate numbers. At the time, an innovation about as revolutionary as the telephone."

Robin noticed that his voice held real admiration. But then Martin turned dismissive.

"Of course, what was really happening was automatism: the subconscious minds of the players guiding them to move the piece to spell out desired answers. Still, there are many accounts of unaccountably precognitive and extrasensory messages, just as we experienced last night." He glanced shyly at Robin, spoke toward her. "Both Freud and Jung attended séances and studied the phenomenon. It's as if the collective concentration on the board somehow heightens perception."

Patrick was already busy rolling a joint on one of the coffee tables. "Well, let's see if ol' Zach can come up with some lottery numbers tonight."

Lisa ignored Patrick, huffed at Martin. "This is all fascinating, Professor, but you're completely ignoring the salient point, which is that we were talking to *Zachary Prince*." She picked up the yearbook, open to Zachary's picture, and shook it at Martin. "He was real. He died here mysteriously" − she mimicked Martin − "in 1920, in fact. And last night, we got him on the *telephone*." She tapped the Ouija board with a crimson nail, then leaned back in her chair, crossed her arms. "Now, tell me that was coming from my mind, or Robin's."

Martin pushed at his glasses. "I don't recall any mention of a Prince—"

"Right, Zachary is just *such* a common name. Must be a coincidence," Lisa shot back.

Martin frowned. "It wouldn't be at all surprising if one of you had heard talk of a student dying – even read the yearbook. It's been here under our noses. It's hardly inconceivable."

Robin suddenly realized Martin was right, and automatism might not have anything to do with it. She hadn't read the yearbook, but Lisa certainly could have. She felt a wave of cold and heat at once, paranoia and humiliation. What if the whole evening really had been an elaborate prank? Plant a Ouija board in the game cabinet, pretend to summon a long-dead student, leave the yearbook to back up the story. For all Robin knew, they were all in on it but her ...

Not Cain, though, her mind countered instantly.

And what about the game scores, the newspaper confirming them this morning? Surely that was proof—

Unless the newspaper had somehow been faked.

The thought sent another wave of paranoia through her, a feeling as shaky as nausea.

But why? Why would they do it?

Robin glanced to Patrick, studied him furtively. Though he was sprawled quite nonchalantly on the couch, he was watching Martin and Lisa intently.

He shifted his eyes toward Robin, caught her watching. The look he gave her was veiled, unreadable.

Martin was speaking loftily to Lisa. "At any rate, we

99

have all night to test the theory and——"

He stopped mid-sentence, frowned around the room as if he'd misplaced something. "Where's Jackson? We need to replicate the conditions."

Lisa fished in a pocket for a cigarette, smiled secretly. "He'll be down."

Patrick lounged back on the couch and fired up the joint. Everyone looked toward him; he lifted his hands. "I'm replicating the conditions."

Martin nodded. "By all means. The altered perception probably contributed to the overall experience."

Patrick grinned, exhaled. "It sure as hell contributed to mine." He extended the joint to Lisa, who took it, put it to her lips for an appreciative drag.

Martin continued. *Almost manic*, Robin thought. "Atmosphere is a huge factor in the efficacy of a seance. We had all the conditions aligned for us last night – the storm, the power outage, the fire ..."

Caught up in her inner tumult, Robin had forgotten the fire she'd started to build. Now Martin noticed the unlighted logs in the fireplace. He reached for Lisa's lighter and knelt rather awkwardly on the hearth beside Robin, sparked the lighter and ignited the newsprint between the logs. Flames licked up the paper, casting orange light on his face.

There was actually something attractive about him, Robin decided: the way he came alive when he was interested in a subject, the take-charge confidence he'd been showing all evening.

Martin turned beside her, meeting her eyes. Robin looked away quickly, flustered.

A voice came suddenly from the doorway, raised in irritation. "Okay, just stop it. It's not funny."

100

They all turned. Cain stood under the archway, looking frazzled. The others looked around at one another, mystified. Cain's voice grated in annoyance. "The pounding? On the pipes?"

Patrick sat up from the couch. "We all've been here in plain sight of each other. Nobody's been doin' any pounding."

Cain looked to Robin for confirmation. Robin nodded, unable to speak.

Martin rose from the hearth, brushed soot off his hands. "What exactly were you hearing?"

Cain glanced back at Robin, then to Martin. "In the ceiling. Loud. Rapping. Knocking—"

Patrick raised his eyebrows at Martin. "Funny, didn't you just say spirits communicated through knocking?"

Lisa's voice came suddenly from the table, breathless. "You guys—"

They all looked over. The planchette was moving under her hands.

Her eyes were wide. "He's here."

Robin felt a jolt of excitement, mixed with unease, doubt, a flood of paranoia again. A prank? A ghost? What were they doing?

Lisa looked up at her from the slowly circling pointer – and under the excitement, there was something helpless, even a little frightened in her eyes.

Robin bit her lips. *Go*, she told herself. *Just go back upstairs* now.

And then the longing to be part of something, something extraordinary, won out.

She sat abruptly across from Lisa, reached out to the moving planchette. Touching it was like an electric shock – there was something so clearly alive there, her breath stopped in her throat. She looked at Lisa in disbelief. Lisa met her eyes, nodded. She felt it, too.

In the doorway, Cain made an exasperated sound. "Oh Christ." He turned to leave.

The planchette suddenly jumped, spelling quickly, urgently. Robin stared down at the unfamiliar letters. Lisa sounded them out one by one under her breath, groping at the words. Latin, Robin realized. Lisa spoke the whole sentence out.

EVIDENTIA   EXCULPARE COUNSELOR ?

Cain froze in the doorway.

Robin wondered about the phrase. *A legal term? Something about evidence?* She remembered that Zachary had been studying law, too.

Patrick snapped his fingers at Cain impatiently. "Well? What's it mean?"

Cain glanced at him. "Exonerating evidence. I was writing a paper about it – just now." He looked at Lisa again with blistering suspicion.

She stared back at Cain defiantly. "*He* said it. I didn't."

Martin spoke up, more to himself than the others. "Telepathy again."

He reached for his legal pad, made a note.

Lisa pressed her fingertips into the pointer, raised her voice. "Zachary, was that you knocking?"

There was a puff and whoosh and a rush of orange light ... as a log caught fire in the hearth. Everyone turned toward it, startled.

Then the indicator leapt to life. Robin could feel the

urgent tug under her hands. Much faster than the night before, and more confident. Almost – cocky.

DID   YOU   MISS   ME
CHILDREN ?

Robin's eyes widened; she felt a prickling on her neck. Lisa looked at her from across the board. Robin leaned forward, intense. "Are you Zachary Prince, who died here in 1920?"

The pointer was still for a moment, then spelled more slowly.

ARISE   ARISE   FROM   DEATH

"That's the inscription from the yearbook," Lisa said softly to the others.

Robin felt a deep chill. There was something wrong here, a creepiness under her fingers, almost heat, like anger. How different it felt from the playful teasing of the night before.

"Zachary, *how* did you die?" Lisa asked.

Robin felt another shock of heat under her fingers as the pointer moved quickly.

BURNED

Robin flinched, and saw Patrick grimace. "That's harsh."

Martin stepped abruptly forward, stared down at the table. He directed his voice toward the board.

"If you're a ghost, what *is* a ghost?"

The pointer stopped, still now.

103

Robin couldn't feel a thing under her fingers. She looked across at Lisa.

Martin spoke again, more demanding. "*Explain* what you are."

The pointer was completely still.

Martin leaned over the board, agitated. "Why won't you talk to me?"

Shadows danced on the walls from the firelight; then the pointer started to move. Random, teasing circles. Finally, it slid quickly from letter to letter.

A S K   N I C E L Y

Martin colored. Cain looked sharply at Lisa, then at Robin. Robin started to shake her head.

Martin cleared his throat, forced himself to speak politely. "I ... would like to talk to you, please."

Robin flinched as the pointer jerked to life, spelling almost violently.

C R A W L

Martin paled, stunned.

Robin gasped, pulled her hands off the pointer.

Cain advanced on the table. "That's enough, Marlowe."

Lisa stiffened. "I'm not—"

"I know you're doing it."

"*I fucking am not.*" Lisa shoved the board away from her.

"She's not," Robin protested.

Silence fell in the room. The logs snapped in the fireplace as flames ate at the logs. Patrick and Cain circled the shadows around the table, the board.

Robin bit her nails, stared down at the black letters, focused in on the burn marks along the edge of the board. Charred. There was something ominous about the black now, something that didn't make sense.

Stop now, she told herself. *I don't like this game.*

Cain stopped across from her, met her her eyes. He seemed about to say something.

Robin suddenly put her hands back on the indicator. Lisa looked at her, slowly reached out to the wooden piece. A garnet in one of her rings caught the light, glowed briefly like a drop of blood.

Robin drew a breath and asked tightly, "Zachary, why are you angry at Martin?"

The pointer circled, slid almost sullenly from letter to letter. Lisa sounded the words out, frowning.

A D O N   O L A M

Robin and Lisa looked across at each other, then at Martin. He stared down at the board as if mesmerized.

"What does that—" Robin began.

The planchette jerked under their hands, scraping violently across the board. Robin and Lisa could barely hold on.

A S K   H I S   C O C K S U C K I N G M A S T E R   O F   T H E   U N I V E R S E

Lisa gasped and stood, pushing herself away from the table. Robin sat frozen, staring down at the board. Martin's face was very still.

"Master of the Universe? Is this a video game now? What the fuck ..." Patrick looked around, bewildered.

"God. It means God." Martin pulled back Lisa's chair and sat heavily down, put his hands on the indicator and stared across at Robin. "Let's go."

Robin jolted, startled by his vehemence.

Cain stepped closer to the table, behind Robin. "I don't think—"

Martin glared at Robin, eyes burning. "Let's go."

Transfixed, she slowly extended her hands to the planchette. Her fingers touched Martin's cold ones. Martin spoke through clenched teeth, unfamiliar, grating syllables: "*Haim ata ru – ach o Qlippah?*"

The pointer jumped violently under Robin's hands and flew off the table, clattered to the stone hearth.

"*Shit*," Patrick yelped, jolting back.

Robin found she was standing – she'd jumped up so quickly, she hadn't realized she was on her feet. Everyone was standing except for Martin, all of them frozen in disbelief.

Cain whipped around toward Martin. His voice was strangled. "What the fuck did you say?"

Martin sat back against his chair. He spoke evenly, his face like alabaster in the flickering light. "I said, What are you, you fuck?"

He stood up with eerie calm, crossed to pick up the pointer from the hearth. He put it back on the board and sat, looked up at Robin intensely. "Come on."

Cain moved forward. "No. That's enough. You're too into it."

Martin nearly shouted over him. "Come on."

Robin flinched, blinked back tears, but she felt for the back of the chair and sat, reached to the pointer.

Cain spoke low behind her. "You don't have to."

Martin's voice cut through his. "What are you?" he

demanded of the air. All scientific detachment was gone; he'd spoken as if to a real person. He pushed his fingers into the pointer, stared down at the board as if he were alone in the room.

Robin touched the pointer with her fingertips. Immediately, the piece began to move. Robin recoiled. There was something different there, not a new energy, but a change in the energy. *So much ... loathing. Malice. Fury.* The malevolence fairly crackled through her fingers.

But the words the pointer spelled were slow, almost teasing.

WOULDNT   YOU   LIKE   TO   KNOW   ?

Martin jerked forward, his voice raised. "*What are you?*" The planchette scraped, swift and violent, across the board.

ASK   YOUR   PORK   LOVING   KIKE   GOD

Robin gasped and pulled her hands away from the planchette. She felt rather than saw Cain move forward behind her; then his hands were gripping her shoulders. Lisa was hugging herself from the edge of the shadows.

Martin pressed his fingers into the wood, white-faced and shouting. "I'm asking *you*. Tell me what you are!"

Everyone was still. The indicator slowly circled under Martin's hands.

Robin watched, paralyzed, squeezing her hands together on her thighs, subliminally aware of Cain's hands on her shoulders. She suddenly thought, with clarity for the first time, *Lisa wasn't moving it. It wasn't ever any of us. Then, oh God ... what is it?*

The letters appeared inexorably under the cut circle of the pointer.

$$TELL \quad ?$$
$$OR$$

Robin could feel the others craning forward, waiting, mesmerized, as the pointer's circles diminished to barely a hover. Then a sudden burst of letters.

$$SHOW \quad ?$$

Robin stared at the board in disbelief, the letters, the word echoing in her mind. No one was speaking the words aloud now; they were all just staring down in numb silence. She had just enough time to wonder, *Show us what? How—*

Martin commanded, "Show us."

Cain spoke instantly: "No—"

The planchette scraped violently across the letters.

$$YOU \quad WANT \quad TO \quad KNOW \quad ME$$
$$TAKE \quad ME \quad IN$$
$$OPEN \quad WIDE$$

In the hearth, the fireplace logs cracked open, showering sparks upward. All five of them spun toward the fire, freaked.

Robin caught movement out of the corner of her eye and glanced up at the mirror above the fireplace.

In the dark glass she saw a pale shape rushing forward, as if coming from a long distance, a tunnel. There was no time to scream, no time to react ... All she had was a glimpse and then—

The mirror shattered.

Lisa and Robin screamed. All five of them jumped back as ugly glass spears shot from the mantel, exploding outward, shining briefly in the air, and then crashing on the floor.

No one moved. All five stood frozen, stunned, suspended in shock.

Patrick gasped out weakly, "Motherfucking shit."

Robin's heart was pounding in her chest. She could hear Martin breathing shallowly beside her, blinking behind his glasses. The room was utterly silent, the shadows long on the wall. Glass shards like knives littered the carpet, glittering in the firelight.

Cain was the first to move. He forced himself forward to the fireplace, stepping carefully around the razor-sharp glass. He reached out (Robin almost called out *"Don't!"* but could not make herself speak) and put his hand flat against the pale circle of wall where the mirror had been.

"It's hot," he said. His voice was far away, as if he were in a trance. "Fire must have ... heated the mirror and it broke."

Lisa turned on him, nearly shrieking. "What planet are you on? It just *happened* to *shatter*? At that precise moment? Gosh and gollee yes – happens every day."

Martin spoke, his voice dry, also sounding very far away. *Or is that me?* Robin wondered. *Am I the one who's far away?*

"Hysteria," he said, almost to himself.

Lisa went wild. "Don't you fucking tell me I'm hysterical!"

Martin pointed at the broken mirror, cold and surreally calm. "That. Hysteria. We made it happen. I was reading accounts of similar occurrences under conditions of extreme psychological stress ...

His voice was flat, monotonous. But Robin noted with distant but crystalline clarity that there was an undertone there: excitement.

Patrick laughed uneasily, big and hulking in the half-light. "We all were pretty ... jacked up." Beside him, Lisa looked dazed, disconnected, shivering. Patrick reached out, kneaded the back of her neck with a big hand. Robin felt a stab of jealousy, then a fragment of a rational thought. *He's used to hysteria. Because of Waverly.*

Shadows crawled up the walls around them.

Robin heard herself speaking from a long distance. "I saw something in the mirror. Just before ..."

Everyone looked at her in the dark, silent room.

"A shape ... it was so fast ... like something coming this way."

The others stood, looking at her almost thoughtfully. They did not speak, perhaps processing. She almost thought they hadn't heard. The candles flickered, and the logs hissed as they rolled with flames. *We're in shock, aren't we?* Robin thought. *That's why everything feels so frozen and far away.*

Cain finally spoke. "Probably just the mirror bending before it cracked." He nodded to himself slightly – Robin was sure he wasn't aware of doing it – convincing himself.

Patrick put an arm around Robin. His arm was heavy,

110

and warm, and real. She leaned into him hungrily, feeling her whole body against his. To the side of her she saw Cain turn away from them, but the body warmth, the heat of Patrick's blood, the sound of his heart beating, the life of him, that was all she could care about.

Martin was speaking, his voice sounding detached from his body. "What were we all thinking about just before it happened?"

The others looked at him. Robin felt Patrick shift and was childishly irritated at the intrusion. Whatever Martin was getting at, she wanted no part of it. She only wanted to crawl inside Patrick and curl up and never come out.

Martin looked around at all of them, insistent. "I think we should talk about it, while it's still fresh in our minds."

Robin felt Patrick turn completely from her. He towered over Martin, who seemed half his size. "Are you crazy? After the way it went off on you?"

Cain turned on Patrick, the anger leaping from one to the other, electrifying the room. "And who was that coming from?"

Patrick whirled on Cain. "Say what?"

Cain faced him, hands clenched at his sides. "Whose subconscious was it tapping? Sounded like right-wing frat-boy bullshit to me."

Their shadows loomed on the wall as the two advanced on each other, voices rising.

"You calling me out, freak?"

"I'm calling what I see, asshole."

Robin suddenly found herself back in her own body, as if jerking awake from a too-real dream. She stepped quickly between Patrick and Cain.

"*Stop it.* It's bad enough, isn't it?"

Cain and Patrick faced off tensely, glaring at each other over Robin's head. The air crackled between them.

But then Cain stepped back.

Robin breathed an inaudible sigh of relief, and felt a stab of disappointment that it had not been Patrick to step down.

"Let's all just ... leave it. Get some sleep," Cain muttered, glancing away from Robin.

Nobody moved.

The wind gusted outside, pushing at the windows, like an animal wanting in.

Lisa's voice was flat, dead certain. "No way am I going anywhere alone."

And Robin knew it was not enough this time for the two of them to stay together for moral support. Two girls were no match for whatever she'd seen in the mirror.

The five of them looked around at one another in the firelight.

"We could stay down here."

Everyone turned to Martin, startled. He glanced at Robin. "Bring some bedding down ..." His eyes indicated the floor, where the glass shards still glittered like daggers.

There was wonder in Patrick's face as he looked at the smaller boy. "You're way into it, aren't you? You're just itching for something to happen."

Martin stared back at Patrick. "Aren't you?"

Robin tensed at the challenge. Patrick bristled. The two boys stared at each other, Patrick big and hulking, Martin small but grimly determined.

112

Cain shook his head, disgusted, and started for the doorway to the hall.

Patrick suddenly called out after him. "Good luck with those pipes, dude."

Cain stopped in the arch of the door, turned slowly.

The five looked at one another again, not moving.

Chapter 12

She was dreaming ... of chaos and fire ... blistering, unbearable light, filling her, scorching her. She screamed with her entire being ...

And exploded, shattering into a million pieces.

Then darkness and the iciest cold. Cast out ... cast off ... she had never felt so abandoned ... so completely alone. Nothingness around her ... howling wind ... howling rage.

My body ... where is my body?

Her discarnate being shuddered with a cry of fury ...

Robin's eyes flew open at the sound of a gasp. She bolted up to a sitting position.

She was in the lounge. A few dying red coals in the hearth illuminated sleeping shapes crashed out on the floor. Robin remembered dragging the mattresses down from the boys' floor, sweeping up the pieces of mirror as best they could, pushing the shards with the janitor's broom into a corner far away from them.

She shuddered through her entire body. *Cold. So cold ...* Her teeth began to chatter.

Something moved in the dark.

Robin twisted around in terror and saw that Patrick and Lisa were wide awake, sitting up beside her. Robin caught her breath, whispered into the shadows. "What is it?"

Patrick swallowed. 'I heard ... somethin'." He looked as disoriented as she felt – uneasy, still surfacing from sleep.

Lisa's teeth were chattering, too; her eyes were wide, glistening in the dark. "I felt something. On top of me. I'm scared. I mean ... really scared."

Robin could barely speak. She forced out "I know," and took in a shallow breath.

Then she stiffened, staring in front of her. Her breath was showing in the air, as if the room were freezing.

Patrick and Lisa were staring at the air in front of her, and she knew they saw it, too.

Lisa gasped out, "God ... what's going on?" Her words came in frosty puffs.

Robin reached out and clasped Lisa's hand, felt her riveted with pure terror.

A soft banging started, like the wind slamming shutters. The three of them went rigid, listening through the shadows.

Suddenly, a shape rose up in the dark in front of them.

Robin flinched back; Patrick jumped.

Then Robin recognized the lean, tensile strength of the body, realized it was Cain, sitting up from his mattress, his hair mussed from sleep. She felt the others relax slightly as they identified him, too.

He lifted his eyes toward the soft banging, whispered into the dark, "It's a window ... I think." He did not sound entirely convinced.

Patrick spoke through stiff lips. "Jesus ... it's freezing." His eyes were glazed; he swallowed through a dry throat. Robin wanted to reach for his hand as she'd reached for Lisa's, but she felt enveloped in a drowsy, almost drugged paralysis.

Lisa whispered, and her words made Robin's blood run cold. "I think ... I think there's something here." She was staring toward the fireplace, her eyes wide as saucers.

Robin turned her head reluctantly, not wanting to see, but compelled.

Above the glowing bed of coals, the smoke in the fireplace was curling strangely, more like the spiral patterns of cigarette smoke than wood smoke. Then as they all watched, mesmerized, something seemed to breathe through the smoke ... long, deep breaths.

All four were frozen in terror in the murky darkness.

Patrick choked out a strangled sound. "I'm out of here."

But he didn't move. *Can't*, Robin thought. *None of us can ...*

And then she thought, *Martin.*

With great effort, she turned her head toward the last mattress – and gasped at the sight of Martin's sleeping form.

The pieces of broken mirror stood on edge around Martin's head, the shards arranged to point at him like a halo of daggers, as if the shattered pieces had assumed malevolent life and crept up on him, poised to kill.

Robin stared, numb. Martin opened his eyes. He seemed to sense her attention and started automatically to reach for his glasses.

Robin cried out, "*No!*"

116

The panic in her voice froze him. He stared up through the shadows.

Cain spoke forcefully, a command. "Don't turn your head. Just sit straight up."

Martin raised his head from the mattress stiffly, carefully, nearsighted eyes blinking.

Robin grabbed his hand and pulled him forward, away from the glass. Cain found his glasses on the carpet and put them in his hand. Martin fumbled the spectacles on and stared down at the glass spears in dazed incomprehension.

Cain twisted around to the others, his voice tight. "Joke's over. This is bullshit." He glared at Patrick. "Someone's a sick fuck, and I think it's you."

"That's it, asshole." Patrick lunged at Cain, and suddenly they were grappling, throwing punches.

Lisa and Robin cried out, grabbed at Patrick and Cain; trying to pull them apart.

The rappings started again, as if titillated by the sudden violence. Clearly not a window this time, but a wave of sharp knocking, coming from the ceiling, from within the very walls.

Cain and Patrick froze mid-struggle, looking up and around them.

The pounding grew sharper, louder, a rising tide, building, thundering, shaking the walls. Someone started to scream; Robin thought it might have been her. She could barely hear herself think.

Cain suddenly lunged for the table, flung himself up on his knees, reaching for the board. Robin had no idea what he was doing, but beside her, Martin cried out, "*No!*"

Cain twisted to the fire and threw the board on the

117

glowing embers.

All around them, the rappings pounded in a frenzy. Now Lisa and Robin both were screaming.

On the coals, the board burst into flame.

And suddenly, everything stopped.

Dead silence.

The five of them sat frozen, staring into the fire as the yellow flames rolled, burning the board to black.

Chapter 13

Hours of eternity later, the first streaks of gray dawn showed through the windows.

Robin, Martin, and Cain huddled in blankets. Unable to sleep, they had forayed, hands linked to belts as if on an Arctic expedition, to the closet the Hall residents called the downstairs kitchen to make coffee, stopping at the bathroom to use it one by one, door cracked open and the others on guard outside.

Now they sat with hands wrapped around mugs, drinking in silence, while Lisa and Patrick dozed beside them in the murky gray light.

Somewhere a door slammed and they all jumped. Lisa and Patrick bolted out of sleep, freaked.

They all huddled, frozen, listening. Robin's blood turned to ice at a rattling, dragging sound in the hall.

Lisa whispered, terrified, "No ..."

They all whirled at the sense of movement behind.

A stocking-capped stoner stood in the arched entrance of the lounge. Robin recognized him from the third-floor boys' wing. Behind him, another stoner in striped jacket and comically identical stocking cap

119

hauled a suitcase, its broken wheels rattling.

The stoners looked around the lounge, taking in the bedding, the overturned furniture, the five students, huddled in blankets, hollow-eyed and haunted, pale as ghosts.

One of the stoners laughed uneasily. "Whoa ... musta been some party."

Patrick managed a bleak smile. "Yeah. Some party."

Robin, Cain, Patrick, Lisa, and Martin all started to collect their bedding.

They did it in silence, avoiding one another's eyes.

Chapter 14

And the rest of the weekend could not have been more ordinary. Residents began to trickle in early Sunday morning, becoming an unstoppable tide. There were midterms to study for, after all, and perhaps there were others who were glad enough to cut the family visit short.

By noon that cloudy day, doors were standing open all over the Hall, music blasting again, residents visiting, making sandwiches out of leftover turkey, passing around foil-wrapped care packages of pumpkin loaf and gingerbread cookies while they moaned about pounds gained, nursed hangovers, and visibly started to panic about term papers and exams.

Back in her room, Robin swallowed two of Waverly's Valium before returning the bottle to the bottom drawer, then slept a black sleep until six that evening, when she bolted up in terror at the sound of her door slamming open.

Waverly breezed in, one of her signature thoughtless entrances. She turned all the lights on full and proceed- ed to fuss about the room, pulling open drawers and unpacking prissily and noisily, with appalling disregard for her roommate.

Robin lay back on her pillows, barely able to move. She was aware through her depressant haze that Waverly would think Patrick was still out of town, and that Patrick would go to pains to make her think he had been. At least Robin wouldn't be alone that night. And for the first time in their short acquaintance, Robin was painfully glad of her roommate's presence. Surely nothing mysterious or out of the ordinary would dare happen around Waverly.

Strangely comforted, she drifted back into a drugged and troubled sleep.

Late that night, when the rooms went dark and all the rest of the Hall slept, two lights were still on.

One was a solitary desk lamp, in a dim room lined with bookshelves along every available inch of wall space. There were no other adornments – not a poster on a closet, not a rug on the floor. The bed was unmade and there was a pall in the room, the numbness of loneliness.

Martin sat at his desk, surrounded by uneven piles of books. His laptop was open and signed on to the Net, but he seemed unaware of anything in front of him; he merely stared into space.

Abruptly, he stood and crossed to his bed. He knelt, reached underneath, and dragged out a suitcase. He un- zipped the brown vinyl flap and looked down at the con- tents. After a long moment, he removed several leather- bound books with gilt Hebrew lettering on the covers.

He seemed to brace himself before he lifted one onto the bed and opened the cover.

*

The other light hung from a cord that surely had never passed an electrician's inspection. The single bare bulb dimly illuminated the basement.

The long, low-ceilinged room was a horror – movie dream, a claustrophobic maze of stacked furniture and metal utility shelves and twisted pipes.

A shadowy figure moved stealthily through the crooked aisles.

There was a sudden hiss and clanging just to the right.

The shadow jumped back – then Cain relaxed as he made out the shape of the old boiler. He crossed to it, knelt to open the control box, studying the gauges inside.

Then his eyes fell on the floor beside him. He frowned, reached out to pick something up off the concrete.

A cold smile creased his lips as he stared down at the object in his hand.

Chapter 15

By Monday, Mendenhall was as full and boisterous as ever, bearing little resemblance to the endless and haunted halls that the five of them had inhabited over the weekend.

The maelstrom of school descended, spiked by the heightened anxiety of midterms. Students studied everywhere, huddled alone in corners with piles of books, gathered in nervously chattering groups at every available table.

Everything returned to normal – except Robin. Instead of sleepwalking through her days under a dark cloud, she was wide-awake.

Somehow the terror of the haunting had receded and she was left with an overwhelming feeling of, yes, excitement, and impatience to know more. No longer envious of groups and pairs of students, she hurried through the halls, flushed and light-headed with her secret. Finally, she belonged to something bigger – something almost unbearably strange and fascinating. In fact, she could think of little else. If not for a dreaded biology midterm that afternoon, she would have gone to the library the very first morning.

Now, one midterm down, curled up in her room with *Ego and Id*, her mind kept wandering back to the long weekend, the board, the veering, delirious, almost sexual sense of being completely out of control. The tug of ... *something* ... responding under her hands.

And the impossible shatter of glass.

She shivered, but not exactly from fear.

Zachary was baffling. From 1920, but as Cain had said, pretty hip for a ghost. Lonely and charming. Sensitive and scathing. Intuitive and playful – and then the vicious fury at Martin, for no good reason.

There was a mystery here, and it tantalized her.

She thought of the sensitive young man in the yearbook (now concealed under her bed, threatened by dust mites but safe from Waverly's prying eyes). Surely there was nothing monstrous in that face. Maybe the scary things, the lashing out, were coming out of his pain. He'd died suddenly, horribly; he was confused, frightened, lost, angry. And he, this lost spirit, had been reaching out to them, to her.

But the anti-Semitism, her mind reminded her. *Those horrible things he said to Martin.*

It seemed unlike him, whoever he was.

But it was part of that whole time, the twenties—

She realized immediately, ashamed, how hollow that rationalization was.

It was vile, no matter how you looked at it.

Nothing good could possibly come from that.

Her eyes fell on her open notebook, and a phrase from Professor Lister's lecture leapt out at her: "Do our demons come from without, or within us?"

She bit her lip, looked quickly away from the words –

then realized that across the room, Waverly was turned around in her desk chair, watching her with a narrow blue gaze.

"What did you do around here for three days?" she demanded, obviously suspecting more than studying.

Robin looked her straight in the eyes. "Talked to ghosts," she said lightly.

Waverly stared at her, then grabbed her overnight bag from the closet and stormed out of the room, slamming the door behind her against Robin's laugh.

Robin almost went to the library that minute, but then a shutter banged against the window and a spike of fear shot through her – a memory of the rapping, and her own screams.

She shivered, and then went back to Freud.

But the longing continued.

She looked for the others, making needless trips to the laundry and the Coke machine, hoping to run into them, but they seemed to have melted back into the woodwork like whatever phantom they had been talking to.

Then on a blustery Wednesday, she was walking through the maples of east campus in the icy and intrusive wind. The sky through the branches roiled with dark clouds; the wind pushed at her, half-lifted her. Every step was like trying to balance against an invisible, chaotic power. But what she felt was exhilaration, anticipation. She stopped to catch her breath on the bridge over the swollen creek, leaned against the wall with her hair whipping around her, and found herself staring up at the weathered stones of Moses Hall, the philosophy building.

Cain stood on an upper balcony. He was smoking,

126

staring off at the masses of dark clouds over the hills, completely unaware of anything below.

Then he looked down, right at her. Her heart leapt, and she saw him start. Their eyes locked across the distance ... electric, and real.

So it did happen. And it's not over, she realized. *Not by a long shot.*

The thought was a shiver of excitement and unease.

Chapter 16

The clock radio buzzed her awake. She had been dreaming of Zachary: she'd been running in the halls, trying to find him, hearing him call her name ...

She settled back on her pillow, thinking back on the dream. It hadn't been scary, she decided. In fact, it wasn't an unpleasant feeling at all.

The clock buzzed again and she remembered with dismay that her Ancient Civilizations midterm was that morning.

She threw on clothes she'd left on the floor the night before and grabbed a portable plastic coffee mug along with her backpack.

She left her floor and hurried down a dark set of back stairs that led toward the second-floor kitchenette. Near the bottom of the narrow stairs, she heard feminine voices from below, raised in a fight. One was shrill, with an unmistakable Southern accent.

"I know y'all were up to something while I was gone ..."

Robin halted in the stairway door. In the kitchenette, Waverly held the brimming Pyrex coffeepot. Her pert features were twisted in a lethal fury; she advanced on Lisa, who leaned against the counter, looking sleepless and drugged. "You cross me, you bitch, and I'll rip your cocksucking tongue out."

Lisa laughed; her voice had a dangerous edge. "And get blood on that little *ensemble*? Not in this lifetime—"

Robin watched in fascination. She could almost feel the animosity rolling off them in waves. Waverly noticed Robin standing in the doorway, and her voice jumped up an octave. "And what are *you* looking at?"

Simultaneously, Lisa turned away, sick of it. "Do the world a favor and drop dead."

And as their voices crossed in mutual malice, the coffeepot shattered in Waverly's hand.

Waverly jumped back to avoid the splash of scalding liquid, but too late. Her silky pink sweater was drenched. She stood speechless, with just the brown plastic handle of the pot clutched in her fingers. All three girls were frozen. Robin's eyes locked with Lisa's. Zachary's name hovered in the air, unspoken between them.

Then Waverly started to screech, holding out her coffee-stained sweater. "*Goddamn* it. This is Nicole Farhi. It's ruined!"

Lisa started to laugh, but there was an edge of hysteria underneath. She bolted from the kitchen, running away down the hall, leaving Robin, wondering, and Waverly, wet and ranting, behind.

Robin's mind kept returning to the incident as she sat taking her Ancient Civilizations midterm in an arena-seated lecture hall. She replayed it again and again: the coffeepot in Waverly's hand, the tension in the room, the sharp cracking, and the sudden explosion of glass. The energy had been the same as in the séances, like static electricity between her and Lisa, before the pot shattered. And unnervingly reminiscent of her dream that night of her own body shattering.

She was certain it had been Zachary. He was still here.

She stole a look back at Patrick, who was sitting rows away from her in the sea of silent students, always bigger and blonder than she remembered. Ever since the midterm had been distributed, he had been sitting without writing, deathly pale, just staring down at the page of essay questions.

Robin felt her stomach twist in sympathy. She knew he needed this grade to keep his football scholarship. If only he had come to her, she could have helped him study, drilled him on the possible questions.

But there was nothing to be done now. She sent him a silent wish for inspiration and forced her attention back to her own test.

A little while later, she glanced up from an essay comparing and contrasting creation myths.

On the other side of the room, Patrick was bent over his blue book in the awkward curl of the left-hander, writing very quickly, his big hand almost flying across the page.

Robin watched him a beat, surprised. Patrick looked up suddenly, straight at her. His eyes were startlingly blank. He stared toward her, not seeming to see her, and Robin jolted. His hand was continuing to write, as if divorced from his body. Robin stared for a moment, then turned quickly away, chilled.

When she glanced back again, Patrick was bent over

his blue book again, writing in a continuous, uninter-
rupted flow.

She found the Mendenhall lounge deserted; apparently
the Hall's residents were too freaked out by midterms
even to zone out to TV. The shadowy groupings of
furniture again reminded her of a stage set, waiting for
the players.

Her gaze went to the fireplace. The hearth was clean;
the shattered mirror had been replaced by a square
modern thing that clashed with the ornate Victoriana of
the room. Either the powers that be had attributed the
breakage to the storm or the Housing Office, out of long
experience, had decided not to bother tracking down
the vandals.

Robin stood in the drafty room on the cabbage-rose
carpet and spoke aloud. "Zachary?"

She closed her eyes, held her breath.

The cold air enveloped her. She strained through the
silence to hear, feel – anything.

Finally, she opened her eyes. The lounge seemed
dreary, dusty, and perfectly, obtusely normal. Not a
trace of whatever had been with them over their long,
lost weekend.

So why was she shivering?

She looked toward the bookshelves, the yearbooks
returned to a neat line. She remained looking toward
them for a long time.

Outside the door of her room, she listened for a good
minute before she slid her key into the lock and twisted
the doorknob cautiously.

The room was blessedly empty.

She turned toward her bed ... and gasped.

The yearbook lay out in plain view on the rug beside her bed, open to the black-and-white photo of Zachary.

Fury at Waverly swept through Robin. *How dare she?*

She stooped to pick up the book.

Her hand brushed the leather cover and she gasped again, pulling the hand back, clutching her fingers closed. She'd been shocked – a crackle, like static electricity.

She was suddenly certain that Waverly had not moved the book at all.

She let herself remember for a moment the terror of that night – Zachary's desperate and inexorable presence. Such fury and ... despair. So tormented. Seemingly trapped for eternity in the agony of his death.

But when she looked down at the photo, she felt again the twist in her stomach, the ache of longing and companionship. The haunted young man ... handsome, sensitive, diffident ... there was no anger or violence there.

He was lost – as lost as the rest of them.

And he was reaching out to her.

Chapter 17

The sky swirled with turbulent clouds outside the cathedral windows in the college library.

Robin walked through the labyrinthine stacks of the periodicals archives, her eyes running along the years listed on the bound spines of old magazines – 1950, 1949, 1948 – a feeling eerily like going backward in time. She passed the thirties, moved through the twenties, thought faintly of Gatsby and flappers and stock market disasters.

And Hitler. "A dark time in general," Martin had said.

She halted at 1920, the date in cracked gilt on a wide, crumbling spine.

She stepped to the shelf, pulled out the thick book of bound yellowed news journals.

In the soporific quiet of a study carrel, she pored over old school newspapers with photos of solemn jocks with slicked-back hair and baggy uniforms; ads for soaps that promised God-like cleanliness, for bottled study-aid tonics that might as well have been labeled "cocaine"; news of war, of students enlisting, shipped overseas. The black-and-white pages had turned sepia, fragile; the musty smell was a sense memory of a time she'd never lived.

She carefully turned another delicate page, and stopped, her eyes widening.

She was looking at a photo of Mendenhall. Not quite the rambling hodgepodge it was now, but the main structure was recognizable – except that the top floor, what had to be the attic, was blackened, charred by fire.

Smoke still curled from the turrets. The headline proclaimed in seventy-two-point type: FIVE KILLED IN FRATERNITY FIRE.

Robin's mind barely had time to register. *Five? Like us. We're five—*

Then her eyes locked on one of the names: "Zachary Prince, son of Dr. and Mrs. Abraham Prince ..."

She scanned the newsprint quickly, the words pounding in her head. "The fire originated in the Mendenhall attic, trapping the five students, who succumbed to the blaze. Fire investigators have no clue how the fire started or why the students were in the attic ..."

Robin looked up, her eyes dark. Her thoughts roiled, with no coherent theme; everything in her body felt numb.

She turned the page of the book to see if the article continued. There was no more on Mendenhall, but a slip of paper was stuck between the pages, yellowed, with a hand-printed verse:

Oh, Harvard's run by millionaires,
And Yale is run by booze,
Cornell is run by farmers' sons,
Columbia's run by Jews.

134

So give a cheer for Baxter Street
Another one for Pell,
And when the little sheenies die,
Their souls will go to hell.

Robin gasped aloud at the viciousness of it.

You don't know what you're dealing with, the voice in her mind said grimly. *You're in way over your head.*

She felt a cold prickling on the back of her neck, spreading down her spine. Suddenly, she was sure that she was being watched.

She twisted in her chair, stared back into the narrow rows of metal bookshelves behind her, searching the shadows between the stacks.

No one in sight.

After a long moment, she turned back to the desk and the book, tried to focus again on the article. But the feeling of intrusion remained on her skin, clammy and unwelcome as a stranger's touch.

The sunset was spectacular and bleak, a thin, piercing silver and black, like a prizewinning photograph. The wind, high and chill, whistled through the spiky, sharp tops of trees.

Lights were on all over the dorm, students hunkered down with their laptops and books in bed or hunched at their desks, wrapped in blankets.

Robin stood at the very end of the third-floor boys' hall, knocking on the door of Martin's room.

She stepped back, a bit breathless, waiting. Under her arm she held the book of newspaper clippings from 1920.

There was no sound from within the room and, now that she noticed, no crack of light showing under Martin's door. Robin hesitated, then knocked again, harder this time, just in case.

Why her first thought was to go to Martin, she wasn't sure. It was an impulse, or maybe more an instinct: in a group of outsiders, Martin was as much an outsider as she was. There was a bond there – of alienation? – that she trusted more than any connection she had with the others.

At the very least, what she had under her arm was a fact; he would appreciate that. He was as determined as she was to *know*.

And there's another connection as well, isn't there?

Her eyes fell on the little metal piece hammered into the doorjamb, its Hebrew letters barely visible in the gloom of the hall. *Mezuzah*, her mind reminded her, though she had no real idea how she knew the word.

Funny – didn't Martin say that first night that he didn't believe in God? But wasn't having this piece, this *mezuzah*, like having a cross beside your door? A reminder of God? Not exactly an agnostic thing to do.

She thought uneasily of the board's fury at Martin.

But it wasn't at Martin, was it?

Her mind flashed back to the board, the savage messages:

ASK   HIS   COCKSUCKING
MASTER   OF   THE   UNIVERSE
ASK   YOUR   PORK   LOVING
KIKE   GOD

136

She stood still. *God ... a Jewish God ... the rage of it ... Zachary's anger was at* God ...

She knew it was meaningful, somehow. And then the thought was gone, and she was back in the corridor, in front of Martin's door.

There was only silence from the room. But somewhere on a floor below, she could hear someone playing electric guitar, fast, hot riffs.

Robin turned, listening. After a moment, she stepped through the stairwell door and followed the sound down the dark stairs. She moved with the sound into the second-floor hall and stopped, as she had somehow known she would, outside the door with the NO MINORS sign.

She stood outside Cain's room for a long time without moving, then raised her hand and knocked.

There was no answer, just the music. Robin had an image suddenly: *an electric guitar plugged into an amp ... the sound surrounding Cain through the headphones he wore, shuddering through him in the dark ... as he played furiously, obsessively ... his eyes dark and strange ...*

Robin stood in the dark outside the door for longer than she knew, the guitar searing through her cells, vibrating her bones, somehow eerily familiar. And then she recognized it.

The sickening, delirious feeling of the energy through the planchette.

Robin backed away, turned, and ran down the hall toward the stairwell.

Flushed but calmer, she stopped off at Lisa's room on the way back and knocked on the door with the desert landscape. There was no answer. She thought briefly, longingly, of going to Patrick's room, but chances were dismally good that Waverly would be with him, and there would be no explaining what Robin was doing there. Waverly was suspicious enough (of orgies, ritual sacrifice, Robin wasn't sure) without any prompting.

In the end, she simply went to bed and lay in the dark, listening to the swirling wind, watching the trees bend outside the dark glass of her window, thinking of the other four, the group of them. Not friends, not even companions. But she'd shared something with them more profound than anything she'd ever experienced. Now she didn't have the first idea how to approach them, or even if she had the right to – but she knew it wasn't over.

It was a long time before she fell asleep.

And the last thought that kept running through her mind in the dark was: Five.

There were five of them, too, in 1920. Zachary and the others.

And they all died.

Chapter 18

"'Each one of us is not even master in his own house, but must remain content with the veriest scraps of information about what is going on unconsciously in his own mind ...'"

In the top tier of the psychology lecture hall, Robin barely heard Professor Lister's lecture. More Freud. Endless Freud.

Her mind was on the oversized book in her backpack, the newsprint images of the attic fire.

Suddenly, students all around her were standing, collecting belongings. Robin realized the period was over.

She looked over the wave of departing humanity, searching for Martin. She'd looked for him at the beginning of class, but he hadn't been there ... and still wasn't.

Robin stood but lingered at her seat, looking down at the whitehaired professor on the dais, who was arranging his notes on the lectern for the next class. *Do it*, she ordered herself. She started down the stairs toward him.

Lister glanced up as Robin approached the dais. She hesitated, and he smiled down at her like some kindly Greek philosopher from the mount.

"Something I can help you with?"

Robin took a breath. How could she say it without sounding like a complete nutcase? "I wondered ... what Freud had to say about ghosts."

The professor raised his eyebrows. Robin hurried on, "I mean ... people did see ghosts back then ... in Vienna?"

"And since the beginning of recorded time," he agreed. He took off his glasses, polished them. "Freud said ghosts are a manifestation of hysterical repression – deep wounds of the psyche slipping past the mind's censor."

He put his glasses back on, and must have caught the blank look on her face, because he elaborated. "At the risk of sounding simplistic, what haunts us is what is haunting us."

Robin frowned. "So, basically, he was saying ghosts are all in the mind."

"Not exactly. I believe he was saying that ghosts are the things we have buried in the mind – coming *out*."

Students were filing into the hall for the next class. Robin shifted.

"But Jung believed in real ghosts."

The professor half-smiled. "Jung believed in ghosts utterly."

He was so matter-of-fact. Robin stared up at him. "What do *you* think?"

He studied her, an appraising look. "I think the question is, What do *you* think?"

It felt like more than a question. But someone cleared

his throat behind Robin, breaking the moment. She turned and saw a lanky, hawkish grad student standing behind her, balancing a briefcase and a stack of files. He looked pointedly at the stairs she was blocking. Robin stepped aside and muttered, "Thanks" in Lister's general direction as the grad student brushed past her, and then she hurried for the aisle.

Outside the lecture hall, she stood on the mosaic marble tiles under the domed rotunda of the psychology building.

No help at all, she thought irritably. "*What do* you *think?*"

The truth was, she'd expected him to dismiss the idea of a ghost outright. Almost hoped it. Instead, this maddening ambiguity.

"*Do our demons come from without, or within us?*"

She felt unbalanced by the notion that Zachary could be something inside her coming out.

She certainly didn't recognize the spirit as something from *her*.

Or did she? Could she have made Zachary up? A student like her, lost like her, reaching out?

She could almost believe it was from her mind – if not for the book of newspapers in her backpack. *Zachary lived here. He died here.*

She was suddenly aware of a prickling on the back of her neck, an unmistakable sense of presence behind her.

She went cold, whirled on the floor.

Martin stood above her on the sweeping staircase, looking down from the shadows.

"God," she gasped.

"I need to talk to you," he said flatly. His voice was hollow in the vast rotunda.

She breathed out. "I need to talk to *you*."

Chapter 19

The north side of campus was built on a hill. A set of terraces connected by staircases descended to the main plaza, each terrace leading off to different paths and buildings, like an elaborate vertical maze.

Robin and Martin walked down the staircases, under oaks and maples, an occasional tall pine, as Robin recounted the coffeepot episode. "It was just like the mirror – that night. It felt the same. This ... tension – and suddenly the coffeepot shattered in her hand."

"And this happened with just you and Marlowe present."

"And Waverly."

Martin stopped on a terrace, leaned against the base of a statue to write rapidly in a spiral-bound notebook.

Robin debated telling him about the yearbook moving from its spot under her bed, then decided against it. He seemed perfectly convinced already; she was gratified that he didn't question her experience at all.

Robin looked down the walkway, lined on one side with brooding Greek statues on stone pedestals. The wind blew her hair in her face and she brushed it away.

"I think he's still around. Zachary. I think he has been – since that first night we talked to him."

Martin stopped his scribbling. "A ghost again?"

Robin bristled. "What else?"

"Purely psychological. Taken one at a time, each incident can be rationally explained. But taken together ... well, we all bought into something bigger. We fed it energy, if you will." He looked up, out over the layers of clouds on the horizon, beyond the tops of the trees. There were high red spots in his cheeks from the cold. "And physical manifestations occurred. The mirror *did* shatter. There were rappings. And now, with the coffeepot breaking, peripheral manifestations."

He flipped back pages in his notebook ... and Robin realized that the whole binder was filled with notes of the Thanksgiving weekend. Dozens of pages, scribbled in his cramped longhand. She saw her own name, and Lisa's, and what she was sure was Hebrew lettering before he shut the notebook.

She frowned. "So nothing more has happened to you since that night?"

"Nothing." Martin's voice was short; he sounded disappointed.

He tapped his pen on his notebook thoughtfully. "But we have all the classic conditions for a poltergeist haunting. You and Marlowe – all that hormonal angst ..." He glanced at her, then away.

Robin flared up. "You guys aren't exactly choir boys."

"That's my point. There's a synergy of ... unhappiness among us. A fusion of 'Discarded Ones.'"

He seemed amused by the term, and Robin felt a

144

chill, although without knowing why. She looked around at the statues surrounding them, blank marble eyes staring down.

Martin spoke beside her. "I bought a new board."

Robin turned and stared at him. "What?"

"How can we not follow up?" he said impatiently. "It's a perfect term paper. My thesis question is 'Can a focused collective emotional energy cause a psychokinetic effect?'"

Robin shook her head almost violently. She unzipped her backpack and pulled out the book of old newspapers. "I don't think it's emotional. I've been doing some research, too." She opened the book on the marble pedestal, turned pages to the article about the fire. (She'd been careful to remove the inserted page with the vile song before she packed the book).

She held the pages down against the wind and stepped back so Martin could read. "It's all here, just like he said. Zachary died in a fire in *Mendenhall*. I think that's why he's so angry and ... lost."

Martin looked exasperated. He stepped closer, glanced over the article.

She watched him read, and was gratified to see a shadow flicker in his eyes. "How do you explain that we were talking to a ghost who called himself Zachary when there was a real student named Zachary who died in that very building in 1920?"

"But that's precisely how these subconscious messages work," he explained with exaggerated patience. "You and I were reading texts from the 1920s. The board we were using was dated from 1920, so 1920 was in the atmosphere between us. We're living in the building where this student died – in 1920. One of us is bound to have heard something about it. We bring all these random facts together on" – his voice dripped sarcasm – "'a dark and stormy night.' The collective subconscious energy puts all those connections together and starts spelling out messages from this so-called ghost."

Robin felt her face getting hotter and hotter. It was almost perverse, the way he refused to see.

"Maybe you just don't want to believe," she said suddenly.

He almost gaped at her. "What—"

"Maybe you're not seeing because you don't want to see. It reminds you too much of religion, when you just rejected everything, right? It's all psychology to you. No God, no religion, no ghosts."

Martin looked startled, and, in fact, she'd surprised herself with her outburst. But he answered her with raw impatience.

"Of course I rejected it. It's so completely archaic. I'm supposed to believe in a religion based on texts from the Middle Ages that seriously acknowledge astrology and numerology and ... demons? It's beyond ridiculous. It's beyond comprehension. Give me Freud any day."

Robin wanted to point out that he had a charm from that archaic religion nailed to his door frame, but she didn't know what good it would do. He was extremely conflicted; that much was clear. She had a sense that he wanted to believe, and was overcompensating in his skepticism. All to do with his rabbi father, no doubt. Positively Freudian.

But before she could say any of that, Martin abruptly switched gears.

"All right, we have conflicting theories. So we test it." He cleared his throat, suddenly seeming nervous. "We could ... do the paper together, from the two different points of view." He looked at her briefly. "'Poltergeists – Psychic or Psychological?'"

Thrown off by the change in tack, Robin stalled. "Have you talked to the others?"

Martin reddened, looked off down the terraced stairs. "I was hoping maybe you could. I mean ... you're so honest and real and ... they like you." His voice dropped. "People don't tend to like me." He looked away from her, blushing even deeper.

Robin herself flushed – both with pleasure at Martin's assertion that the others liked her and confusion at the realization that *he* liked her.

Martin stood awkwardly, in an agony of embarrassment. She reached, grasped his arm, and shook it gently. "I'll talk to them. But not for a term paper. To find out why Zachary's here, what he wants. We can't just play around." She looked off toward the edge of campus, toward the Hall, and her face was troubled. "He's not playing."

The sky was already streaked with dark when she left Martin at the bottom of the stairs on the main plaza. She did not see that he turned to watch her as she went ... holding his arm where she'd touched him.

She turned off the plaza and walked along the footpaths that meandered through the oak grove, her feet crunching on the slippery dry leaves. Branches entwined over her head, enclosing the path. Her thoughts were stormy. Martin might have convinced himself that he could find a scientific explanation, and maybe write a brilliant and groundbreaking thesis in the process, but there was something else behind this obsessive pursuit of

147

the facts. In his own way, he was as caught up in the mystery as she was. He was only being hyperacademic because it was comfortable, or reassuring, or safe. And he was obviously rejecting anything that resembled faith – so hell-bent on not believing that he was ignoring what was right in front of him. That wasn't only stupid; it might even be dangerous.

And, she suddenly intuited, she had the distinct feeling he wasn't telling her everything. He was – maybe not lying, exactly, but he was definitely holding back. Her mind went to the Hebrew lettering she'd seen in his notebook. Significant, but she didn't know why.

Ahead of her was a small copse of trees, a circle within the grove, with a bench inside the circle. Her steps slowed and she realized that she had been headed here all along, although she'd never thought much about the place before.

She moved off the path and waded through a tangle of vines into the quiet circle of trees, approaching the curved marble bench.

She'd passed it before and noticed the inscribed names, but she'd never really looked; there were many such memorial benches and statues scattered about campus, gifts from wealthy alumni, sometimes from an entire class or club or fraternity. But there was something about this one, a heaviness – the isolation of it, maybe, or the formality of the circle that enclosed the bench.

She brushed past the rough trunk of an oak, stopped in front of the bench, and looked down at the lettering in the marble. The date made her shiver.

CLASS   OF   1920:   IN   MEMORIAM

There were five names engraved underneath in alphabetical order. She reached out slowly and touched the fifth.

ZACHARY PRINCE

And as she stood with her fingers against the cold, smooth stone, she felt a breath on her cheek, exactly as if someone was standing beside her.

She whirled, staring around her in the shadowy grove.

The trees were tall and still, the air heavy.

There was no one there.

But there *was*. She could feel it, a presence like eyes, like touch.

"Zachary?" she whispered.

The slightest wind breathed through the shrubbery around her, brushed teasingly at her clothes, slid into the cloth like fingers. Robin gasped.

The breeze lifted her hair, caressed her cheeks, breathing into her ear.

Robin closed her eyes, turned her head into the touch, even her heartbeat suspended.

The wind rustled again through the trees – and was gone.

Robin opened her eyes.

The grove was still, and suddenly colder, the sky almost completely dark.

Her face was flaming, but she trembled with cold. And then, suddenly terrified, she turned and ran from the circle of trees through the grove.

She pulled the heavy front door of Mendenhall closed

behind her and stood beside the wall of mailboxes in the dim hall, flushed with strange feelings, not all of them fear.

It was Zachary.

The longing – she'd felt it. It was real, and intense, and—

Pleasurable.

Her legs felt light and weak and her breasts ached as she remembered the touch of wind under her clothes.

Someone touched her back in the dark and she twisted around, freaked.

A shadow towered in the dark hall.

She shrank back against the coatrack, barely bit back a scream – and then she recognized Patrick.

His face was tight in the shadows of the entry hall, his voice curt, distant. "We need to huddle. All of us. The Columns at eight."

Robin nodded, speechless. And then for a moment, something flickered in Patrick's eyes – stark, intimate—

Terrified.

Her gaze locked with his.

Then he turned sharply and walked off, leaving her in the dark.

Chapter 20

On the north edge of campus, just before the woods, lay the overgrown ruins of sunken gardens. Low walls rimmed a crumbling stone plaza; dead vines crawled up the twisted columns of an arbor. In daylight, it was a haunted forest, in moonlight a dryads' circle, a place of ghosts and broken hearts and fever dreams.

Being of no obvious practical use, in comparison to a sports facility, for example, the Columns had long ago fallen into disrepair. The regents saw no reason to funnel money into rebuilding the structure. But students knew and loved the Columns for their desolate privacy, and found any number of illicit uses for the spot, as evidenced by the glitter of broken glass, the wrinkled ends of smoked-out joints, the pale deflated balloons of used condoms.

As if by some mutual unstated agreement, the five of them had all gone over separately. Patrick was there alone when Robin arrived. She stood in the dark of the arches, watching him sip from a flask as he tended a small fire he'd built in the middle of the flagstones.

She stayed back, hidden by a tangle of vines, and

watched as the others appeared, materializing one by one in the arches of the arbor, pale in the darkness, like ghosts themselves. She knew their shadows instantly: Lisa, with her wild mane of hair; Martin's small stooped silhouette; Cain, moving between the weathered stones with lanky, catlike grace.

Then Patrick looked up the wide, low steps as if he'd known all along Robin was there. She stepped forward with a surge of excitement and anticipation.

None of them spoke as they gathered in the dancing light of the fire. But their eyes met and held, a silence more intimate than words.

Patrick looked around at them in the ruined courtyard. His voice was flat. "Things are still happening, right?"

"Yes." Robin spoke first, and Lisa echoed her.

"Oh yeah."

Martin nodded once, and Robin frowned toward him. He'd said nothing had happened to him. Had he lied to her? Or was he just going along to encourage the others to talk?

A cold breath of wind gusted through the courtyard. Robin shoved her hands deep in her pockets and shivered.

Cain turned toward Robin with that direct gaze of his. "What happened with you?"

Robin thought of the grove, the feeling of being touched.

She knew she was blushing and looked toward Lisa, who was crouched beside a granite column, smoking. "Yesterday we were in the kitchen ... with my roommate ..."

Patrick looked quickly across at her in the firelight.

Cain shot an oblique look at him. "His girlfriend."

Patrick bristled at Cain's accusing tone. "Yeah, so?"

Robin continued hastily, hoping to defuse them. "Waverly was arguing with Lisa — and the coffeepot shattered in her hand." She looked at Lisa, who leaned back against the granite pillar and smoked without speaking, veiled and withdrawn.

Something's wrong, Robin thought. *What?*

Cain sounded skeptical, as usual. "I've seen glass break on hot plates before."

"Hell of a lot of stuff breaking," Patrick retorted.

Cain ignored him, turned back to Robin in the shadows. "Anything else?"

Robin thought of the grove again, the intimate touch of the wind, the overwhelming sense of presence. But how could she explain it? She knew only that she hadn't imagined it.

"It's just ... a feeling," she began.

"Someone *watching*. All the fucking time," Lisa said vehemently from the steps. She took a shaky drag from her cigarette, then ground it out on the flagstones. She wouldn't meet Robin's eyes.

Martin looked from Lisa to Robin, eyes intent behind the glimmer of his glasses.

Robin watched Lisa, wondering. "Yes ..." she said, slowly. "Tonight I swear I felt someone in the grove. Really ... like a presence." She blushed again in the dark.

Cain studied her in the firelight, frowning. "Maybe there *was* someone in the grove." He looked pointedly at Patrick. Patrick flipped him off.

"But it felt real," Robin protested. "I mean, *not* real. Not ... human. But there ..." She trailed off lamely.

153

Patrick stepped forward. "Well, this is real." He tossed a blue book down on the rough stone of a low wall.

Robin recognized the Ancient Civ test. "Rupert's midterm."

Patrick opened the book toward the light of the fire to show her the inside cover. A big A+ was marked in red, followed by several exclamation points and a paragraph of glowing comments. Robin looked up at Patrick.

"That's great."

"Yeah, great. Only I didn't write it." His face was pale. "I thought I fell asleep. When Rupert called time, I totally freaked. Then I looked down and——" He flipped through the pages of the blue book. Robin stared, startled.

The whole book was filled with dense, small, perfect writing, even the back cover.

Patrick lifted uneasy blue eyes to Robin's. "It's my writing – but it's not."

They all crowded around to read:

The Terem of the Shattering was in the first Tzimtzum when the light of the Einsof entered the Kelim of the ten Sephirot. The first Partzufim could not bear the illumination of Chochma and were shattered into pieces, resulting in the expulsion of the broken Kelim below the worlds to the Churu Klipot, the place of darkness below Malchut. After the shattering of the Kelim the light departed from the Chalal and rose above, returning to the Emanator, while in the Achar Kach, the Aviut of the Klipot remained, touched by the light of Chochma, like a smear of oil upon the lamp . . .

It went on and on, pages and pages, incomprehensible.

154

"What does it mean?" Robin said finally.

"Fuck if I know." Patrick spat on the stones.

Martin bent over the booklet on the granite, flipping through the pages.

Robin looked at Patrick, spoke slowly. "I saw you writing. Really fast. I only filled half the blue book."

Cain turned from the wall to stare at Patrick. "What kind of idiot do you take me for?"

Before Patrick could respond, Cain looked around at the others in the moving firelight. "Haven't you ever wondered why this guy's not in a frat, where he belongs? Because he got kicked out. For a prank. He and that girlfriend of his broke into the Beta house and sawed through the legs of the dining room chairs. So the brothers would sit down for breakfast and all fall down. Cute, right? Only one kid almost lost an eye."

Patrick glared at Cain, truculent but silent. Robin felt as if she'd been struck, but she knew instantly Cain was telling the truth; she'd had a vague idea that Waverly had been kicked out of her sorority for some escapade with Patrick.

Cain wasn't finished. He spoke softly, his eyes never leaving Patrick's face, his jaw tight with cold. "I talked to the janitor, frat boy. Seems the pipes in Mendenhall have a tendency to bang if the boiler overheats. He said the thermostat was turned way up over the Thanksgiving weekend. So I went poking around the basement. I found this on the floor by the boiler."

He reached into his jacket pocket, flipped a pack of Zig-Zag rolling papers onto the wall. "He faked this. He faked all of it. Another frat boy prank."

Patrick muttered, a low growl. "Okay. So I turned the boiler up."

155

Robin stared at him in stunned betrayal. Lisa and Martin looked shocked. Patrick spread his arms, turning on the flagstones in their midst. "But that's all I did. I didn't move the furniture. The mirror – you all saw it. How could I have done that?"

Cain shook his head. "I rest my case." He started for the crumbling stone steps leading out to campus.

Lisa whirled on him. "Wait a minute. Wait just a goddamn minute." The fury in her voice halted Cain. He paused on the step, glanced back.

Lisa advanced on him, looking up the stairs, trembling with tension. "Something's been in my room. Watching. I can *feel* it." She jerked her head toward Patrick. "No way is *he* doing that."

Cain looked her over, unbending. "Any witnesses?"

Lisa's eyes blazed at him. "Fuck you. I know what I felt!"

Cain pointed to Patrick. "Or maybe you're in on this with him."

"Bull fucking shit." Patrick's face was ominous now. He towered behind Lisa, gestured at the blue book as he glared up at Cain on the steps. "I never heard of the shit I wrote in there."

Cain took a step down. "You found it somewhere and copied it. That's what the Net is for."

Robin moved across the grassy stones, closer to Patrick, alarmed by the escalating fight. But Martin spoke from the wall, his calm voice interrupting.

"You've heard of it. Your conscious mind – such as it is – didn't register it." Patrick stopped his advance on Cain almost obediently, and Robin thought again, admiringly, how easily Martin was able to defuse Patrick's temper. Even Martin's little barb about

Patrick's conscious mind didn't seem to bother him.

Martin moved out on the plaza into the circle cast by the fire, looked around at all of them. "My theory is that the séance dissolved subconscious blocks. Gave us access to knowledge – and power – we don't usually have." He lifted the blue book.

Patrick nodded slowly, considering.

Robin took a breath. "But what if it's *not* psychological?" She opened her backpack, took out the oversized book of newspaper articles, and laid it open on the wall. Patrick and Lisa crowded in to look at the book in the firelight. Martin stood apart, watching, as she spoke, nervously.

"The year Zachary Prince died, there was a fire in the Mendenhall attic. Zachary and four other students were killed. He died *in the dorm*."

Lisa glanced at her quickly, her eyes dark. Someone moved by Robin's side and she realized Cain had come down from the steps. He and Patrick kept on opposite sides of her as they looked over the article. Robin studied their faces, saw the jolt in their eyes as they read ... heard Patrick murmur, "Fuck me ..."

Patrick and Cain looked up, glancing around at the others in the orange firelight. Wind rustled the brush between the arches. Everyone pulled their coats closer around them.

Patrick turned to Martin. "So what's the story? We've been subconsciously picking up a ghost?"

Martin stepped forward. "Whatever it is, there's one way to find out." The firelight turned the lenses of his glasses to flame. "Let's try it again."

The others looked to him, jolted. The night seemed to darken around them.

Robin was impatient suddenly, tired of Martin's academic posturing, tired of Cain's hard-nosed skepticism. There *had* been a real Zachary, and he *had* lived in the dorm and died brutally there. None of them had known those things when they contacted him. What more of an explanation did they need? And he had reached out to them – no, not to them, to her – for a reason. Zachary had reached out to her, and she felt a responsibility to help him. Her mind pushed back the terror of Thanksgiving. Instead, she deliberately focused on the softness of the presence she'd felt in the woods.

She looked around at the circle, finding their faces in the dark, appealing. "Maybe Zachary's been doing these things because he wants something. Maybe he needs our help."

The others stood in the silent courtyard, silent, considering. Emboldened, Robin ventured, "We could do the séance in the attic, where they all died."

Four pairs of startled eyes jumped to hers. "To ask Zachary ... what he wants," she finished.

She saw Lisa go still, intent. A breeze ruffled her hair and Lisa flinched. Robin caught it again: the strong sense that something was wrong. And then Lisa nodded tightly.

"You're right. We need to find out what's going on."

Patrick backed up, staring around at all of them. "Whoa, hold the phone. Y'all have some short memories. That motherfucker is one pissed off ghost. We all pretty much lost our shit that second night."

Patrick's blue eyes fixed on Robin's. For a moment, she was back in the terror of the night – the shape rushing forward in the mirror, the paralyzing cold.

And the rapping.

158

She pushed it all down. "Think of the way he died," she urged Patrick. "Of course he's tormented ... but maybe we can help – release him or something." She was aware of Cain shaking his head, disgusted.

Martin was studying Patrick. Now he said almost pleasantly, "Are you afraid? That's interesting."

Cornered, Patrick blustered. "Hell no. I'm down. I got two more midterms to take before Christmas break. Bring it on."

"Friday night," Martin said. "It has to be all of us. It doesn't work otherwise." He looked at Cain pointedly.

Cain smiled without humor. "Oh, I'll be there. I'm not missing this little show."

They looked around at one another in the dying firelight, a silent bond of agreement.

"Friday night," Martin said again, sealing it.

Patrick kicked at the remnants of the small fire, scattering ashes and extinguishing the embers. The others turned to leave the courtyard. Cain remained standing by the wall.

Patrick, Martin, and Lisa kept moving toward the stone stairs, but Robin hesitated, looked back at Cain in the dark.

"So nothing's happened to you at all?"

He paused a beat too long and she stared at him, realizing.

He shrugged almost angrily. "I've been writing songs. A lot of them. They're good."

Robin suddenly remembered the searing, unearthly music she'd heard in the hallway outside his door, and the hair on the back of her neck rose. Before she could say anything, he began to rationalize, defensive. "Look, *I* wrote them. A ghost didn't. Martin had a point – we

159

freaked ourselves out and jarred something loose – subconsciously. A by-product of O'Connor's little show."

As ever protective of Patrick, Robin retorted with some heat. "If you think Patrick did it all, why did you even show up tonight?"

Cain's grin twisted at her. "You got me." He shrugged. "I'm hooked. Who what when where how? I mean, what the hell? I need to know."

They looked at one another in the dark. The wind picked up, whispering along the stones, and Robin shivered.

Cain nodded at the book of newspapers under her arm. "Can I take a look at those?"

Patrick's voice called behind her. "Robin. You comin'?"

She turned and saw the others waiting for her at the top of the worn stone stairs. She stepped forward and handed the book to Cain. Their eyes held for a moment as he took it.

Robin turned and walked across the dark courtyard for the steps. But before she climbed, she turned and looked back.

He was watching her – as she'd known he would be.

Chapter 21

The walk home was cold and largely silent as they made their way through the tall shadows of trees back to the Hall. It was as if once they'd made their decision, there was nothing more to talk about.

Lisa walked stiffly, sunk into herself, and Robin had to bite her lips not to ask her what was wrong. Whatever it was, Lisa obviously didn't want to talk in front of the others. *Or me, either, I guess.*

Once the building was in sight, they separated. Lisa and Patrick hung back to smoke, but there was more to it – a feeling that they shouldn't be seen together. *And why is that? Guilt? Or possessiveness? Do we just not want to let anyone else in on it?*

Even Martin paused at the mailboxes, fumbling distractedly with his keys, so Robin could go in ahead, without him.

Her room was empty, thankfully no Waverly to deal with.

Robin stripped off her coat – the wool smelled like cold air and smoke from Patrick's fire – and threw it on her bed. She stood for a long time in the center of the rug before turning and leaving the room again.

She moved blankly down the hall toward the bath-room, but near the open bathroom door, she slowed, listening, her pulse quickening.

Scrabbling sounds came from within, and a labored breathing.

She froze, then after a moment stepped warily to the doorway and looked in.

In the sickly light of the girls' bathroom, Lisa was rummaging ferociously through her locker. She grabbed for an orange prescription pill bottle, twisted it open.

Obviously empty. Robin flinched as Lisa hurled the bottle at the wall, slammed her locker closed.

Then Lisa glimpsed Robin in the mirror, a shadow in the doorway behind her. Lisa whirled, freaked.

Robin stepped forward into the light. "It's me."

Lisa breathed out silently, then bent over the sink to wash her face, so as not to look Robin in the eyes. The red string was like a slash of blood on her wrist.

Robin moved slightly closer. "Are you okay?"

For a moment, Robin thought Lisa wasn't going to answer. She buried her face in a towel, and when she looked up again, her eyes were distant, sunk into pale flesh. But abruptly she spoke. "I'm dreaming about him. I mean, I'm dreaming about him fucking me." She turned and looked Robin in the eyes.

Robin stared at her, jolted, not knowing what to think. She was always wary of Lisa's grandstanding. But Lisa had been so quiet all evening, not herself at all. And she was pale and jumpy, her usual bravado gone. In fact, she looked sick.

Could it be true? Is she actually being – Robin's mind skittered away from the word.

Robin's face must have changed to reflect the sick jolt of horror she felt. Lisa immediately closed off. She tossed her hair, smiled that mocking smile. "Oh, look, he's good. What can I say? I come." She threw her towel into her locker and pulled out a hairbrush, attacked her hair viciously.

Robin tensed, wounded by Lisa's tone and roiling with mixed emotions – distrust, the old paranoia, and something else, too.

Jealousy?

No, of course not. But – but what?

The truth was, she'd thought Zachary was only appearing to her.

"Well. Great. How nice for you," she replied tightly. She turned to go.

Lisa spoke suddenly. "He's not doing it to you?" There was a slight tremor in her voice.

Robin turned back to look at her, shook her head.

Lisa smiled thinly. "Lucky me."

The mirrors reflected them both ... multiple images. Robin spoke carefully into the silence. "Do you want me to stay with you?"

Lisa's smile twisted. "Why? You want a piece of the action?"

Robin flushed, deep red. Stung, she turned to leave.

Lisa called out shakily, "Robin."

This time there was no mistaking the desperation in her voice. Robin turned back, almost afraid to know.

Lisa dropped the hairbrush into the sink. She faced Robin and slowly unbuttoned the high collar of her shirt. Robin gasped.

Lisa's throat and chest were covered with bruises and scratches.

163

And bites.

The girls looked at each other in the glare of the fluorescents, too frightened to speak.

A few candles burned in Lisa's room, since neither girl had wanted to sleep completely in the dark. Robin had been sure she'd be wide-awake all night (*and better that way*) but she'd drifted off and now slept fitfully on one side of the bed.

So it was just on the edges of consciousness that she heard it start – a low rhythmic bumping somewhere in the room.

Robin frowned in her sleep, stirred.

The bumping grew louder.

Robin's eyes fluttered open. Through the haze of sleep and shimmering candlelight, she saw shadows battling on the wall. A huge dark mass, crouched over a feminine form.

The bumping grew louder, beginning to shake the bed, pounding, violent.

Robin jerked up, wide awake now.

The shadows were gone. But Lisa's side of the bed was shaking and bouncing as Lisa flopped up and down on top of it, crying out in terror, fighting at something invisible.

Robin cowered. The room was like ice; the presence beside her was thick, palpable, a choking sense of malevolence, paralyzing her with an almost-blinding terror.

Her mind recoiled, folding in on itself – a swooning madness – then she pulled herself back from the brink and screamed aloud.

"Zachary, stop! STOP!"

Lisa spasmed, then suddenly ceased flailing and collapsed on the bed.

The candles on the bed stand flickered, flaring up.

To Robin's horror, she felt the presence there, the dark energy, turn its attention to her.

She could feel the hair on her arms rise, her whole body going numb as she felt cold breath on her face, smelled a sick, rotting stench.

She pressed herself back against the headboard, her eyes wide and glazed. The presence leaned in to her; her body could *feel* the mass of something huge and alive, throbbing with malevolence. Invisible breath stirred her hair ... and she heard herself whimper like an animal.

Then it was gone.

The shadows in the room softened; the air was no longer freezing. And there was no sense of the fist that had seemed to squeeze her heart.

Lisa lay beside her, shaking with terror. She broke into raw sobbing.

Robin shook herself free of the paralysis and leaned over to hug Lisa, holding her. She could feel Lisa's spasms through her whole body. Her own teeth were chattering from adrenaline.

"God ..." Her words were choked. "Has that been – is that the way it's been?"

Lisa shook her head, swallowing. "Never like that."

Robin clenched her nails into her own palms, fighting to keep control of herself. "We can't do the séance. It's too dangerous. We don't know what we're dealing with."

Lisa pulled away from her. Her eyes were dilated, glazed. "We have to do *something*. We have to get rid of him."

They looked at each other in the wavering candle-light.

Lisa spoke, her voice low and fierce. "Don't you dare tell anyone."

After a moment, Robin silently nodded.

Chapter 22

Robin watched the campus recede from the window of the bus, on her way to Ash Hill Cemetery.

Lisa had sworn her to silence about the attacks, but that didn't mean she couldn't do some more investigating on her own. Before they went any further (she thought of Cain briefly), she was going to check some facts.

It had been a relief to leave campus. Simple enough to call directory assistance and learn that yes, there was a graveyard just outside of town, and when she'd pretended she was seeking the grave of a relative, the grounds manager readily confirmed that a Zachary Prince who had died in 1920 was buried in the older section.

The bus route that connected the school to various towns along the interstate ran right by the cemetery. Wedged in a window seat, Robin saw the town really for the first time. Central Ash Hill was a good jaunt from campus, and she'd not had a set of friends to coax her to prowl about the main street's few shops and restaurants and its one cinema.

But she barely noticed as the main drag turned to clapboard houses with wide porches; she was sunk into herself, brooding over the night with Lisa.

What she felt – it had come to her at some point, beyond the horror, beyond the revulsion, and the sheer psychotic unreality of it – was betrayal. She'd somehow been able to rationalize the terror of the initial hauntings (now that they were past) as the cry of a lost spirit, angry and confused.

But what had happened to Lisa was vile, unforgivable. Robin felt violated herself. She could not believe it of Zachary – not the haunted young man from the yearbook, not the Zachary of her mind, the Zachary who called to her in her dreams. There was gentleness in that face, and compassion. None of the smirking entitlement of a predator.

Yet she'd seen the attack with her own eyes.

Could death – admittedly a horrible death (she thought of fire, of melting flesh, and shuddered) – change the character of a soul? Somehow she couldn't believe that. Of course, she had to admit, the seductive banter of the board hadn't sounded much like the words she would expect from the troubled young man in the photo, either. And neither had the degrading things the board had said to Martin.

So which was the real Zachary?

She had unquestioningly accepted what the board, and Zachary (or whatever presence had been speaking through it), had said to them.

Now she felt tricked, *lied* to. And because Robin had been fooled, she was more determined than ever to find out what was really going on.

But for all the terror of the moment when the presence had turned to her, she had had a puzzling sense – no, a certainty – that she wouldn't be attacked in the same way. That was something she knew, though she couldn't quite get to why.

It gnawed at her as she watched the outer streets of the small town turn to expanses of woods and fields through the bus windows. Something that Lisa had done.

From the start, Lisa had been brazenly flirtatious with Zachary. More than flirtatious, even. Inviting.

Inviting.

Robin sat up on the seat. That was it. Something Lisa said that first night, like Mae West – an invitation: "Well then, come up and see me sometime."

And he had.

Robin didn't know why it was important, only that it was.

The bus groaned to a halt in front of a high granite wall. Robin pulled herself up on the steel bar of the seat in front of her and walked a little unsteadily to the door. Three deep metal steps down and the automatic doors were flapping shut behind her.

The bus roared off, spewing black exhaust, leaving her alone outside the imposing iron gates of the cemetery.

The wind was strong, gusting under layers of clouds in the sky; too high for rain, but dark enough to make her wish she'd asked one of the others to come with her. It wasn't merely the promise she'd made to Lisa that had held her back, though. Asking Patrick to go along was out; Waverly had been watching him like a hawk ever since Thanksgiving. Lisa was too shaken. Martin was so openly contemptuous of the idea of a ghost that

169

there was no point in involving him unless she got something definite. And Cain—

She didn't know what to think about Cain.

But of course he didn't believe in anything. So what was the point?

Still, anyone would have been better than facing a whole cemetery alone.

Robin shivered in the wind, then grimly straightened and pushed the tall gate open, flinching at the iron squeal of rust against metal.

The more modern part of the cemetery was well tended, the grass, already turned winter brown, clipped and smooth. Most of the graves were modest; many of the headstones were simple marble rectangles set flat into the ground.

What's the point of a flat headstone? she thought as she walked along the smooth packed-dirt paths, past curved marble benches under clusters of oaks. *So discreet, it doesn't even seem like death.*

The older part of the cemetery made up for it, though, with statues and monuments crooked and streaked with age, cracked by moss that spread in patches like some pestilent disease. Wind gusted around her, whispering dryly through overgrown grass and bare trees. There was a feeling here ... the heaviness of arrested time. Her steps were slower and slower; she found herself wishing for the polite modernity of the polished flat stones.

Too late to turn back, though. She made herself move forward through the haphazard maze of stones, paused under a row of bent cypress to puzzle over the directions the grounds manager had given her over the phone.

There was supposed to be a gate separating one

section of the graveyard from the one she was in – the north section, the grounds manager had said, although he'd hesitated before he said it, in a way that made Robin think he'd meant to say something else.

She turned and squinted through the line of cypress, and then she saw it – rusted bars and crumbling foundation posts. She moved toward it through the trees.

Inside the gate, these grounds felt even older than the rest, tombstones crowded together and falling over. As Robin stepped through the iron arch, she had an instant impression of a different cemetery altogether. She moved slowly in through the stones. Here and there, she saw little piles of small rocks placed on the gravestones ... some ritual she seemed to recall from a movie, but she didn't remember which or what it meant.

There were no crosses, either, she realized. And something was different about the writing.

She turned in a circle, looking around her at the tombstones. Many were in English, but every third or fourth one bore a strange alphabet, square and archaic.

And then she saw it: a weathered granite oval, three feet high. She registered the name first, so familiar to her now.

ZACHARY PRINCE
1 9 0 1 – 1 9 2 0

But what made her gasp was the Star of David carved into the top of the stone.

Jewish. He was Jewish.

Looking around her now, she could see the same stars on other graves around her, the little rocks – a ritual she'd seen in a Holocaust movie. The alien lettering was

171

Hebrew. It was the Jewish section of the cemetery, that's what the grounds manager had been reluctant to say. Segregated – in 1920, it would have been.

She stepped close to the worn stone and read the inscription beneath the name. Her eyes widened at the epitaph:

GENTLE   BROTHER,   LOVING   SON

It all hit at the same time: the finality of the grave of a nineteen-year-old boy, barely older than she was. The bewildering inscription – as far from the angry personality they had encountered as she could imagine. And the paradox of raging anti-Semitism coming from a Jewish ghost.

Robin looked around her under the darkening sky, shivering. She spoke low. "Zachary? I'm here."

She stood very still, listening to the dry whisper of the grass. She knelt on the grave and reached out, put her hand against the rough stone.

"What do you want?"

She was barely breathing. The light around her slipped lower, darker; the movement of wind was almost imperceptible. But nothing and no one answered her.

She sat back on her heels, withdrawing her hand from the stone and resting both hands on the ground beside her. And then something stung her palm, a dull but discernible prick. She pulled her hand back instinctively and stared down into her palm. There was no mark.

She frowned and scanned the ground in front of her. Scattered beside the base of Zachary's headstone were some small rocks like the ones she'd seen piled on other tombstones. Perhaps they'd fallen from the headstone over the years. But the sting hadn't felt like a rock. Then she saw it, lying half-buried in the dirt.

Gently, she picked it up – a small flat piece of silver, blackened with age. She broke the encrusted dirt from the delicate bars and looked down at the medallion: a Star of David.

Zachary's? Had someone left it for him, all those years ago? Had he meant for her to find it?

She sat very still, holding it – until she realized she was waiting for the touch of the wind. And then she jumped up from the grave and ran as if chased through the acres of stone.

Chapter 23

Back at the Hall, Robin stood in the dim corner of the third floor boys' wing, knocking hard on Martin's door, wishing that she'd thought to bring a camera to the cemetery to document the gravestone. But she had the Star of David (she felt for it in her jeans pocket, reminding herself it was there). And surely Martin would believe her, and think it as strange as she had, the proof Zachary was Jewish.

She stood back, waiting, and focused on the little metal scroll nailed to the door frame, with its Hebrew lettering ... remembered Zachary's raging, the fury not just at Martin but also at the Jewish God.

Zachary was Jewish. Martin was Jewish. Despite his outward denial of his own faith, Martin had spoken in Hebrew to the board. There was a connection here, something she didn't understand, but somewhere at the heart of it was the answer.

She was absolutely sure that Martin knew more than he was telling.

She reached to knock again.

A hand touched her shoulder from behind and she whirled, gasping.

Cain stood behind her in the dark corner of the hall. He looked down at her pale face, frowned. "What's wrong?"

Cain's room was illuminated by two circles of low light cast by a desk lamp and another on the bed stand. Robin paced the floor through the pools of light while Cain sat on his bed, watching her.

"I found Zachary's grave."

She blurted it out, and was gratified at his startled look. "He's buried in the cemetery just outside of town." She met his eyes. "In the Jewish section. There's a Star of David on the headstone. I found this on the grave."

She fished out the Star of David and handed it to him. Cain examined the tarnished metal piece, then looked up at her in disbelief; she recognized the same jolt of confusion that she had felt in the cemetery, looking down at the grave.

"He was Jewish?" Cain said slowly.

She nodded intensely. "So he would never have said those things to Martin." She hesitated, then continued impulsively. "But actually I don't think he was saying them to Martin. I think it's really somehow about God—"

"Wait a minute, wait a minute," Cain said, interrupting her. "You said Zachary lived in Mendenhall. But Mendenhall used to be a fraternity. The frats didn't let Jews in on this campus in 1920. There was a quota system for Jewish admissions, even – the school cut the Jewish students down by half over two years."

Robin was shocked, though she knew she shouldn't be. "How horrible."

175

Cain gave her a cynical look. "Yeah, well, this school wasn't the only one.

Robin's eyes clouded as she thought it through. "Maybe he was hiding being Jewish, then, so he could get into the college. And putting on the anti-Semitism, to pass as" – she had to search for the word – "Gentile."

She sat abruptly in the window seat. "What a terrible way to have to live. No wonder he's so angry."

Cain frowned and started to speak. Robin was sure he was about to say something scathing about the nonexistent ghost. But he stopped himself and sat for a moment, silent. Finally, he looked across the room at her.

"I know something else about your friend Zachary." He stood, extending the Star of David. She took it and watched as he moved over to his desk. The volume of bound newspapers she'd given him was on top. Cain opened the old book to a page he'd marked with a concert flyer, glanced back at her.

Robin rose and moved to his side, looked down at a Law Review article. She read the title aloud: "'*IRS vs. the Baltimore Talking Board Company.*'" She looked at Cain, confused ... but there was a prickling of significance along her neck. "Baltimore Talking Board."

"Yeah. Same as the one we were using." He spoke rapidly, running his hand through his hair. "This is a real legal case from 1920. I looked it up. This Talking Board Company had the patent on alphabet boards and was really churning them out, because of that Spiritualist craze that Martin was talking about. The IRS got a look at the profits and started taxing the boards as games, so the manufacturer took the case to court, trying to get out of the tax by claiming religious

176

exemption. They argued that the Ouija board isn't a game, but a form of spiritualism, and therefore exempt from federal income tax." He smiled thinly. "The game company lost, of course."

Robin looked at him, still not understanding. He nodded to the book.

"Look who wrote the article."

Robin turned to the author's name, and caught her breath. "*Zachary.*"

Cain's smile twisted. "I figure he decided to do his own research."

Robin's eyes were dark as she realized what he meant. "So he tested the board to see if it really worked." She drew in her breath. "'That was *his board* we were using. Do you think that's why his ghost is attached to it?"

But she frowned at her own theory, realizing intuitively that there was a logical flaw. In fact, the whole idea of Zachary with the board made her extremely nervous. *The burn marks on the board. He was using the board. Did they* die *using the board?*

She lifted uneasy eyes to Cain's, allowing her secret fear to come to the surface. "Do you think that what we're talking to might not be Zachary?"

He half-laughed, a harsh sound. "I never thought it was Zachary. This ghost thing is just oh so romantic ..." His knowing gaze blistered her, and she looked away, flushed and angry, caught out. "But it's bullshit. Someone's playing a game here. And I know O'Connor's been pissing around – that stuff with the water heater, and that bogus midterm."

Robin's hackles rose at the same old attack on Patrick. She took a step back, about to retort; then her

177

gaze fell on the nightstand beside Cain's bed, and she lost her train of thought.

Next to the base of the gooseneck lamp, there was a torn yellow strip of paper, folded in a square.

Robin's eyes widened. She recognized the paper: It was one of the strips they had written that first Thanksgiving night, at Martin's suggestion – and after Cain had left the room. The purple pen identified it as her strip.

Which meant that Cain had gone back down in the night to get it. Which meant ...

"You," she said aloud. "It was you." She turned on him. "You went back that first night. You moved the furniture."

Cain stared at her. "What are you talking about?"

She took three quick steps to the bed stand, grabbed the yellow square of paper, held it out accusingly. "How did you get this? What are you doing with it?"

Cain looked trapped, then angry. "What were you doing writing it?" he slammed back at her.

Robin faltered, suddenly remembering what she'd written. *Something no one knows about me ...*

They stared at each other, both flushed. Then Cain's face closed off.

"Fuck it. Play your games. You're all crazy. I don't care."

Unable to look at him, Robin turned quickly and bolted out the door.

She ran down the hall, startling a couple of students who stood talking beside another door, and ducked into the stairwell.

In the narrow, dark passage, she stopped to catch her breath, and slowly unfolded the paper to stare down at her own purple writing, the words accusing her from another lifetime:

I want to die.

Chapter 24

It was long past midnight, and Robin saw no one in the halls as she made her way up the stairs to the narrow passageway that led into the attic.

She had never been in the attic, had only been vaguely aware it existed. It was surprisingly large: high-raftered enough in the center for even Patrick to move about without having to watch his head, then sloping down to almost nothing in the corners. But claustrophobic nonetheless, with its unfinished walls and the amazing array of discards, much of which must have been forgotten, gathering dust for years.

Four of them, minus Cain, now hovered in the rat warren of furniture from various time periods, paintings, dusty stacks of boxes with God knows what odds and ends, racks of old Glee Club jackets, even, weirdly, a headless dressmaker's dummy. Cobwebs hung from the sloped corners; everything seemed ominous in the shadows.

Martin was setting up the new board he'd bought, the familiar commercial version, on a heavy round table he'd found among the detritus. Patrick obligingly lighted the candles Martin had brought with his Zippo lighter.

Patrick likes Martin, Robin realized, surprised and rather touched by the thought. *At least he's fond of him, in some abstract way. Maybe because Martin's not afraid of him.*

She looked over to where Lisa stood off by herself, chain-smoking in the flickering candlelight. *Now I know what they mean by "a shadow of herself,"* Robin mused, worried. *She looks like a ghost.*

But that's why we're here, isn't it? To stop all this?

She had not told anyone but Cain of her discovery in the cemetery. She wanted to question the board herself, without suggesting any answers to the others.

She knew Cain was wrong about Patrick – or anyone – setting up a prank. What was happening was far beyond a prank. Cain was clinging to that to protect himself – irrational rationality.

But he was right that there was a game going on. She was sure now: it was Zachary who was playing it.

Almost as if he'd picked up on her thoughts, Martin turned from the board and looked directly at her.

"Where's Jackson? It's almost one-thirty."

Robin started, her heart beating a bit faster. It was quite possible Cain wouldn't show, and she didn't know if anything would happen without him.

And would that be such a bad thing?

And then the door opened behind Lisa, and Cain stepped in. He looked around the candlelit attic.

Martin cleared his throat. "We were beginning to think you weren't coming."

Cain glanced briefly at Robin, said nothing.

Martin shrugged. "All right, then. Let's do it." He stepped to the table and turned on a mini-tape recorder, then picked up a clipboard. "We'll start with the girls – they're the best receptors."

Robin thought, *Taking charge again. What does he want out of this?* But she sat slowly in one chair, looking at the shiny, smooth, burn-free new board. *Will it work with a modern board? Will Zachary come?*

Her skin prickled.

Do I want him to?

Martin pulled out the other chair, looked to where Lisa sat on her box. She ground out her cigarette, stood and crossed to the table, and sat, her limbs heavy, her face set. Martin stood beside them with a clipboard and pen.

How official we are.

Robin looked across the table at Lisa, trying to project calm and reassurance. They both stretched out their hands to the planchette in the center of the board.

The pointer moved immediately, almost before they touched it.

Robin drew in a startled breath. She could feel Lisa flinch through the wood of the planchette.

The board spelled out quickly

H E L L O   C H I L D R E N

Martin read the words aloud dispassionately. For the tape, Robin realized. She and Lisa looked at each other, unnerved, as the indicator kept moving under their hands.

I V E   B E E N   W A I T I N G

The candles flared, hissing with dripping wax. Martin looked at his watch, made a note on his clipboard.

Robin spoke sharply. "Waiting for what?"

Under their fingers, the pointer flew across the board.

MISSED   YOU

Patrick exhaled a cloud of smoke from the joint he'd just lighted. "But you've been around, haven't you?" He spoke it flatly, to the air.

ALWAYS

Robin could feel Cain behind her, prowling the perimeters of the attic, watching everything like a hawk. She spoke aloud.

"And all these things that have been happening to us ... that was you?"

She could feel a peculiar intensity, almost a heat in the energy coming through the planchette under her fingers as it moved.

IM   LONELY   TOO
SWEET   ROBIN

Robin tensed; she saw Lisa stiffen across from her.

Martin stepped forward, spoke beside her. "Did you write O'Connor's midterm?"

I   HELPED

Martin scribbled ferociously on the clipboard. Robin leaned forward, intent. "Why?"

The pointer hesitated ... then skimmed lightly over the letters.

Martin deadpanned the words and everyone laughed, startled at the sudden humor. Patrick did a double take, growled back, mock-insulted. "*Hey.*"

Robin could feel the others relax. It was a game again, playful and fun, the same easy intimacy they'd had that first night.

Oh no, Robin thought grimly. *Not this time. I'm onto you.*

Patrick stepped up now. "Were you inside me?"

The planchette moved once.

YES

"I'm not sure I like that, pal," Patrick warned. He was mostly joking, but the planchette moved swiftly, emphatically.

I LIKED IT PAL

Patrick went rigid. Robin felt cold. The candlelight flickered, and everyone looked at one another uneasily.

Focus, Robin ordered herself. *Find out what we need to know. But be careful – draw it out.*

"How did you get inside him?" she asked aloud.

HE ASKED

Martin read it out, looking at Patrick. Patrick stared back at Martin. "Like hell I did."

Martin met his gaze levelly. "You did. That first night." He mimicked Patrick, a remarkably good imitation. "'How, Zach? You gonna take it for me? Eleven o'clock next Friday ...'"

Robin had the fleeting, totally chilling sensation that Martin was speaking for Zachary, continuing the conversation of the board. Then the pointer was moving under her fingers again.

I M   H E R E   T O   H E L P

Martin read that aloud, too, and Robin again got an eerie feeling of schizophrenia.

"What do *you* want, though?" she demanded.

The pointer circled slowly, as if considering. *It's playing with us*, she thought very clearly, and the thought was terrifying. *Not he* – it. What is it?

The pointer moved from letter to letter. Martin lifted his head to speak the words. His voice was hoarse.

Y O U R   S O U L S

The attic was deathly silent, candlelight flickering on the dusty walls. Robin could only move her eyes, but from what she could see, everyone had gone as white as ghosts.

Then the pointer leapt to life, spelling quickly.

J O K E

Then it began racing back and forth between two letters, faster and faster.

H A H A H A H A   H A H A H A H A H A

Robin jerked her hands away from the planchette. The pointer stopped. Lisa remained with her hands pressed into the wooden piece, as if unable to move.

Patrick spoke grimly. "Very funny, Zach."

"It is not funny." Robin's face was set as she put her fingertips back on the pointer. "What do you want? Why are you ... bothering Lisa?"

The pointer was still.

Then Lisa gasped. Everyone turned to look at her, and Robin gasped, too.

Lisa sat frozen in her chair, her hair floating around her head as if lifted by invisible fingers.

Patrick jerked forward, slashed at the air with his hands. Lisa's hair dropped to her shoulders again. She hugged herself, staring up into Patrick's eyes in helpless terror. He put his hands on her shoulders, pressed himself against the back of her chair like a bodyguard. Behind them, Cain looked stunned.

Martin spoke suddenly. "Feel that. Cold."

Robin realized she was shivering violently. All of their breath showed, white puffs in the freezing air.

Robin leaned across the table and took Lisa's hands, looking into her face. "We can stop *right now*."

Lisa shuddered but shook her head. "Ask him what he wants." She placed her hands on the pointer, stared, hollow-eyed, into Robin's gaze.

Robin's fingers slipped into her pocket; she felt the sharp points of the Star of David.

All right. Now.

Robin put her fingers back on the planchette, asked the question she had been thinking ever since she knelt at Zachary's grave.

"You're not Zachary Prince, are you?"

Everyone but Cain looked at her, startled. The pointer was still.

"What are you talking about—" Patrick began.

"Wait," Robin commanded. She stared down at the board, clenched her jaw. "*Answer me.*"

She felt the pointer jerk under their fingers, a sharp jolt of angry energy. Lisa's eyes widened. Then the pointer spelled out the words slowly, almost sullenly.

MY   CLEVER   GIRL

Robin spoke evenly to the air. "I'm not your girl."

The pointer leapt to life, scraped across the board in violent jerks.

AND   IM   NOT   A   GODDAMN

Robin gasped, realizing what was coming. Martin read the last word through clenched teeth.

JEW

Everyone flinched at the epithet. Lisa pulled her hands away from the planchette as if burned, but Robin remained with her fingers touching it, determined. Beside her, she could feel Martin staring fixedly down at the board, stiff with tension.

Patrick spun to Robin. "Hold the fuck up. What's goin' on?"

Robin took her hands off the planchette, a gesture like lowering her voice, as if whatever they were talking to wouldn't be able to hear if she broke contact with the board.

"I went to the cemetery today. I found Zachary's grave." She looked to Martin. "There was a Star of David on the headstone."

Martin stared back at her, stunned. "He was Jewish?"

Robin nodded, glanced at the board. "So he would never be spouting this anti-Semitic ... filth."

Lisa's face was transparent. "It's not Zachary?"

Patrick wheeled around on the attic floor. "Then who the fuck are we talking to?"

Robin looked to Cain. "We know Zachary wrote an article on the Baltimore Talking Board – the board we were using over Thanksgiving weekend. We think Zachary and some of his friends were using that same board themselves."

"Oh my God," Lisa whispered. "And they were talking to ..." She stared down at the board.

They looked around at each other in the freezing half-light.

Robin put her hands back on the planchette. Lisa reluctantly reached forward, too. Robin spoke tensely to the board. "Why did you lie? Who are you really?"

The pointer circled, eerie, slow sweeps, not spelling anything. The slow circling was worse than any message. Robin could hear everyone breathing harshly in the cold.

She tried another tack. "Why did you pretend to be Zachary?"

The pointer spelled immediately.

F U N

Robin swallowed, disturbed. "Did you know Zachary?"

O   YES

"What happened to him?

The planchette trembled as if with laughter, then moved under their hands, slow and taunting, now Martin read the word.

GUESS

Robin's voice was raw in the silence. "He used the board to call you?"

YES

"Why?" She asked quickly.
The pointer circled, as if considering, then spelled

SOMETHING   IN   COMMON

Robin frowned. "What did you have in common?"
She felt a malevolent heat coming through her fingertips, a feeling of pure rage. The pointer flew across the board.

ADON   OLAM

The words were unfamiliar, but before Robin could ask, the board went on, the indicator making vicious sharp sweeps.

OUR   FUCKFACE   KIKE   GOD
OUR   LYING   CHEATING
WHOREMASTER   GOD
GOD   GOD   GOD

The pointer began to rattle violently on the board. Lisa gasped.

Martin suddenly stepped forward under the rafters, spoke tightly to the board. "*Haim ata Qlippah?*"

The pointer stopped rattling instantly.

Robin's eyes widened at the unfamiliar language, with the one familiar word.

"What does that mean?" Cain demanded. "What the fuck are you saying?" Patrick growled simultaneously.

"Shut up!" Martin snapped, startling both of them.

The pointer was moving, forming incomprehensible letters. Robin felt a different energy through the wooden piece – a cunning. Lisa sounded out the letters one by one.

A T A   Y O D E A

Martin stared down at the board, not moving.

Cain grabbed Martin's arm. "What's with the Hebrew? What did you say?"

Martin pulled away from him, "Just *wait.*" He spoke to the board. "What do you mean? *Explain* what you are."

The pointer moved. This time the words were recognizably English, but mystifying.

A   S M E A R   O F   O I L   U P O N   T H E   L A M P

Robin read out the sentence, which seemed eerily familiar. Martin had gone very still. "Explain," he said tightly.

The pointer moved again.

I AM ENERGY

Martin had stopped reading and was just watching the board, fixated on the emerging letters. Lisa and Robin sounded the words out haltingly.

YOU ARE MASS

Patrick moved closer, staring down at the letters forming. Martin spoke harshly. "*Go on.*"

I CAN USE YOUR MASS

Robin felt someone move beside her and was surprised to see Cain at her elbow, staring down at the board as intently as the rest of them.

YOU CAN USE MY POWER

They looked at one another in the candlelight. Martin hadn't taken his eyes off the board. He demanded skeptically, "Power to do what?"

ANYTHING

The whole energy of the attic room had changed. Robin could feel it – the intense, curious focus of the five of them, and a sense of almost conspiratorial intimacy from the board. She felt vaguely that they were being lulled, that whatever they were talking to was working toward something. The thought made her cold with fear.

She jumped slightly as Martin leaned forward intensely. "Let's see what you can do, then."

The pointer moved, and spelled:

$$J U S T \quad A S K$$

The five of them were deathly silent. Patrick spoke first, his voice sounding far away. "Move the table."

Robin looked down with the others as the pointer spelled out the next sequence.

$$T O U C H \quad I T$$

They all looked around at one another. The darkness shimmered with candlelight under the slanting attic beams.

Robin wanted to say *NO*, to stop whatever was happening, but she, too, was lulled, almost hypnotized.

Martin reached down and put his hand on the table. Patrick placed his big palm flat on the surface. Then Cain reached out and touched the edge.

The table suddenly slid five feet across the floor.

Robin and Lisa sat frozen in their chairs, empty space between them. The boys stood stupefied, motionless, not breathing.

Martin came to life, marched across the empty space, grabbed the edge of the table, and dragged it back between Robin and Lisa. Robin noticed through the dreamy edges of her shock that he had to use his entire strength to move it, it was that heavy – yet moments before it had slid across the room as easily as if it had been on wheels.

Martin spoke loudly to the air. "No more circus tricks. What can you *really* do?"

Across the table from Robin, Lisa's eyes were

dilated, her hands clasped in her lap. Robin saw something jolt in her face, a grimace that was almost a sneer, and then, just as quickly, a look of confusion. She put her hands back on the pointer as obediently as a child.

No, Robin thought. *No more.*

She shoved her chair back, about to get up, and then felt a push in her head, something feeling around the edges of her mind, whispering, trying to get in. Robin felt a stab of revulsion. She pushed back, and the presence was gone.

She looked down in a daze and was jolted to see her hands were back on the moving planchette. *What's happening?*

The guys were crowded up against the table, Martin and Patrick sounding out the letters.

I LL SHOW YOU

The pointer kept moving.

*ZE MA SHE UCHAL
LEHAROT LECHA*

The words were so utterly unfamiliar, the others were sounding the letters out one by one, but Robin could hear Martin speaking the whole sentence under his breath. "*Ze ma she-uchal leharot lecha—*"

Cain noticed, as well. He turned on Martin. "What's happening?"

Martin stared down at the board, breathing shallowly, mesmerized. Robin thought with clarity, *It's getting at him. It's almost got him.*

193

Martin spoke with strained excitement. "*Im ata Qlippah, tochi-ach et ze.*"

Robin pulled her hands off the pointer. "No." She stood, facing Martin. "*Stop it.* What are you doing?"

Martin stepped back, looked around at the others, dazed, as if he'd been jerked out of sleep. "Just ... asking it what it means."

Robin stood, breathing hard. They could stop now. She knew they should, but they were so close, so close to knowing.

She sat, ground her fingers into the pointer, stared fiercely at the board. "*I'm asking you.* What are you saying? What do you want from us?"

She looked up at Lisa. Lisa extended her fingers and touched the piece, looking across at Robin.

The pointer trembled under their hands – then went crazy, scraping savagely from letter to letter. Robin and Lisa could barely hold on.

LIFE   BREATH   WARM
BODY   BLOOD

The words were flying so fast, Robin was registering them almost subconsciously.

BODY   HUMAN   BODY   BLOOD
LIFE   ALL   OF   IT   ALL   OF
IT   ALL   OF   IT

The table began to rock, jumping on its legs, bucking wildly on the planks of the floor.

The girls bolted up from their chairs, springing away.

"Holy shit." Patrick pulled Lisa backward, away from

194

the rocking wood. Robin backed up and ran into Cain and Martin, who both steadied her. In the center of the floor, the table kept up its wild shaking dance.

The door slammed open behind them.

The table stopped dead. The five of them spun – to see Waverly standing in the doorway.

Robin drew a breath, for a stunned second thinking Waverly had seen the table shaking. But her roommate was totally fixed on Patrick.

"You cunt-hunting scum." Waverly's words were slurred. She was swaying slightly, drunk, as she turned a venomous gaze on Lisa. "I knew I'd find you with this *whore* – and the rest of this trash."

The five stared back at her, flushed with adrenaline and anger at the interruption.

Waverly turned on Robin, blue eyes flashing fire, Southern accent thick as tar. "And *you*, with your tail up, panting after him. 'Oh, Patrick, let me do your paper while I go down on you.'"

Robin felt herself flush with fury. "*Get out—*"

A candlestick with a burning candle flew across the room, barely missing Waverly's head.

Waverly whirled from Robin, staring at the rest of them. "Who threw that?"

Dead silence.

Behind Waverly on the floor, the candlestick rolled against a stack of dusty old newspapers. The pile suddenly ignited, flames licking up shockingly quickly.

"Look out!" Cain shouted. He leapt to pull Waverly away from the fire and stomped the flames out.

The six of them stood in dazed shock. Then Martin turned coldly to Waverly. "You should go now." His voice was quiet, deadly. The whole group of them stared at Waverly from their semicircle.

Waverly looked at Patrick. He stood still, as if rooted to the plank floor. She shook her head in total disbelief. "You're really going to stay here with these freaks?"

Patrick turned on her. Robin saw something twist in his face, though his eyes were as blank as a sleepwalker's. His voice was a snarl, strangely accentless.

"Fuck off and die, you bitch. Just die—"

Waverly staggered back, stunned, then turned and ran from the attic.

Patrick shuddered, and for a moment he looked dazed, almost sick. He strode across the floor and slammed out after Waverly.

It had all happened so fast, Robin couldn't move. Cain and Lisa seemed equally paralyzed.

Martin walked forward almost calmly, picked up the candlestick, turned back to the table, pale and resolute. "Come on. Let's keep going." He straightened the candle in the holder, fumbled out matches to light it. Robin saw his hand was trembling.

Cain stared at him. "You've got to be kidding."

Martin's face was feverish. "Don't let *her* ruin it." He seized Robin's hand, tried to pull her back to the board.

Cain grabbed Martin's wrist hard, stopping him. He pulled Robin free, stared Martin down. "I don't know what you're after, but we're done."

He slid an arm around Robin's waist. Robin leaned into him, releasing herself into his protection. Cain's arm tightened around her.

Martin stepped sharply back, stared at the two of them, jolted, a look oddly like betrayal.

Cain took Robin's hand and led her toward the door.

196

Anywhere, she thought. *Anywhere but here.* She reached out for Lisa, touched her arm, and Lisa moved obediently with them.

Just before the door closed, Robin caught a glimpse of Martin standing alone under the rafters.

The candles flickered beside the board on the table behind him.

Chapter 25

The moon sailed through drifting clouds. Wind billowed through trees, swirling leaves on the street outside the dark dorm.

In the black of her room, Robin slept fitfully in her blankets.

Something was moving in the room ... sliding through the silence, a thick, animate presence. Its gaze searched the dark, finding and fixating on Robin.

It slithered toward the bed—

Robin woke from her dream with a gasp – and realized she was not dreaming. Something was on her, a foul dead weight, impossibly heavy, flattening her to the bed. Her whole being recoiled from the presence above her – malevolent, hungry, crushing her down.

She flailed out, thrashing against the weight, convulsing and contorting her body in an attempt to throw it off.

Through her terror, she was aware of a thud from somewhere in the room. There was a sharp slam, and a piercing scream.

Robin pushed upward with all her strength and threw the weight off her.

She gulped for air, able to breathe again, free — and then bolted up at a sudden banging crash.

Then there was total silence.

Robin's heart was knocking at her ribs; her breath came in panicked gasps as she looked wildly around her in the dark.

The room was empty, the door to the hall wide open. Beside her bed the windows were open, too, the curtains billowing inward.

And then somewhere outside, the screaming started. Voices shouted frantically: "Oh my God." "Call an ambulance!"

Robin threw back her blankets and jumped out of bed, ran to the window to look out.

Lights were going on all over the dorm; half-sleeping students appeared at windows.

A crowd was forming below, dazed students gathering, running out of the dorm, stopping in horror.

A broken body lay on the bricks in a pool of blood, blond hair spread around her head like a halo, sightless eyes staring up.

Robin pulled back in terror.

It was Waverly.

Robin burst out through the front door, hurried down the steps.

More and more students were gathering in the windy street, wearing nightclothes, in shock. The flashing red lights of electric security carts illuminated the plaza; sirens were screaming from somewhere, approaching. Someone in a uniform started yelling at the students to get back.

Robin scanned the onlookers. She saw Cain first, slim

and still in the white lights; then all the rest of them were there, finding and fixing on one another, drifting together through the crowd as if magnetized – Martin, Patrick, Lisa. Robin eased her way up to them through a group of sobbing girls.

Patrick's eyes were wide, glazed with shock. He stared toward Waverly's body.

"What happened?" Robin asked numbly.

The four all looked at her strangely in the moonlit dark, lights from the security carts flashing on their faces.

Lisa was the first to speak, her voice low and harsh. "Don't you know? She went out your window."

Robin jolted. "*What?*"

Lisa looked upward, indicating the curtains billowing from Robin's and Waverly's open window.

Robin started to shiver. She had only pulled on jeans and a sweatshirt; the wind was icy and groping.

Cain spoke roughly beside her. "We better get our stories straight." He was moving slightly, away from the crowd, so they couldn't be heard.

Everyone moved with him, subtly pulling away.

Robin glanced at Cain quickly, swallowed. "We have to tell the *truth*—"

Lisa interrupted, a vehement whisper. "What truth – we were doing a *séance*? And have these backwoods cops fry us for satanic murder?"

Robin looked at her, stricken.

Martin's face was pale, oddly blank in the moonlight.

Cain turned on Patrick, his voice low and tight. "Where were you when she went out the window?"

Patrick looked at him without speaking. He seemed dazed, his eyes rimmed with tears.

Lisa flared up, protective. "What are you talking about?"

Cain jerked his head toward Patrick. "I want to know where he was when this happened."

Lisa's eyes blazed. "*He* was with me."

Robin stared at her, stunned. *Lisa and Patrick.* Lisa looked away from her. "I was scared. I ... I didn't want to be alone."

Cain was looking from Patrick to Lisa, his eyes narrowing. "Wait a second. The *two* of you—

Martin spoke over him, a hoarse rush of words. "We were in the attic. We were doing a psych interview for class. Word association. I say *apple*; you say *orange*. *Wet, dry. Hot, cold.* We heard screaming and we came down. We never saw the bitch."

Robin looked at him, startled at the word – when Martin suddenly hissed, "Shut up and *lie*."

Robin looked toward where he was staring. A couple of uniformed deputies – bulky farm boys with crew cuts, were pushing through the crowd, coming their way.

They bore down on Robin. One of them pointed an index finger at her.

"You're the roommate?"

Robin nodded, swallowing.

"Sheriff wants to talk to you." The deputy spoke curtly.

Robin looked back at the others. They stood at the fringes of the crowd, staring after her under the moonlight as the deputies led her away.

The halls of the administration building were silent and empty, its long, polished floors gleaming in the dark.

Robin sat in the stark conference room under harsh

201

fluorescents. A deputy watched from the doorway, standing guard as if to keep her from escaping – a physical impossibility, since she felt completely incapable of moving. Across the long table, a hard-eyed sheriff regarded her skeptically.

"You were in the attic? Working?"

In her panic, Robin had told the story Martin had fed the group, instinctively realizing that it was important to say they'd been in the attic, in case anyone had seen the lights or had seen them go up there.

She answered as calmly as she could manage. "It was quiet. We were running a test for psych. The TV's always blasting in the lounge ..." *Too many details*, she thought. *Let him ask the questions.*

The sheriff leaned forward. "I thought you were working on a term paper."

Robin felt faint. She tried to control the trembling in her voice. "A ... term paper for psych. Based on ... word-association tests." The sheriff sat impassively, waiting. "We ... heard screaming and came down ... Everyone was gathering outside ... and Waverly ... she was dead."

"So you weren't in your room." He stared into her face.

Robin faltered, didn't answer.

"Because someone said they saw you come out of your room."

Robin forced herself to raise her eyes. She looked at him without answering, her face pale under the sickly fluorescent lights.

The sheriff appraised her. "You and her get along?"

Robin lifted her chin. "No. She didn't like me."

"And why was that?"

She spoke with effort. "She'd been suspended from her sorority and, well, she didn't like being here, I guess."

"Tough to live with." Sarcasm fairly dripped from his voice. "And did you like her?"

Robin took a shaky breath. "No." Her voice was barely a whisper. The sheriff looked at her hard. Robin tried to hold his stare, but she couldn't. She dropped her eyes.

The sheriff scraped back his chair, stood. His voice was heavy with irony. "Don't go anywhere, Ms. Stone."

Robin pushed out through the heavy front doors, bursting from the building.

She stopped on the wide portico, staring out into the dark, her thoughts a black storm of noise.

They think I did it.

Did I?

When that thing was on my chest, and I pushed ...

She shuddered, forced her mind away from the thought. Rain brushed her skin, a fine mist that haloed the streetlamps.

Robin froze, staring down at the lights.

At the foot of the wide, pale steps, a shadow stood under a lamppost, holding a duffel bag, waiting.

He looked up toward her; the light caught his face.

Cain.

Robin didn't know what she felt, but it wasn't surprise. She went down the steps, stopped in front of him. They looked at each other in the pale wash of lamplight.

"What happened?"

She glanced back up at the one light on in the building. "He didn't believe me. He told me to stay in town."

"They always say that." Cain threw his cigarette away. It exploded in tiny sparks on the wet pavement.

Robin shivered violently. "I can't go back there."

Cain took her arm. "We're not. We're getting the hell out of here."

Chapter 26

The rain had started in earnest, pounding into the railroad tracks at the edge of town, pooling on the boarding platform of the Ash Hill train station, the town's gateway to the outside world.

Cain drove his dented Mustang across the iron tracks and turned into the parking drive of a drooping two-story railroad hotel across the street from the station.

He parked in front of the office and turned off the engine, looked at Robin briefly in the reddish neon light. They turned away from each other in the same moment, got out of the car without speaking, and ran through the sheets of rain for the door.

The Mainline office was as seedy as Robin would have expected from the hotel's reputation on campus. She avoided the filthy sprung couch, hovered by the door as Cain put bills down on the battered counter.

The red-eyed, rail-thin night manager scooped up the twenties. He leered toward Robin, smirked at Cain, dangled the room key from a finger. "Happy trails."

Robin's cheeks were burning as they went out into

the rain. The sagging screen door slapped closed behind them.

In the boxy little room, Cain pulled faded chintz drapes across the window. He turned, caught Robin staring at the lumpy bed.

She lifted her eyes from the bed to his face.

The room flashed with blue light. Thunder cracked, booming through the sky. Rain spilled down outside, another torrent.

Robin breathed out and sat shakily on the edge of the mattress. The box springs squeaked under her weight.

Cain sat on the windowsill, watching her. "So what really happened – back there – in your room?"

She looked up at him with haunted eyes. "I don't *know.*" She shivered, remembering. "I thought I was dreaming ... but I woke up and there was something on top of me." She nearly lost her breath again, feeling the foul dead weight, the black terror. "I was fighting it – and then I heard a crash and screaming ... and when I went to the window, I saw her ... I saw her ..."

And then the thought that she had been fighting all night long to suppress finally bubbled to the surface, and she looked at him, stricken. "Oh my God. What if I really did kill her?"

The whole horror of it overcame her. She put her face in her hands and began to cry.

Cain moved swiftly to crouch in front of her. He took her arms hard. "You didn't kill anyone. Robin." He shook her slightly. "Was there *something* on top of you? Or *someone*?"

He touched her chin, made her look at him. "Listen.

206

jock boy yells at her. He follows her out. And then suddenly she's dead."

Robin pushed him away, her eyes suddenly blazing. "It's not Patrick. You know it's more than Patrick doing —"

"I *don't* know!"

She exploded to her feet. "God, why? Why? Why do you hate him so much?"

Cain wheeled on her, shouting back, "Because he cheats on everyone. The way he treated his girlfriend ... and *you* – he's got you waiting in line for it ... and you don't see. He has no idea who you are ... what you are ... what's really there. He doesn't care. And he never will."

Robin stood still, looking at him in shock. "Oh," she managed, in a small voice.

Cain walked forward and pulled her roughly against him, his mouth coming down on hers. Robin breathed in and kissed him back fiercely. Heat flooded through her body. She pushed her hands up under his shirt, feeling the skin of his back, the taut muscles trembling as he crushed her closer, kissing her mouth, her throat. Her nails dug into his skin.

He whispered into her neck, shaky. "I don't want you to die."

She whispered back, "I don't want to."

They kissed and kissed, mouths fused, hands slipping into clothes to find skin, arms and legs intertwining. Reason melted away and there was only her body and his, his breath in her mouth, the pulse of his blood through her skin.

Life ... blood ... body ... warm ... life ... blood ... life ...

207

Their legs became too shaky to stand ... and they were sinking on the bed ... then falling ... riding the waves of sensation and fierce, exultant heat.

She woke to pitch-blackness and the sound of the rain, and her heart pounding, and the all-too-familiar feeling of terror.

Someone was whispering in the room, a slithery, electrical sound.

Robin's eyes went wide; the hair at the back of her neck rose. She sat up slowly, trying not to breathe.

A dark shape suddenly rose from the floor. Robin gasped, cowered back.

Cain's face came into focus as he leaned on the bed, contrite. "Sorry. Sorry. It's me." He pulled off headphones connected to a digital tape recorder. The slithery whispering vibrated from the earpieces.

Cain put the recorder aside and lay back on the bed with Robin, holding her, burying his face in her hair. For a moment, the fear receded. She pressed her cheek against his chest, her heart racing again, skin flushed with the awareness of his body, the newness of him. She felt sore and deliciously alive. *So this is what it is ...*

He held her tighter, but she could feel him tense against her. Immediately, the dread was back, like an icy wind. She whispered, "What were you doing?"

He pulled away slightly; his voice was reluctant. "I taped that attic séance, too. I had this feeling Martin was working on his own agenda."

She sat up to look at him. He shook his head, but reached for the recorder.

"He's been speaking Hebrew to – whatever it is, and

it spoke Hebrew back." He clicked the recorder on, rewound the tape to find Martin's voice. He pulled the headphones out so the tape played aloud.

"*Im ata Qlippah, tochi-ach et ze.*"

Robin stiffened at the Hebrew. "There. That word. Qlippah?" She looked at Cain. "The board said something like that the very first night."

"Yeah. But that's not all." He felt on the floor, pulled up a familiar box, yellowed with age. The cover had a graphic of the alphabet board, and the label: BALTIMORE TALKING BOARD.

The box, Robin realized. *The box the board was in.*

Cain nodded. "I went down and looked in the game cabinet in the lounge, after we left the attic. We burned the board but not the box."

You *burned the board*, she thought, remembering Cain grabbing it, flinging it onto the fire while the walls pounded all around them.

Cain's face was taut, as if he were remembering, too. "Look at this." He removed the lid of the empty box and showed her the inside cover. Her eyes widened.

There was writing in the box – old and faded, but still readable, except the words were unfamiliar, spelled out in uneven capital letters.

Then she caught a glimpse of a phrase that looked familiar: ADON OLAM. And another word jumped out at her: QLIPPAH.

She drew in a breath as she realized what she was looking at. Cain met her eyes.

"They took notes on their séance, right? Back in 1920? And it was saying the same things to them that it was saying to Martin."

They looked at each other in the darkness. Martin's

voice spoke eerily from the tape recorder, like an ancient chant. "*Ze ma she-uchal leharot lecha*—"

Cain reached down to the floor for his pants, his face set. "We need to know what it means."

Chapter 27

Isolated at the end of a residential street at the edge of town, Temple Emanu-el was a product of sixties architecture, built in a series of white arches that looked weirdly like a huge white shell.

It was early morning, but inside, the synagogue felt as dark as night, only a few ghostly safety lights casting oval pools of illumination beside the pews.

Cain and Robin moved into the resonant silence. Robin looked up and around at the high arched ceilings, the Hebrew lettering in the stained-glass windows, took in the mosaic tiled floors under their feet. Somewhere, a cantor was chanting, a haunting dissonance. Robin hadn't been in a church in years, but this place felt older than any church she'd ever seen. She felt the strange sensation of slipping backward in time.

She jolted as a voice came sharply from the darkness in the front of the synagogue. "Yes? Is there something you want?"

Cain and Robin spun, searching the shadows.

A set of heavy curtains rippled and a rabbi stepped through a curtained door by the side of the dais –

formal and severe in his black coat and white shirt, yarmulke and black-rimmed glasses.

They'd worked out their cover story in the car, agreeing to say as little as possible. But faced with the reality of trying to explain their dilemma to an adult human being, Robin faltered.

"We're working on a school project," she stammered.

Cain spoke over her, taking control. "We need someone to translate this." He walked forward in the long aisle, turned on the recorder. Martin's voice echoed in the temple.

"*Im ata Qlippah, tochi-ach et ze.*"

The rabbi had seemed about to refuse them, to question the intrusion, but his face changed at the sound of Martin's voice. He frowned deeply, seemingly more perplexed by the words than by the students' uninvited presence in the synagogue.

He looked blankly from one to the other. "'If you are Qlippah, prove it to me'?" He shook his head. "That makes no sense."

Cain spoke quickly. "Why? What's a Qlippah?"

The rabbi shrugged, spread his hands. "It's a ... a potato peel, or an orange rind."

Cain glanced at Robin. Robin's heart sank. That didn't make any sense at all. Maybe Martin just didn't know that much Hebrew.

"Are you sure?" Cain asked. He rewound the tape, played it again.

"*Im ata Qlippah, tochi-ach et ze.*"

The rabbi listened intently, then gestured impatiently. "Qlippah. A peel. A rind. An ... eggshell."

Robin jolted. "A *shell?*"

The rabbi nodded to her. "Or a husk. The part of

something that you throw away. The discards."

Robin's pulse quickened. She had a sudden flash of Martin on the windy hill, smiling secretively to himself. She looked at Cain, spoke softly. "Martin called *us* that – the 'Discarded Ones.'"

The rabbi looked startled at the phrase, almost disbelieving. He moved farther up the aisle toward them. "The Discarded Ones – you mean the Qlippoth? The old creation story?"

Robin and Cain locked eyes, a jolt of energy passing between them. Robin turned to the rabbi, trying to keep her voice calm. "Could you tell us about it? It's for a term paper."

A strange look passed over the rabbi's face, conflicted. "From the Kabbalah."

Robin felt another shock of recognition at the word. Martin and Lisa had used it the first night.

The rabbi's eyes were clouded. "The Sepher Zohar tells a story ... that the Master of the Universe made several failed attempts at creation before our present world. He threw the broken shells of those first defective beings into the Abyss."

That's it. This is what it's about. Robin's skin prickled with the knowing. *The broken shells of those first defective beings.*

Cain was equally still and intense beside her. "Are those shells ... alive?" he asked cautiously.

"Not alive. Antilife." The rabbi paused. "Evil." The word hung in the darkness of the temple. Robin shivered.

"You mean like ... demons?" Cain demanded.

The rabbi shifted, suddenly defensive, uncomfortable. "It's a myth. How could God fail at creation?"

213

Cain spoke roughly. "The ... *Sepher Zohar* – does it say how to get rid of one?"

Robin knew instantly Cain shouldn't have asked. The rabbi stiffened.

"Get rid of one? What game are you playing?" He looked sharply from Cain to Robin. Neither of them spoke.

The rabbi pulled himself up, offended. *And maybe a little scared*, Robin thought – which chilled her more than any of the rest of it.

"The Zohar is sacred knowledge. Secret knowledge. Not for children." Robin saw the dark flicker in his eyes again. "Not a game," he added curtly.

He turned on his heel to walk down the aisle. Easier to take offense at a joke than to believe it was a serious question. But that fleeting, frightened look on his face gave Robin a last desperate hope. She broke free from her paralysis, grabbed the game box from Cain, and ran to follow the rabbi.

"Please. It's not just a story."

Perhaps struck by the anxiety in her voice, the rabbi hesitated, looked back at her. She pulled off the lid of the box, thrust it toward him, displaying the writing inside. "We have to know what this says."

The rabbi glanced at the lettering and jolted. He turned over the lid and his face darkened as he looked down at the graphic on the box.

He shoved the box lid back at Robin, wiped his hands against his coat. "Burn it. No good comes from such toys." He turned abruptly and strode away from her.

Cain was suddenly at Robin's side. "Come on." He took her hand, steering her up the aisle.

Robin resisted, looking back. The rabbi had already

disappeared behind the curtains. "But we have to find out what—"

Cain pushed through the doors into the dark foyer, pulling her with him. "We're going to." She gasped as he pulled her into a dark doorway. He put a finger to his lips and pointed upward.

Above the door frame was a sign with an arrow: LIBRARY.

Cain eased the door open and they slipped through.

They were in a long, dark hall.

The cantor's chanting was louder; light spilled from a half-open door. Cain pointed past rows of closed doors to a double doorway down the hall.

He took her hand and they ran light-footed past the lighted door, heading toward the library.

Robin had just grabbed the brass handle and pulled open the door, when she felt Cain freeze behind her.

The corridor was unnervingly silent; the unearthly singing had stopped.

"You there! What are you doing?" a man's voice shouted from the darkness at the end of the hall.

Cain pushed Robin through the library door. "Go." He whipped around and ran down the hall.

As the door whispered shut behind her, Robin backed up into the dark library, scanning for a place to hide. Footsteps thudded in the hall outside, but the cantor's steps thumped past and down the corridor, after Cain.

Robin turned in the dark room and strode for the bookshelves, moving quickly past modern paperbacks with vapid titles: *Judaism and You; The Soul of the Torah.*

She spotted a shelf of leather-bound volumes behind the heavy front desk, hurried toward it – and caught

215

sight of a taped label on a box: *Sepher Zohar: The Book of Splendor.*

The Mustang was idling down the street as Robin slipped out the front doors of the synagogue. She ran down the long front steps, clutching the book under her jacket.

Cain shoved the passenger door open from inside and she tumbled into the seat, knocked off balance by the bulky book.

"Okay?" he asked tersely.

She nodded, gasping.

He was still breathing hard, too. "Think I'll quit smoking." He floored the accelerator, skidding off down the street, as she shook the leather-bound volume from its box and opened it.

"Oh no," she gasped. Cain braked sharply, startled.

"What?"

She held the book open on the dashboard, displaying the pages. The book was entirely in Hebrew.

"We'll have to go back." She swallowed, sick with disappointment.

Cain's eyes narrowed. "I've got a better idea." He shifted back into gear, whipped the car around.

"Where are we going?"

Cain smiled at her thinly. "To the repository of secret knowledge."

They drove into dim morning light.

Chapter 28

Ash Hill was a small community, but every college town makes its reluctant concessions to technology, and Main Street did boast a cyber café.

Trees bent in the wind under an ominous sky as Robin followed Cain through the black glass door of a long storefront building.

The warehouse room was painted black, as well; heavy curtains kept light from coming through the front windows. Stage curtains hung at intervals, creating semi-private "rooms" with low area lighting, spotlighting a few tables each. Several pay terminals were available for Internet access, and there were plugs and phone lines for laptops, as well.

Robin and Cain wove through the maze of drapery. In a curtained corner, Robin pulled up an extra chair while Cain set up his laptop.

It was almost surreal how easy it was. Cain signed on and in under ten seconds his initial search for "Qlippoth/Kabbalah" yielded over a thousand hits.

Cain gave Robin an almost amused look, then began clicking through the sites.

From Wikipedia, they got a definition of Kabbalah: "An interpretation of the Torah (Hebrew Bible); the religious mystical system of Judaism; a unique, universal, and secret knowledge of God, the laws of nature and of the universe."

A page appeared with odd symbolic images: a diagram of triangles and wands labeled "The Ten Spheres of Creation"; a black snake coiled up through the tree of life.

Cain clicked onto a link titled "Qlippoth – the Discarded Ones."

Robin leaned against his shoulder to scan the text, which was illustrated with chilling images of formless swirls of energy with malevolent eyes. She recognized familiar words, read aloud.

"'The *Sepher Zohar,* or *Book of Splendor,* maintains that there were several failed attempts at creation before the present one. The first beings were unable to hold the light of God and shattered into pieces—'"

They both looked at each other in the same moment.

"This was in Patrick's midterm," Robin said. Cain nodded slowly.

"It was right in front of us; we just didn't see it."

"*We* didn't. I think Martin did."

Robin shifted her eyes to the screen again, found her place. "'The Master of the Universe threw the broken shells of these first defective beings, the original Sephiroth, into the Abyss.'"

Cain murmured, "Rabbi knows his Zohar."

Robin continued. "'The Qlippoth, these husks, or shells, are not alive, but touched with life, like a smear of oil upon the lamp.'"

She stopped, recognizing the phrase from Zachary.

I am energy. You are mass.

But it wasn't Zachary, was it? It was one of these.

Cain scrolled down, and they read in silence, trying to process the information. Sometimes the text was too obscure to grasp, but Robin got an unsettling picture of the Qlippoth as inchoate energy, spirits without bodies from the beginning of time, hovering always at the edges of the living world. Another disturbing sentence caught her eye: "They manifest as malevolent autonomous forms throughout the universe."

Cain stopped on a piece of text and read aloud.

"'Like the fallen angels of the Bible, banished from Heaven, the Qlippoth are enraged with their exclusion from creation and inflamed with a desire to invade and pervert mankind. "Shape without form, shade without color, paralyzed force, gesture without motion"; they long for life, and are responsible for all the evil of the world.'"

Robin felt queasy, a weird, disconnected feeling of unreality. *How can this be happening?*

And yet, there was something familiar about the words she was reading. *Defective. Cast out. Envy of the chosen. Rage at exclusion.*

Like me. Just like me.

Do our demons come from without, or from within us?

I guess it doesn't matter. Either way, it's here.

She looked at Cain in the dim light of the computer screen, shaken. "Inflamed with a desire to invade and pervert mankind ..."

Cain had scrolled down and stopped on another sentence. "Jesus. Listen." He read, "'The malevolent intent of the Qlippoth has been made manifest through-

219

out human history, as in the case of Hitler and the Nazis, who through séances and other occult practices opened the door to widespread Qlipponic possession. See *Key of Solomon.*'"

Robin sat still, stunned. Cain's face was bleak. "None of this is good news." He turned back to the keyboard, and typed "Key of Solomon" into the search engine.

The links appeared and he clicked on the first. A text Web site came up: The Greater Mysteries of the Key of Solomon.

"So much for secret knowledge," Cain muttered. He scrolled through the text.

Robin looked at the section titles flashing by: "Invocation," "Protection," "Banishment."

"Stop," she said suddenly. They both leaned forward to read ... and then both looked at each other in the same instant.

"Holy shit," Cain whispered.

Cain veered the Mustang onto a side street at the sight of the police barricade at the school gates.

He pulled over to the curb, parked under a spreading oak. The sky through the windshield of the Mustang was dismal, drizzling icy rain. Robin stared out through the glass, past the remains of a McDonald's breakfast scattered on the dashboard.

The road into the college was blocked with posts; police and sheriff's cars lined the road. A steady stream of cars and buses took students out of the college, onto the highway.

Cain shook his head. "They shut the whole place down." He switched on the radio, searched for a news channel, while Robin scanned the silhouettes in the cars, hoping for a glimpse of a familiar profile.

Cain stopped on a station and they listened to the TV announcer: "Baird College has released students early for Christmas break after the suspicious death of a coed. Two missing students are wanted for questioning ..."

Robin looked up, startled, at the last. Cain reached and turned off the radio. He looked out at the stream of cars leaving the campus through the veil of rain.

"They could be miles away by now."

Robin shook her head, sure. "Don't you remember how we met? None of us *go* home."

She reached into Cain's backpack for his cell phone, started to dial.

Robin and Cain were the only customers in the dim Main Street diner. They sat edgily in the cracked red vinyl window booth, staring out plate glass at the flooded downtown street. The drizzle of rain had turned into a gale. Wind bent the trees on the sidewalk, gusted against the glass, so that water poured down in sheets.

A bulky Toyota 4 Runner pulled up to one of the diagonal parking spaces outside the diner. Two figures emerged from the car and darted across the wet sidewalk, hurried in through the front door of the diner.

The door blew shut with a jangle of bells. Patrick and Lisa shook water off their clothes. They saw Cain and Robin at the window booth and stopped still for a moment before crossing the restaurant to sit across from them.

Robin met Lisa's eyes, but before anyone could speak, the waitress came to fill their coffee cups.

"Wet out,' she remarked stoically. She handed out

menus, then departed.

The four of them looked at one another warily.

Cain spoke first. "Where's Martin?"

Patrick matched Cain's curt, neutral tone. "We tried his room before they closed the dorm down. No one there."

Robin looked across at Lisa. "We called his parents' house. The housekeeper didn't even know school was let out. You haven't seen him at all?"

Lisa started to speak, then her eyes widened; she stared out the window.

A sheriffs car was cruising slowly down the muddy street outside the diner.

All four of them hunched down in their seats, not breathing until the car cruised on, disappeared around a corner.

Patrick sat up again, his face grim. "Sheriff came by Mendenhall looking for you all."

Cain straightened, looked across the table at Patrick. "Why did you stay?"

Lisa looked at Robin. "We had to make sure you were all right."

Robin felt a sudden ache in her throat. She glanced out the window, in the direction the sheriff's car had disappeared, then back to Lisa, haunted. "They think I killed Waverly."

Lisa swallowed. "Was it ... Zachary?"

The four of them looked around at one another. Lightning flashed outside, branching fire in the dark sky. They all flinched, and then Cain exhaled. "We think we know what 'Zachary' is."

*

Outside the wide window, rain pounded into the rutted

parking lot of the Mainline. Inside the dim room, Cain and Robin had the diagrams and texts they'd printed out in the cyber café spread out on the bed for Patrick and Lisa to see.

Robin watched their faces as Cain gestured, explaining.

"The *Key of Solomon* is full of truly weird shit. Spells for just about everything. Demons, exorcism, rituals of invocation and banishment. People really believed this stuff — it's amazingly matter-of-fact."

Robin recalled Martin's words on the steps, that windy day: "I'm supposed to believe in a religion based on texts from the Middle Ages that seriously acknowledge astrology and numerology and ... demons?"

She turned to Lisa, who was standing frozen, pale with disbelief. "But you've heard of this, haven't you? You and Martin were talking about Kabbalah that first night."

Lisa twisted the knotted red thread on her wrist. "The morning after — when we found the game scores in the newspaper — he asked me what I knew about Kabbalah and" — she breathed in sharply, remembering, "the Qlippoth thing. But I never heard of any of *that*."

She looked down at the red yarn, as if just noticing it. "This was something I saw in a magazine. It was for fun."

She suddenly, savagely pulled the yarn from her wrist, breaking it and flinging it away from her.

"I didn't know," she whispered, looking sick.

"None of us did," Cain said. He indicated a diagram of a starlike arrangement, then bent and quickly sketched out a table with five figures around it in the same arrangement. Robin noticed fleetingly that Cain's trademark cynicism was gone; he was strangely comfortable with the ancient symbols.

"Look. We've been creating a pentagram all along – the five of us in this shape. Five is a magic number. A pentagram is a gateway. We made an opening—"

"And this ... this shell thing came through," Patrick finished grimly.

Robin turned dark eyes on the others. "Zachary Prince and the kids who died in the fire were doing a *séance* in the attic – with the same Ouija board that Lisa found. They wrote the answers the board gave them." She showed them the faded writing in the lid of the box. "They called up the Qlippah." Her voice dropped. "And it killed them."

Lisa blanched. "Why? What does it want?"

Cain sat on the edge of the radiator. "The Kabbalah texts say the Qlippoth want life."

Lisa turned to Robin. "But you just said it killed those people."

"And Waverly." Patrick spat.

Robin nodded. "That's the thing. It wants life – it's jealous of all human life. But it can't *have* life. It can only destroy."

Patrick paced in the small room. "The truly fucked-up thing is that I believe it."

"What do we do?" Lisa's voice was small and wan. Robin felt like crying herself.

Patrick stopped his restless prowling. "We head for the tall grass. The fuck away from here."

"We can't leave Martin," Robin protested.

"Every man for himself," Patrick retorted.

Robin whirled to Cain, her eyes appealing.

"We don't know he's anywhere near here," Cain told

224

her. His voice was gruff, but he looked away from her gaze.

Robin stared around at all of them. "Martin wouldn't have left. You know he wouldn't. He's obsessed. He doesn't *think*. He's still in Mendenhall with ... that thing."

Lisa hugged herself. "What if he's dead?"

Robin flared up. "What if he's not?' Her voice rose. "We all let this thing out. What if it can move? It killed Waverly. What's it going to do next?"

An uneasy silence fell between them. Thunder rumbled again, then the not-so-distant crack of lightning.

Cain picked up some printed pages. "There's one more thing. We found a banishing ritual. It's pretty wild. But at least there's a precedent."

Lisa was suddenly very still. "You mean we could get rid of it? For good?" she asked cautiously.

Cain looked troubled. "I don't know. But somebody thought so ... This stuff has been passed down for ages." He looked around at them. "We all have to do it, though, or the ritual won't work."

They looked at one another in silence. Then Patrick growled. "Shit on the mumbo jumbo. This thing kills. We go in, we get Martin, we get out. End of story."

Four pairs of eyes locked over the strange diagrams on the bed. And slowly, they all nodded agreement.

Chapter 29

The day passed in slow motion. Going back onto campus with all the police everywhere was out of the question. They decided to try for ten at night, figuring the campus would have been completely cleared by then and the police would relax their vigil.

Patrick and Lisa went out for supplies, since Robin and Cain couldn't risk being seen. Robin dozed fitfully, waking several times to find Cain poring over the ritual. She watched him, fascinated. *For all his rationalism, he's in his element now, caught up in the mysticism. Maybe we all want to believe.*

They ate pizzas that Patrick and Lisa brought back. Patrick drank beer after beer and rolled joints, which he smoked, too, the look on his face precluding any protest.

Robin sat with her back against the wall, her thoughts a tumult. *Waverly's dead. She's dead, and we could be next.*

She thought of Martin, alone in the dark halls with some unimaginable thing, and shuddered.

Suddenly, Cain was crouched in front of her, taking her hand, looking at her questioningly. She shook her head, trying to smile, and he sat beside her against the wall, warm and real.

Patrick took in the two of them, and when Robin met his gaze, he nodded. Approval, or maybe a blessing.

"The Discarded Ones," he said aloud.

Everyone looked at him.

"That's us, right? Damaged goods. It came straight to us — because it knew."

Cain squeezed Robin's hand. Lisa put her head on Patrick's shoulder.

The four of them sat in silence, listening to the sound of the rain outside.

Waiting.

The campus seemed vast in the dark as Patrick drove his SUV without lights into the woods, heading toward the Columns. After much heated debate between the boys, they'd decided it was best to get to the dorm through campus.

They left the 4Runner in the woods and then moved through the oak grove, nervous as cats, wearing dark clothing and each carrying a duffel. The rain had abated, but the dead leaves under their feet were damp and slick, and wind lashed through the trees, intermittently showering them with droplets.

They stopped on the path, looked through a tangle of bushes to the silhouette of Mendenhall.

The dorm was towering, a huge dark shell. Robin thought she could hear a shutter banging somewhere in the building.

Cain started forward, then Patrick hissed, "Wait."

Lights swept the pavement of the circular drive in front. All four of them hit the ground behind the bushes, waiting, not breathing. A sheriff's car cruised by; the lights passed over them, dappling light through the bushes.

Robin pressed her face into the damp leaves, heart pounding, breathing in the loamy rot.

Then the patrol car turned the corner of the drive, moved away down the street. Robin felt Cain's hand on hers, closing around her fingers, pulling her up.

The four of them slipped from the wet bushes and hurried around to the side wall of the building, halting at a door hidden under the fire escape.

Cain fished out his dorm keys and tried the lock. The key turned, but as they'd all expected, the door was bolted from inside.

Patrick stepped back, looked up at the slatted metal fire escape ladder above their heads, calculating the height. He turned to Lisa, spoke in a low voice.

"Up on my shoulders."

Cain stooped, locked his hands together to boost Lisa up. She stepped into his hands and Patrick grabbed her by the waist; both of them lifted her up at once to kneel on Patrick's shoulders. Lisa put her palms on Patrick's head, then, balancing carefully as an acrobat, unfolded herself to a standing position.

Patrick grabbed her ankles, steadying her. She reached up for the bottom rung of the ladder, grasped it, and yanked hard. The ladder refused to budge.

"It's stuck," she whispered down. She gave another hard tug, then ordered Patrick to let go.

Robin watched admiringly as Lisa tucked her legs up to her chest and slung an ankle over the rung of the ladder, then hoisted herself up over the ladder and onto the platform.

Her Nikes squeaked on the wet metal as she stood and shoved down on the ladder, pushing and straining, but no amount of force would unstick it.

Cain called up softly. "Break a window and come down and let us in."

Lisa looked down at them over the railing. Her face was hard. "No way am I going in there alone."

Cain looked to Robin, raised his eyes to the ladder, questioning. She nodded, and he laced his hands for her.

Robin tried to copy Lisa's moves as Cain lifted her and the two boys boosted her up. She felt Lisa's hand grab her wrist, and Patrick's hands gripping her ankles, pushing up.

Adrenaline flooded through her as Lisa hauled her up over the side of the platform. Robin scrambled, grabbing at the metal screen of the platform until somehow her whole body was lying flat against the metal. She was trembling all over. Lisa was crouched against the wall, panting, but she managed a ghost of a smile.

Robin got to her feet, brushing herself off. She pulled the flashlight from her pocket, wrapped her scarf around the flashlight and her hand. Lisa backed up against the railing. Robin smashed the flashlight through the window.

She used the flashlight to push the jagged glass out of the frame, then cautiously stuck her head through the opening. She turned her flashlight on and shone the beam down one side of the Hall, then the other. She stared into the darkness, her pulse racing – but there was no movement. The Hall was dark and utterly silent.

She looked back at Lisa, who was hovering behind

her on the fire escape, and slung a leg over the windowsill.

Inside, the Hall was pitch-black compared to outside. Glass crunched under Robin's feet. She turned to the window and helped Lisa through.

Lisa straightened and the girls looked at each other, faces pale in the dark.

Robin felt along the wall, found the light switch, flicked it. Nothing.

"Electricity's off," she said uneasily, then remembered they couldn't turn the lights on anyway, not with police patrols out there.

Lisa shivered. "Let's go fast."

Robin turned her flashlight on, keeping the beam low, below the window level, as Cain had instructed earlier. Lisa took Robin's hand and they ran together down the dark hallway.

The hallway opened onto the landing above the main staircase. Below them, the well of the staircase gaped open like an enormous black cave.

Lisa and Robin crossed the landing and hurried down the sweeping stairs, Robin's flashlight bobbing wildly. At the bottom, they turned into the shadowy front hall.

In front of her, Lisa pulled up short, gasping in terror. Robin froze.

A hooded figure stood by the door in the hall.

Robin felt herself screaming in her mind, her sanity wobbling.

Then something clicked in her head as her eyes adjusted to the dark.

She choked out, "Coatrack." She shined her flashlight beam over the figure.

Someone had left a heavy coat draped over the

human-size rack. A hat perched on the top completed the illusion of a shadowy stalker.

Lisa exhaled shakily, leaning limply against Robin.

"Back door," Robin managed.

They turned away from the front door, moved slowly down the murky hall, gingerly passing by the open bathroom, the curtained fire door, the narrow kitchenette. Everything seemed animate, ominous. Lisa was clutching Robin's hand so hard, her bones hurt.

The open archway of the lounge was next. Lisa slowed as they approached, reluctant.

A muffled thud came from inside the room.

Both girls stopped dead.

Robin swallowed, spoke quaveringly into the dark. "Martin?"

They were still, not breathing, just listening.

A tapping sound began somewhere in the building, faint, rhythmic, mocking. Robin tried to focus through her terror. Where was it coming from? From the lounge? Or somewhere else in the house?

Lisa grabbed Robin's hand and they both ran, past the lounge doorway, toward the back of the house. Robin couldn't help glancing into the lounge as they pounded past. In that one glimpse, the big room seemed empty, dark, still.

The girls dashed through a doorway into the narrow back entry hall. They halted at the back door, panting. Robin's blood was pounding in her ears, but the tapping had stopped.

Robin shot the inner bolts and used her house key in the dead bolt, swung the door open.

Cain and Patrick hustled inside, carrying the duffels.

Outside, wind shivered through the dark trees,

whipped the branches into a frenzy. For a moment, Robin stood in the doorway, grateful for the air on her hot face. The wind pushed at her, and Robin slammed the door shut.

The darkness was immediate, intimate.

With the door closed, Robin could barely see anyone – just the glistening of people's eyes. But she could feel Cain's wiry tension and Patrick's warm bulk beside her, could smell the cold outdoors on them, and she was momentarily comforted.

Patrick turned on the flashlight; the sudden strong beam startled them all.

"Stay away from the windows with that," Cain warned him.

"Dude, I lay you money I've broken into more houses than you have," Patrick retorted. He took a dark sock from his pocket and pulled it over the flashlight, muting the beam.

Cain turned to the girls. "Everything okay?"

Robin nodded briefly, though of course it wasn't okay; she had no idea if anything would ever be okay again. It didn't feel like breaking into a building. It felt like landing on another planet. The Hall seemed completely cut off from the rest of the world, as if they'd entered another dimension or a parallel universe and were lost to anyone from the real world.

Is it here? In the air? In the walls? What does it look like?

Cain squeezed her hand, as if he'd heard her thoughts. "Any sign of Martin?"

Robin bit her lip, looked at Lisa. "We heard something. In the lounge."

Patrick reached into an inside pocket of the heavy

jacket he wore and pulled out a .38-caliber handgun. The others stared at him, shocked.

"Hey—" Cain started to protest.

"Hay is for horses," Patrick said flatly. "This shell thing killed Waverly." He cocked the gun, held it at his shoulder, then flashed Cain a crooked grin. "Southern gun culture."

Cain smiled grimly back.

Patrick turned, and the three of them followed him through the narrow doorway into the main hall.

They stood in a block, looking warily down the dark corridor toward the lounge; Patrick and Cain in front, Lisa and Robin pushed in behind them, so close that they could feel one another breathe. Robin felt life and comfort in their warm bodies, and she was seized with a sudden fierce affection for the people around her. They were hers, she realized; they were like blood.

Patrick looked at Cain, then took a step forward, and they moved in a clump toward the arched entrance of the lounge.

At the doorway, they all paused, looked in warily.

A dark shape flashed on the other side of the room, opposite them.

They all jumped back, jostling into one another.

"Shit," Patrick muttered, sounding annoyed at himself.

Robin realized they were staring into their own reflections in the mirror.

They all relaxed at the same time, sheepish. Robin looked around the dark cavern of the lounge. Rain beat against the outside of the arched windows. The dark shapes of trees swished and swirled in the wind.

They all jumped again at a sudden fast banging, like the report of a gun, pounding through the ceiling and walls. Robin felt the sound reverberate through her whole body, like someone touching her from inside. Lisa's revolted gasp beside Robin told her Lisa was feeling the same thing.

Patrick and Cain spun almost angrily, looking up and around them at the molded ceiling.

The banging abruptly stopped. The silence seemed even more ominous.

"Upstairs," Cain said tightly, moving toward the door.

The four stepped out of the lounge. Robin heard Cain's intake of breath when Patrick's flashlight skimmed the coatrack, then felt him relax as he recognized the shape.

They crossed the wood floor to the staircase and started up the stairs, dimmed flashlights bobbing in the dark, eyes darting nervously into every corner. The carpet was spongy beneath their feet, a slightly loathsome sensation. Robin flinched at a creak.

At the top of the stairs, Lisa froze, a scream choking in her throat.

To their left, the hallway door was opening and closing slowly, rhythmically, as if the door was breathing ... in ... and out ...

The four stood mesmerized, watching.

Cain suddenly strode to the door and pulled it open. A strong breeze ruffled his hair, and Robin gasped.

"It's the wind. Coming in the broken window."

Robin pushed up behind him, looked down the long, dark hall. She could feel the draft from the window she'd broken.

She leaned against Cain, and he put a strong arm around her waist, holding her tightly against him.

Patrick shoved forward, marched past Robin and Cain. "Let's fucking get on with it." He slammed into the stairwell.

Cain moved Robin forward, touched Lisa's arm, and the three of them followed Patrick through the door.

The stairwell was dark and hollow, resonant with their breathing as they climbed up after Patrick's bobbing flashlight.

"O'Connor, hold up," Cain whispered upward, and the light paused at the third-floor doorway.

The three of them caught up with Patrick on the small landing in front of the door. Patrick pulled the door open a crack and peered through into the third-floor hall. Robin could feel him untense slightly. He nodded behind to the others, then silently swung the door open into the hall.

They followed Patrick into the murky corridor, looking down at a string of silent doors, all closed.

Robin felt a rush of impatience. She moved suddenly ahead toward Martin's corner room. Cain fell quickly into step with her, staying close by her side. She could feel Patrick and Lisa right behind.

Robin stopped at the last closed door and stared at the door frame. The mezuzah had been ripped off, leaving a slash of exposed wood.

Robin swallowed, then set her jaw and knocked hard. She jumped slightly as the sound seemed to echo through the floor. *Now it's heard us*, she thought bleakly. She had a flash of swirling formless energy ... chaotic malevolence ...

"Martin?" she called softly. "Are you in there?"

The other three crowded closer to listen. There was only silence behind the door.

Patrick tucked the gun into the waistband of his pants and put a hand on Robin's elbow. "Out of the way," he ordered. Robin and Lisa shrank back against the opposite wall. Patrick raised his leg and kicked at the door below the knob. Robin saw a flash of a thigh as thick as a tree trunk; then the door crashed open against the wall inside.

Patrick pulled the gun out of his pants, cautiously stuck his head inside the black room, leading with the gun.

Robin peered around the side of him from behind. She could see no movement, no Martin, only shadows.

Patrick shoved into the room. The others followed with flashlights.

The curtains were drawn, but even in the thick darkness, the clutter was unnerving. Books were stacked in teetering piles; the bed was in chaos. Food wrappers and soft-drink cans were scattered everywhere, as if Martin had been living out of the snack machine for weeks instead of just a day and a half. Robin cringed at the rank, rotted smell.

Cain trained his flashlight beam on the mirror. Robin drew in a breath. Hebrew letters were scrawled on the glass and the wall beside it: thick, dark smears of something that looked suspiciously like blood.

Lisa gasped behind them and they all turned instantly. Her flashlight was aimed at a desk pushed into the middle of the room, with a chair in front of it.

The Ouija board was laid out on top of the desk, the planchette in the center of it. Martin's miniature tape recorder was beside it, and fat candles were set up around the board, burned halfway down, hardened wax pooled around them.

Robin focused on a pile of books, open on top of one another, stacked on the chair, with more on the floor beside the desk. Half of the titles were in Hebrew. She glanced at Cain.

He moved forward, staring down at the board. He pulled out his lighter, lighted the candles. The flickering flames seemed to make the room colder, not warmer.

Cain switched on the tape recorder on the table. Everyone jumped as Waverly's voice screamed out of the small speaker: "You're really going to stay here with these freaks?"

Robin had a swift shock of déjà vu at the sound of her dead roommate's voice, then she realized. "It's the tape Martin made in the attic. He left it running."

Patrick's voice rasped from the tape, an ugly sound. "Fuck off and die, you bitch."

Patrick blanched in the candlelight. "Turn it off," he said thickly.

"Wait." Robin fast-forwarded the tape past Waverly's feminine twittering to find Martin's voice again.

"Come on. Let's keep going," Martin was saying.

Then Cain's voice, incredulous: "You've got to be kidding."

"Don't let *her* ruin it."

Robin flinched at the obsessive intensity of Martin's voice. They all stared at the tape recorder.

Cain's voice cut Martin off curtly. "I don't know what you're after, but we're done."

Robin looked up at Cain. His face was tense, fixed on the tape recorder. Patrick shifted uncomfortably. "Okay, so—"

Cain said sharply, "Wait."

They all stood around the desk uneasily, listening as the tape continued to play. There was the sound of people moving, footsteps on the wooden floor, a door opening, then closing.

Then silence ... just the hiss of tape.

And then the sound of the tape being snapped off. But before anyone could even take a breath, the tape started again. Robin stiffened.

On the tape was the squeak of a chair being pulled out ... and Martin's determined voice, speaking aloud.

"Are you still there?"

The four of them stiffened at the familiar scraping sound of the planchette moving on the board.

Then Martin's voice again, low with excitement: "I'm here, too."

Patrick looked up. "Shit. He did it himself."

On the tape, Martin spoke with a touch of longing. "Are you really ... Qlippah?"

Robin jolted, whispered. "He did know. He knew what it was." Cain met her eyes, tense.

There was a brief scraping on the tape, and Martin's voice reading the message. "'Yes!'" A pause. "And ... you were there ... at the beginning of creation?"

There was a longer scraping, and Martin's voice, reading out the reply. "'Before the beginning ...'"

Another pause, then more scraping. Martin spoke suddenly, so intensely that Robin flinched. "I *do* want to know more."

The scraping came again, faster now. They could hear Martin's breathing on the tape. "What do you mean, I could *see*?"

The scraping.

238

Then Martin's voice again, rising in disbelief. "See *God*?"

Patrick moved in the dark beside Robin, an explosive gesture. "What the fuck—"

Martin's taped voice cut through his. "Yes. I want to see God. How?"

Robin felt faint with the sound of the scraping of the planchette. There was a long silence on the tape. *I'm going crazy,* she thought. *I really am going to go crazy.*

Martin's voice came again. This time there was a distinct note of wariness.

"I don't know ... what would you do ... if you were in me?"

Robin's eyes leapt to Cain's face. He stared back at her across the candles, jolted.

"Sweet Jesus," Patrick mumbled. Lisa pushed in to him; he put an arm around her waist blankly.

On the tape, Martin was sounding out letters, stumbling over unfamiliar words. "'*Nayah, horeh, yiyeh* ...?'"

The four looked around at one another, uncomprehending. Then Martin's voice continued, full of longing as he read slowly over the scraping of the planchette.

"'I can show you all that was ... that is ... and that will be ...'"

Robin was frozen with fear. She whispered aloud, "No, Martin, don't ..."

Martin's voice suddenly blasted from the tape.

"All right, then – come inside me. I ... I *invite you.*"

Lisa's eyes were wide with terror. "No ..." she choked out.

They all stiffened at a strange, strangled sound on the tape. Martin was choking, gurgling. Then there was a horrible, triumphant howl. "Ahhhhhhhh. Ahh. Ahhh."

Robin felt her skin crawl. Her legs were so watery, she could barely stand.

Martin's voice was purring with an almost sexual pleasure.

"Oh, yes ... oh, the body ... the body, now ..."

And now a savage glee, an alien voice, hair – raising. Robin felt her gorge rise. The others looked equally sick as the voice cackled on.

"In the body ... in the body now ... the body ... in the body ..."

There was a scuffling sound on the tape and then the sound of the door opening and closing.

Then silence. Nothing but the hiss of blank tape.

Cain reached out and turned off the recorder. They all looked at one another in the wavering candlelight, deathly pale.

"That's what it wanted," Cain spoke thinly, and everyone looked to him. "A body. The bodies the Qlippoth were denied by God. It even said so. We just weren't listening."

"It was just playing with us all along – trying to get in somewhere," Robin spoke aloud, realizing. *And it tried with Patrick first*, she thought, remembering the midterm. *And with Lisa. But Martin let it in.*

Something clicked into place. "It was Martin in my room that night," she murmured.

"He killed Waverly." Patrick's blue eyes were like ice.

Outside in the hall, doors began to slam rapidly, up one side of the corridor and down the other. They all spun in terror. A horrible, insane giggling echoed through the building, freezing their blood.

The doors slammed outside, the sound coming closer ...

Patrick leapt at the door, bracing it closed with all his strength. Some incredible force began pounding on the door from outside; the knocks reverberated through the wood, shaking the frame. Patrick's arms were jarred with the raps.

The knocking abruptly stopped.

Then the door slowly buckled inward, an enormous pressure caving it on its hinges. Lisa's eyes widened; she began to scream.

Cain threw himself against the door, straining with Patrick to hold it closed.

The door suddenly thumped back into place.

Outside, the doors slammed again, a rapid staccato wave, angry and thundering. Robin was screaming with Lisa.

The slamming abruptly stopped.

Dead silence. The four stood frozen, Patrick and Cain still braced against the door, afraid to move. The front door, two floors below, seemed a continent away.

Lisa was trembling all over, her teeth knocking together. "God ... God ... what do we do?"

Patrick hefted the gun, grim. "We nail him." He started to open the door.

Lisa shrieked, "*No!*"

Robin grabbed Patrick's arm. "You can't just kill him."

"The fuck I can't."

They were all talking at once then, fast, their voices overlapping, charged with adrenaline and hysteria.

"*Think.*" Robin dug her nails into Patrick's forearm. "And then what – you end up in prison for murder?"

"Better than dead," Patrick shot back. "Kill the

fucker before he kills us. *He killed Waverly.*" He towered in the dark; the veins were standing out in his neck.

"Not Martin," Cain said. He sounded short of breath. "That thing inside him."

Lisa's voice was shrill, almost a scream. "He *asked* for it. You heard. He invited it in!"

Robin wheeled on her. "So did you, Lisa. You found the board ... right?" Robin faced the other three, pale and resolute. "But we all wanted to play. We *all* kept going. We *all* called it."

They were silent, the truth sinking in.

Cain spoke more slowly now. "Even if we shot Martin, we don't know that *it* would die."

Patrick kicked the wall beside him savagely, caving in the thin plasterboard. Lisa flinched.

"Motherfucking shit. So what now?" He looked at the others, helpless. The candlelight flickered on the walls around them, playing over the crude Hebrew letters.

"Catch him," Robin said slowly, looking at Cain. "Do the banishing ritual."

"Catch him?" Patrick's voice rose in disbelief. "He's got a *demon* inside him."

"And you've got a gun," Cain said steadily. "Clip him in the leg and I'll jump him."

Lisa's eyes leapt wildly from one to the other. "You got that ceremony off the *Net*. What if it doesn't work?"

Cain looked grim. "Then we tie him, call the cops, and run."

They all looked around at one another. It seemed an eternity before anyone spoke. Robin realized the silence was acquiescence.

Patrick shifted unhappily. "Don't blame me if I miss and blow off his goddamn head."

Cain turned on him. "You better not. I mean it, cowboy. Because we need *all five* of us for the ritual to work."

Chapter 30

The door of Martin's room silently opened into the dark hall. Patrick's bulk filled the door frame. Gun held to his cheek, he looked both ways down the corridors.

Empty. But there was a standing armoire halfway down the hall, where someone could be hiding, inside or behind. Patrick looked at the armoire, looked back at Cain. Cain nodded grimly, acknowledging.

The four of them moved out into the hall in a clump, Patrick in front, head swiveling.

Staying pressed together, they moved down the hall toward the armoire.

Patrick put out an arm to stop the others, eased forward himself, then darted around the armoire, gun at the ready. Robin held her breath as he stopped dead; then he relaxed slightly and turned, gestured the others forward.

They all moved ahead together, hovering at the stairway door as Patrick checked the shadowy stairwell, looking up at the stairs, then down to the next landing.

He motioned the others forward again and they moved silently into the dark stairwell, proceeding carefully down the stairs – Patrick leading, with Cain in the rear, his eyes trained warily up. Their breathing seemed harsh, unnaturally loud in the echo chamber of the stairwell.

Robin looked past Patrick, down the steep concrete decline. The door was closed at the bottom of the stairs.

Near the bottom, they paused as one. Patrick took a breath, and then kicked the stairwell door open. It slammed up against the wall in the hall outside.

Gun raised, he spun out of the doorway, swiveled around in the dim landing, eyes darting around him.

No one.

Patrick stepped back into the stairwell, whispered, "It's okay."

They moved out onto the murky landing. Ahead, the main staircase plunged down to the ground floor.

"Downstairs," Cain whispered. "Make him come to us."

He stopped, staring down at the floor. Robin followed his eyes, caught the glitter of shattered glass on the carpet. She looked up, barely registered the broken fire-emergency case on the wall . . .

The door of the stairwell slammed open behind them. They spun in terror as a whirlwind of darkness darted out from the stairwell. Robin caught a glimpse of mad black eyes, the gleam of a raised ax flashing down.

The blade sank into Cain's shoulder with a sickening thud.

Robin screamed, and kept screaming as Cain fell backward, tumbling down the stairs.

Patrick raised the gun and fired three rapid shots, but the shadow spun and darted back into the darkness of a side hall. The shots slammed harmlessly into the wall.

Patrick seized Lisa and pulled her into the stairwell. Robin was left frozen on the balcony. Her heart pounded in her chest, the sound filling her head.

She stared down the stairs at Cain's crumpled body on the landing below.

She jerked forward and scrambled down the stairs, fell to her knees beside him, sobbing.

In the stairwell, Patrick and Lisa huddled together against the door in the dark, choking on their breath.

Above them, a mocking voice boomed. The slithery alien sound of it echoed in the stairwell, through the halls.

"Are the children of light frightened? Are they afraid of the dark?"

Patrick and Lisa spun around, freaked, looking upward.

The voice reverberated around them in the gloom, a hoarse, raw giggling.

Patrick shouted upward, enraged. "You want to play, limp dick? I'll play a bullet through your lame-ass head."

"Don't—" Lisa begged, a frantic whisper. Patrick looked down at her. She was shaking all over, her eyes glazed.

He took her chin, looked down into her face. "Get down to the others. If you don't hear me yelling I got him, you all get the hell out."

Her eyes were wide, terrified. "Pat, no—"

He bent quickly, kissed her roughly. "Go on now."

Lisa sank, trembling, against the wall. He lifted the gun and started back up the stairs.

Cain's face was deathly pale. Blue veins stood out in his forehead; blood oozed from a deep gash on the top of his shoulder. Robin touched him carefully, afraid to hope.

He stirred under her fingers. Her heart leapt. He opened his eyes and she gasped out in relief.

"Oh my God ..."

"It's not ... so bad," he managed. "I twisted away."

Robin pulled off her sweat jacket, wound it tightly around his shoulder. She was shaking, barely able to speak.

"Got to ... get you out of here ..."

Patrick climbed the stairs. The alien voice floated down to him, around him, bizarre and mocking, a Southern parody in an insect tongue.

"Does the big boy have Daddy's gun?"

Patrick flinched as if he'd been struck, a look of stunned recognition in his eyes. His gaze darted up the dark stairwell.

The voice dropped lower, gruff and guttural. "Come make Daddy feel good ... Do it like Ah taught you ... Do it good, boy, or Ah'll whup you raw." The alien laughter rang in the stairwell.

Patrick snarled in rage and ran up the last steps. He burst onto the second floor, spinning wildly, the gun extended in both hands.

The laughter had cut off completely. The hall was dark, silent, just the neon EXIT light above the stairwell and the bluish glow from the snack machine in the laundry room.

Patrick shouted out. "Where are you, shit-licker?" He spat, gripped the gun, moved forward in the hall.

A sound came from the laundry room, a low animal-like whimpering.

Patrick turned and dashed for the laundry room – but

247

stopped still in the doorway, stunned.

Martin was slumped in the shadowed corner, crumpled in half, holding his side. He was drenched in blood, crying. He looked up at Patrick, dazed.

"Patrick? It ... got me." Martin's hands clutched the handle of a bloody ax sunk into his torso.

"Shit. Martin ..." Patrick gasped, sickened.

"I'm hurt ... I ... think I'm dying."

Patrick raised the gun, stepped toward Martin.

A floor below on the landing, Robin had Cain propped up against the banister. She tightened her jacket in a tourniquet around his shoulder. Her throat was raw from screaming; she tasted blood in her mouth. But she forced herself to breathe through her panic. *All I have to do is help him down the stairs and out ... We can go out the door ... We'll be free.*

But Martin.

Was there even a Martin anymore? She saw again the mad figure dashing out of the hall, raising the ax.

Her mind rebelled against the picture. But she knew that beyond the black eyes it *had* been Martin, brandishing the ax with mad glee on his face.

Robin was jerked back to the present as three shots rang through the dorm. She froze with Cain; both of them looking up toward the sound.

There was a terrible silence.

"Oh no ..." Robin whispered.

In the stairwell, Lisa twisted around, and shouted up the stairs. "Patrick ..."

Silence.

Lisa screamed, *"Patrick!"*

She stared upward in terror, unaware of the door opening slowly behind her ... a hand reaching out ...

Lisa spun, screaming, at the touch.

Robin grabbed her arm in the dark. "Shh ...

Lisa crumpled. "Oh Jesus—"

Robin dug her fingernails into Lisa's arm to silence her. She looked up the stairs.

Patrick shouted from above them. "I got the mother."

Both girls sagged in relief at the sound of his voice; then Robin's pulse spiked with horror as she registered his words. *Did he shoot Martin? Is he dead?*

Then something in her mind spoke clearly: *Trick.*

Lisa was already dashing upstairs. Robin followed madly on her heels, shouting, "Wait—"

She burst into the second-floor hall – and was greeted with silence.

The hall was black, murky with shadows. The blue light from the laundry room glowed faintly. She couldn't hear a sound.

"Lisa?" Robin gulped. Her eyes focused in the dark passageway. It was completely empty.

She plunged across the hall to the laundry room – and ran into Lisa, who was stopped in the doorway, frozen. Robin stared past her.

Patrick's body lay on the floor, the ax sunk into his side, blood pooling on the linoleum around him.

Martin crouched over the corpse, his eyes black. He swayed on his haunches, giggling, a mad thing, barely human, vacantly squeezing the trigger of the empty gun.

Robin and Lisa were frozen in horror.

That's not Martin, Robin's brain managed, through her terror. *It's something much more than Martin now.* She stared in paralyzed fascination. Darkness seemed to roll off it in waves.

The thing that was not Martin reared up, yanked the ax from Patrick's body.

Lisa screamed as the ax flashed down. The mad thing inside Martin aped her scream, its eyes shining black.

Then Robin sensed a movement on the floor, and Martin's body jerked backward. The ax blade just missed Lisa's neck, slicing a thin cut of blood on her shoulder.

Robin seized Lisa, pulling her away from the blade. Martin lunged at them again, snarling, then staggered again.

Patrick lay on the floor, blood pumping from his side, one big hand locked around Martin's calf.

He opened his eyes and looked up at Robin. "Go," he whispered.

Martin spun, raised the ax.

Robin and Lisa bolted as the ax flashed down again. They stumbled into the hall, ran into each other, righted themselves, and dashed into the stairwell, both hyperventilating with sobs.

The door slammed against the wall behind them and Martin shoved through, blocking the downstairs route.

In a split second of decision, the girls scrambled up the dark tunnel of stairs, powered by adrenaline, breath rasping in terror. The creature's laugh echoed in the stairwell. It followed them up with shocking speed.

Robin and Lisa burst out the third-floor door into a long hall of rooms: the boys' wing. In the narrow corridor, they tugged each other in opposite directions, whispering frantically, terrified.

"Stairwell off the kitchen," Lisa choked out, her eyes black, pupils dilated to the edge of her irises. Robin could actually see her heart knocking against her chest.

"What if it's locked?" Robin hedged, but Lisa jerked free and was running down the hall.

Robin froze at the sound of clattering footsteps on the stairs. She looked around her frantically at a hallway of locked doors. The kitchen seemed an eternity away. She turned instinctively for the bathroom door, ducked in.

She shoved the swinging bathroom door shut on its hinge, then her heart plummeted as she saw there was no lock. She glanced around her and pulled the trash can in front of the door.

He'll shove through that in a second, she realized. She surveyed the mirrored bathroom in a frenzy, looking for anything that could work as a barrier.

At the end of the hall, Lisa ran into the kitchenette and threw herself at the door to the back stairwell, twisting the knob.

Locked.

Lisa yanked at the door, clawing at it like an animal, sobbing. "Shit shit shit …"

The alien voice came from down the hall, taunting. "Lisa. Lii-saa. You *know* you want me."

Lisa whirled, eyes glazed. She lunged for the counter, pulled open a drawer, and pawed through it, searching for a knife.

Nothing but plastic spoons and spatulas, tangled twist ties.

The voice was closer in the hall, crooning. "I looove how you think of your brother when you *come*."

Lisa screamed and pressed her hands to her ears.

A shadow appeared in the doorway. Lisa jerked back against the counter.

Martin stood swaying, holding the bloody ax. He grinned at Lisa wolfishly, lifted the ax to his mouth, and licked the blade.

Lisa grabbed the coffeepot from the counter and hurled it at him. It bounced off his head, splitting the skin. Blood spilled down his face, but he started toward her as if he hadn't felt a thing.

Lisa threw herself at the counter, grabbing for anything loose, flinging the toaster, a coffee can, the silverware rack. The objects bounced off Martin with sickening, pulpy thuds, but nothing stopped him; he was almost on her.

She was backed, cowering, trembling, into the sharp corner of the counters ... trapped.

Martin's eyes were black as he smiled. He raised the ax.

A voice called out behind him.

"*Martin.*"

Martin jerked around, bobbing slightly on his feet, as if he didn't quite have control of his body.

Behind him, Robin hovered in the hall, pale as ice.

Martin grinned slowly. "Martin who?"

Robin swallowed, sickened by the vacant look on his bloody face. She was so light-headed, she was afraid she would faint. *Just get him away from Lisa*, she thought.

"Zachary, then," she suggested, her voice low, inviting. "Whatever you like." She forced a smile, then ducked teasingly into the hall.

Martin appeared in the doorway, a swaying shadow. He held the ax loosely in both hands, stared down the hall toward Robin. They both stood still for a moment, eyes locked.

Robin was hit by a wave of terror so primal, she felt her mind loosing from its moorings. The thing in front of her was nothing like human. There was an emanation from it of pure evil. It was like chaos barely contained in a thin sheaf of body, like a swarm of angry black insects loosely held by a bubble of skin.

She fought down nausea and panic, lifted her eyes to its grinning face, trying not to show her fear.

Don't think. Talk. Do it now.

He took a sudden step forward and she flinched back.

"Afraid, sweet Robin?" the thing purred.

Robin lifted her chin, looked straight into its eyes. "Afraid of what? You won't kill me. It's something else you want."

She took a slow step back, raised her hands to her neck, and started to unbutton her shirt.

Martin licked his lips, moved forward.

Robin eased her way backward as she fumbled to open her shirt. Martin stared, mesmerized, at the loosening buttons.

"You were in my room that night. Waverly came in and saw you and you pushed her out the window."

The Martin-thing grinned, a horrible sight. Its voice was sibilant, loathsome. "Stupid bitch, with all her screaming. Hardly the mood."

Robin forced herself to smile, to make her voice seductive. "I'm here now. We can do anything you want." She moved infinitesimally back. "Don't you know I was jealous, when you were coming to Lisa instead of me?"

The thing in front of her cocked its head. "You didn't ask. You have to ask."

Robin pulled her shirt off. "I'm asking now."

The Martin-thing lunged at her, incredibly fast. Robin turned in a flash and tore down the hall toward the stairwell.

The creature was right behind her, feet scuttling on the floor like insect claws, rasping breath hot on her neck as it gained on her. She felt hands in her hair, a sharp pain – and she was yanked backward.

Robin cried out. The thing shoved her against the wall by the stairwell door, pinning her between its hands, and shoved the bloody ax against her face. She could smell blood. Patrick's blood.

And more horrible: Martin's face was right up against hers, twisted and grotesque. A stench like burning rolled off him; the alien voice purred against her ear. "Sweet Robin. It was you, you know. It was you who let me through."

Robin's eyes jumped to meet the creature's black gaze. The ravening thing stared into her eyes and she thought she would go mad.

"You wanted to die Thanksgiving night. Your darkness let me through. A perfect gateway."

Robin's throat was tight. Her eyes spilled over with tears. "No ..." she whispered.

"You caused it all."

Darkness opened in Robin's mind, a rush of nothingness.

The thing raised the ax. She could barely register the dull gleam of the blade. Her legs gave way and she began the slide into unconsciousness.

Then the Martin-thing suddenly whipped its head to the side. "Not one step," it hissed.

It raised its arm, brandishing the ax.

Robin turned her head and saw Lisa halted in the hallway, gripping a carving knife. She looked at Robin, eyes wide.

Both girls were frozen. The creature smiled.

The stairwell door flew open and smashed into its head.

Cain burst through the doorway, holding a baseball bat with both hands. He shoved the door hard against the wall, pinning Martin behind it. Robin jerked free.

Lisa ran forward and threw her weight against the door, trapping Martin to the wall. Robin lunged and leaned her weight against the door with Lisa.

The Martin-thing writhed under the door, snarling and foaming like a rabid animal. The girls strained to hold it.

Cain staggered back, lifted the bat, and slammed it against the side of Martin's head.

Martin's eyes rolled up and the thing went limp against the wall, still pinned by the door. The ax fell from his hand, thudded on the floor.

Robin and Cain found each other's eyes.

The only sound was their ragged breathing, and Lisa's sobs.

Chapter 31

Logs burned in the hearth, rolling orange flame.

In the center of the lounge, the round table was set up with five chairs.

Candles flickered at the points of a pentagram chalked on the surface.

Martin's limp body was propped up in one of the five chairs. Lisa and Robin were winding clothesline around and around his torso, tying him to the chair. They wrapped him over and over, a thick coat of ropes, threaded through the slats of the chair – but they had no idea of the strength of the thing inside him or whether the ropes would hold at all.

They had thrown blankets over the arched windows to block the firelight, and they'd rolled back the cabbage-rose carpet. Cain was on his knees, shoulder wrapped, drawing a large pentagram with chalk on the bare floor around the table while keeping a wary eye on Martin; the ax, wiped clean of Patrick's blood, was close by his side. A Coleman lantern beamed a star of yellow light from a side table. Rain fell in a steady curtain outside. It all had a sense of unreality.

Robin tried to focus entirely on the rope in her hands. With Patrick lying dead two floors above them, any kind of thought was unbearable.

Cain finished the last line of the pentagram and stood up, brushing chalk from his jeans.

Robin bent over Martin to tie another knot ... Lisa suddenly cried out behind her, "*Robin!*"

Robin glanced down. Martin's eyes were open beneath her. She gasped and pulled back, her heart pounding madly.

Martin looked up at her, his eyes hurt, dazed. The side of his face was bruised, pulpy from the blow of the bat. He muttered weakly, "Robin? What's ... happening?"

The others gathered warily, Cain brandishing the bat. Martin looked around at them all shakily. "I was in the attic. You left. Then ... what? I don't ... remember."

He gasped, seeing his own blood – soaked shirt. "Oh my God. *Robin* ... " He looked up at her, trembling, terrified.

Robin hesitated. "Martin?" She stepped carefully forward. Cain said sharply, "No—"

Robin leaned in toward Martin and slapped him hard across the face.

Martin's eyes popped open wide, flaming black. Quick as a snake, he lunged up at Robin's throat, mouth wide, teeth bared, cords straining in his neck.

Robin jumped away just as Martin's teeth closed on air with a sickening crunch.

Lisa jolted back, freaked. All pretense of humanity was gone. The Qlippah writhed in Martin's body, sliding in the chair, hissing and spitting. "You dare? YOU DARE? *Let me go!*" It strained at the rope, chest bulging, eyes popping, bellowing like a bull.

Cain raised the bat high, ready to strike. Martin bucked, the ropes scraping at his skin, opening flesh. But the Qlippah seemed to be contained by Martin's physical form — the smallish body unable to break free of the layers of rope.

The table began to shake, rattling on its legs. Lisa and Robin froze in disbelief.

Cain shouted, "You're going all right. Back to the Abyss."

The table stopped. The Martin-thing grinned up at him, a chilling sight. "No precedent, counselor. You've lost your fifth. The star is broken."

Cain's face hardened. He turned, shot Robin a look through the flickering yellow light.

Robin nodded, took Lisa's hand, pulled her toward the doorway. "Come on."

As they passed Cain, she whispered to him, "Be careful." Their eyes met and he brushed her fingers with his before turning back to the thing that had been Martin.

Robin pulled Lisa out through the arched door, into the hollow darkness of the main hall.

Lisa was sobbing through clenched teeth as she and Robin climbed the shadowy main stairs. "I can't stand it. I can't."

Robin stared upward into the dark. "Just a little bit more," she said, hoping her voice was steady.

On the second floor, Robin and Lisa stepped into the blue light of the laundry room.

Patrick's body lay on the floor in a pool of blood, his eyes wide and staring.

Lisa crumpled into sobs again. Robin's eyes filled

with tears, her heart twisting in her chest.

They both knelt beside him on the warped linoleum. Lisa cradled the blond head in her lap. She passed her hands tenderly over his eyelids, shutting his eyes, then stroked his face and hair.

Robin held his hand in hers and thought fiercely, *You saved us. I'll never forget what you did. I'll never forget you. Never. You're part of me forever.*

They were both silent for a time, holding him. Lisa seemed almost calm, dreamily stroking his hair. Then Robin met Lisa's eyes.

"He would want us to, you know."

Lisa nodded. Robin looked down on Patrick's body, swallowed through the ache in her throat. "We need you, cowboy."

In the long, shadowed space of the lounge, Cain gritted his teeth against the throbbing in his shoulder and bent to light candles at each of the five points of the chalk pentagram on the floor.

The Qlippah watched from Martin's body, its head lolling grotesquely against the chair back. "Don't forget the fairy dust," it gibbered. "You have to sprinkle it on me and knock your heels together three times."

Cain stood, fought a wave of dizziness at the pain. He breathed in shallowly, slid his left hand into the front pocket of his jeans for his lighter, stepped to the fire-place to light the candles on the mantel.

The Qlippah watched greedily with Martin's eyes. "You know you don't believe this bullshit. Can't do kike rituals if you don't believe. Better men have tried."

Cain ignored the leering thing. He stooped to one of the duffels, pulled out the printout of the ritual they'd lifted off the Web. The title at the top read, "The Greater Banishing Ritual of the Pentagram."

The Qlippah looked straight into the fire. The flames suddenly leapt up, blazing, showering sparks into the room. Cain jumped back from the burning pinpoints.

The Qlippah smiled loftily with Martin's mouth. "Are you a priest now? A *rabbi*? You, who believe in nothing! Son of a syphilitic whore, and not just in a manner of speaking."

Cain stiffened, his hands clenching.

A smile twisted across Martin's face. The Qlippah's voice became cunning, crafty. "Want to know who your father is?" it crooned. "I can tell you. It's not pretty, but at long last you would know."

Cain turned on it. "Shut up," he whispered. In his hand was a switchblade. He snicked it open. The blade gleamed silver in the firelight.

Martin's face rippled and dimpled, as if snakes were moving under the skin. The Qlippah's whisper was sibilant, inhuman. "You'll fail. You'll fail because you come from dirt. You come from scum. You are not worthy."

Cain's face was drained of color. The hand holding the knife dropped to his side.

Something thudded on the main stairway.

Cain came back to himself, spun toward the sound, brandishing the knife.

There was another thud, another, and then a soft dragging, coming toward the doorway of the lounge.

Robin and Lisa appeared in the doorway, pulling Patrick's body between them on the polished floor, panting at the strain of the dead weight.

For a moment, an animal rage played across Martin's face, then the Qlippah bared its teeth in a hideous grin.

"Ah. Company. Daddy's best boy."

Cain stepped forward to help the girls drag Patrick's body to the table. The three of them stooped and, straining, lifted the corpse into a chair Cain had placed on one of the points of the chalk pentagram, across from Martin's splayed form.

The corpse slumped heavily in the chair. Lisa wrapped her arms around Patrick's torso and held him up from behind. Robin wound rope around him, tying him up into a sitting position, trying not to think too hard about what she was doing. She glanced at Lisa, saw her face was deathly pale but determined.

Across from them, the Qlippah squirmed and jeered in Martin's body, the ropes chafing flesh. "Clever children. Extraordinary children. But doesn't it say in your little do-it-yourself manual? It doesn't count if he's D E A D!"

The Qlippah bellowed the last word, an earsplitting shout. All the windows rattled, as if some huge force were shaking the Hall.

Robin recoiled. Beside her, Lisa sucked in her breath, eyes wide with terror. The rattling continued all around them, deafening.

Then it abruptly stopped. Nothing but the sound of their own tortured breathing.

The Qlippah grinned around at them ferally, tongue lolling from Martin's mouth. "It doesn't count if he's dead," it crooned again.

Cain stared down at it grimly. "It doesn't say that. It says we all need to be here." He looked at Robin and Lisa, flanking Patrick's lifeless body. "We're all here."

He picked up the printout of the ritual, then hesitated, glancing at Robin, a stark, uncertain look. She met his eyes, mouthed *Yes*.

With an almost graceful formality, Robin, Cain, and Lisa all took their places at the points of the pentagram Cain had drawn – the Qlippah squirming in its chair on the fourth point, Patrick's body tied to the chair on the fifth.

Robin stared down at the chalked pentagram, and despite her apprehension, she felt a rush of something like excitement. There was a palpable energy about the ancient symbol – a sense of power and infinity. *It worked for someone, all those years ago. Maybe it can work for us.*

Cain looked down at the printout they had made of the *Key of Solomon*.

"First we mix our blood."

Robin and Lisa blanched as he lifted the knife and cut his palm, then stepped forward and let the blood spill into the bowl he had placed in the pentagram on the center of the table.

"Why don't we all hump instead?" The Martin-thing suggested, pumping its hips upward spastically. "That'll bond us."

This is what evil is, Robin realized. *So close to human, but a perversion of all that is human. I understand now.*

Cain passed the knife to Robin. The blade gleamed ... She clenched the knife in one hand and sliced into her palm. The sharp pain was almost surprising. She thought briefly, *After all this, I wonder if I'll ever feel again.*

She held her palm over the bowl, felt her pulse throb in the wound. The blood flowed black into the metal bowl, mixing with Cain's.

Robin looked to Lisa, unsure of how she'd handle it, but Lisa didn't hesitate. She stepped forward and slashed her palm grimly, looking down at Martin with eyes like ice.

Then Cain took the knife from her and cut into Patrick's stiffening palm, squeezed the dead flesh together to force blood into the bowl.

When he turned to Martin, the Qlippah started to thrash in the chair, ranting. "Nooo ... stay away, scum ..." Its voice turned to a deep, mindless bellow, like the lowing of an ox.

Cain grabbed one of the hands bound tightly to Martin's chest and cut into it. Robin stepped quickly beside him to catch the dripping blood in the bowl.

The Qlippah's bellows turned to crooning. "Ahhh ... lovely ... deeper. . . cut me ..."

Cain turned with the bowl of blood and placed it on the table, then stepped back to stand at his point of the pentagram. Robin and Lisa moved into their points.

Cain lifted the book and read in a strong, clear voice.

"We come together in the name of the Unknowable Unknown to banish this unclean thing from the body of our friend Martin Seltzer."

The candles flickered on the mantel as if on an altar. With fingers pressed together, Cain touched his forehead, the center of his chest, his right shoulder, and then his left shoulder as he recited from the book, his eyes intense as a priest's:

"Ateh ... Malkuth ... ve Geburah ... ve Gedulah ..."

The Qlippah spat at them, writhing in its chair. "This little Jewish ritual didn't help poor little Zachary and his poor little friends, though, did it?"

Robin and Lisa looked into each other's eyes and

263

followed Cain's hand motions on their own bodies, speaking over the Qlippah in concert with Cain.

"*Ateh ... Malkuth ... ve Geburah ... ve Gedulah ...*"

The Qlippah convulsed in Martin's body, screaming over them in a rage.

"They *burned* ... They *screamed as they burned* ...

Cain looked straight at the squirming creature, clasped his hand on his chest, speaking over it.

"*Le-Olahm, Amen.*"

Robin was struck by the power in his voice, even as she and Lisa clasped their hands on their chests, repeating firmly, "È."

The rappings started again, a wave of knocking in the ceiling and walls. The chair underneath Martin rattled in tandem, bucking on the floor.

Lisa backed off her point of the pentagram, staring around at the walls, her eyes wide and glazed. The walls bulged with the pounding.

The Qlippah giggled horribly. "You're next, Lisa. I'm coming for you. Coming all over you—"

Cain shouted, "Lisa!"

Lisa whirled to face them, unseeing. "No ..." She bolted toward the arched door of the lounge. Robin lunged and grabbed her arms. Lisa struggled against her in sheer terror. "It can't — we can't — it can't work."

Robin shouted in Lisa's face, her voice rising above the rappings, above the laughter. "Lisa. Think. None of this is possible at all, but it's happening." For a moment, Lisa's eyes seemed to register.

Martin's eyes grew crafty, the Qlippah shining through them, rippling on his face. "You're going to *die* to save this pathetic Shell? He betrayed you. He knew what I am, and he used you to call me—"

Lisa flinched, looked toward Martin's heaving body. He flung his words at Lisa. "He used you, and Cowboy *died* for it."

Robin spoke fiercely, her voice raw. "Don't listen. *It lies.*" She dug her fingers into Lisa's arms. "We have to believe it. We have to do it. For Patrick. For Martin."

Behind them, the Qlippah bellowed. "LISAAAA ..."

Lisa twisted out of Robin's grasp with a guttural cry, but she faced the Qlippah, eyes blazing. "*Fuck you.*" She stalked back to her point of the pentagram. Robin followed and the three of them took the same breath.

Cain stepped forward to the table, dipped his fingers in the bowl of blood.

He turned to the east and traced a pentagram in the air in front of him. Then he extended his hands in front of him, palms outward, clenched his hands, and pulled them suddenly open, as if pulling aside a set of curtains. He called out fiercely, *"We open the portal of fire!"*

Fire jumped in the hearth, blazing upward with a roar. Robin and Lisa gasped. All around the room, the candles flared up. Even the light in the Coleman lantern leapt, beating against the glass.

Martin started to spit and writhe in the chair, bellowing inhumanly. Lightning cracked in the sky outside, lighting up the corners of the blankets covering the windows.

Cain and Lisa stood still, stupefied. Robin stared around her at the rush of light, the live fire.

She realized Cain was looking at her, waiting for her to continue. She forced herself to unfreeze, to move. She stepped forward to dip her fingers into the bowl of blood.

She turned to the south, traced a pentagram in the air, and called out clearly, "*We open the portal of air!*"

She extended her hands in front of her, clasped them, and pulled them apart, as if ripping aside a set of curtains.

A wind rushed through the room, a roar in her ears ... as if a huge door had opened to the elements. Robin had to brace her feet on the floor and lean forward against the wind. She saw Cain and Lisa doing the same. She was dizzy, almost deaf from the howling.

It's working, she thought in wild disbelief. *We're doing something ...*

Martin twisted, convulsing, moaning in pain.

Cain called out over the howling of the wind. "Lisa!"

Lisa struggled forward through the wind, dipped her fingers in the bowl of blood, and turned to the west. She was shaking as she traced the pentagram, but her voice was strong.

"*We open the portal of water!*"

She extended her hands in front of her and pulled them apart.

Outside, thunder boomed, shaking the sky. Rain started to fall in a torrent, driving into the ground. The rapping started again, intensifying. The Qlippah bucked in its chair, howling with the wind.

Robin felt herself start to go numb with the unreality of it, her mind almost pleasantly detaching from the bizarreness around her. From far away, she caught a glimpse of Lisa's face, white as a sheet but abstracted, puzzled ...

It's shock, she thought. *We're all going into shock.*

Robin forced her mind back into consciousness, shouted, "*Lisa!* You guys!"

Lisa looked at her, startled, focusing.

Cain jolted back to awareness, shot Robin an admiring look. "*Come on!*" He stepped behind Patrick's chair, and the two girls joined him.

They turned Patrick's chair around to the north, and all three dipped their fingers into the bowl of blood. They all put one hand on Patrick's shoulder and used their other hand to trace the pentagram in the air. Simultaneously, they shouted to the air, "*We open the portal of earth!*"

All three made the gesture of pulling curtains open.

Beneath them, the ground started to shake, rumbling as if in an earthquake.

Lisa gasped, stumbled. Robin fought for her own balance, grabbed Lisa's arm to steady her. The Qlippah shrieked with laughter.

Cain shouted at them through the chaos, "Help me. Get him around."

He grabbed the back of Patrick's chair with his good arm. The girls leapt forward and the three of them strained to turn Patrick back to the table. The earth rolled and shook beneath them.

Cain pulled back and shouted, "Back to your points!" They all stumbled to their places on the pentagram and faced Martin, teetering for balance on the shaking floor. Cain picked up the bowl of blood and hurled the contents at Martin, splashing him with blood. The Qlippah screamed with rage.

Through the wind and rumbling, the three of them started to chant. "We banish you with fire. We banish you with air. We banish you with water. We banish you with earth."

The Qlippah shouted over them. "You can't get rid

of me. I came from *you*, Robin. You called me and I came."

Robin flinched, but she kept chanting with Lisa and Cain, eyes locked on Martin in the firelight.

"We banish you with fire. We banish you with air. We banish you with water. We banish you with earth."

Martin's gaze burned into Robin, the Qlippah shining through them, rippling on his face. "You can't get rid of me, because I'm you. Your envy. Your fury. Your hatred."

Robin faltered, looked into Martin's bottomless eyes. The Qlippah smiled.

"You hated her. You wanted her dead. I made her dead. *I am you.*"

Robin cried out in anguish.

And at that hesitation, all three were suddenly blown backward by some immense force. Robin felt her breath knocked out of her. She was lifted and hurled; there was a crash and blinding pain.

The three of them slammed into the wall and slid to the floor.

Robin lay against the baseboard, bright lights swirling in her head, her skull throbbing from the blow. Beside her, Lisa was holding her arm, staring down at it. It dangled at a sickening angle.

Martin started to laugh wildly, the hideous insect voice of the Qlippah.

The rapping raced through the ceiling. The walls bulged out sickeningly, like flesh; the ceiling cracked. White flakes were falling; Robin stared at the powdery dusting on her arm, mesmerized. *It's snowing,* she thought in vague disbelief. *The roof must have ... split open ...*

Cain pushed himself up to sitting and grabbed Robin's arm, twisted her around to face him. "It's not working," he shouted over the chaos. "We have to bail."

Outside, thunder boomed, shaking the building. The Hall groaned as if the entire structure was coming loose from its foundation. Something like rocks began to thud on the floor around them.

In a daze, Robin looked up and realized the ceiling was raining down in flakes and chunks around them.

Robin turned and stared across the pentagram at Martin, who was still tied to the chair. His bloody face was twisted with glee, the Qlippah rioting across his features. The spirit writhed inside his body, laughing at them through the chaos of elements. It shrieked at her. "I am you. I am you. I am you."

Robin screamed out, "*No.*"

Cain staggered to his feet and lunged for the fire ax on the floor. He jerked it up, drew back his arm to swing the blade at Martin's head.

Robin leaped to her feet and seized Cain's arm, fingernails digging into his flesh. "*No.* Wait—"

Cain looked at her frenzied face and fell back. She advanced on the Qlippah, her voice raw.

"You lie. I have friends. I have love. I have life."

Light.

Her mind flew through what she knew. The Qlippoth had broken because they could not hold the light. They couldn't hold life.

Light.

Love.

Life.

She stared at the hideous thing in the chair. Martin was alive in there.

If they could reach his being, fill him, love him ...

She grabbed Cain's hand. "The Qlippoth shattered because they couldn't hold the light. They can't bear light." Cain looked back at her, questioning. Robin faced the Qlippah, braced herself against the wind ripping around them, and spoke aloud.

"Martin, I know you're in there."

The Qlippah cackled. "Martin's *dead*! Cowboy's *dead*! You're all going to die!"

Robin took another step forward against the wind, forced herself to stare into the mad, demonic face. "I know you're in there, Martin. Come back to us. We're here for you ... We're here."

Cain was suddenly beside her, looking at Martin's face intently. "Come out, Martin. Come back."

Robin spoke with him. "You're not alone, Martin. You have us. We're here. We love you. Come to us. Come back."

Lisa pushed herself to her knees, wincing as she stood. She stepped beside Cain and Robin, holding her useless arm, and called against the wind.

"Please come back, Martin ..."

Without realizing, without meaning to, the three of them spoke it at once.

"*Martin*."

And for a fleeting second, Martin's own face flickered through the mad visage of the Qlippah. His eyes, desperately unhappy, stared up into theirs.

Robin jolted, then called to him urgently. "Martin. It's in your body, Martin. It's *your* body. Send it out."

Cain took up the call, overlapping her, "Send it out, Martin."

Lisa's eyes blazed and she ground out, "Send it the fuck out."

270

All three of them shouted, "*Send it out.*"

The Hall shook to its foundations. In the chair in front of them, Martin spasmed, choking, flesh and mind rebelling against the cruel invasive spirit. And then Martin's features emerged from the horrible slack formlessness of the Qlippah's face. His own eyes met Robin's in desperate appeal, and unfathomable courage, and Martin gasped out in his own voice, "Leave ... me ..."

A terrible struggle raged in the flesh of Martin's face ... human features racked with a rippling evil, nerves and muscles contorting with the battle.

A whoosh of energy rose from Martin's body, invisible but palpable. Robin froze, overwhelmed with the sheer force of it. She saw Cain and Lisa staring upward, paralyzed. The energy ripped through the air and cycloned around the room, gusting through the flames in the hearth, shaking the windows, blowing the curtains into a frenzy, overturning everything in its path.

Robin held tightly to Cain. He grabbed Lisa and they clung to one another as furniture rattled and jumped around them. Above them, the ceiling beams groaned.

Lisa was screaming. Robin couldn't tell if she was, too.

The energy spiraled, raging around the room. The couch flipped over, and books exploded out of the shelves, pages flying. The mirror shattered above the hearth, raining glass.

In the midst of the tumult, Robin heard a small, frightened voice.

"What's happening?"

She whipped around. In the chair, Martin sat with eyes wide open, staring in terror at the thundering chaos around him.

Robin gasped, fixed on his face. "Martin?"

271

He looked back at her, small and lost. "What's happening? Where are we?"

His voice was hoarse, but the horrible alien sound was gone. Robin stared at him, hardly daring to hope. There was no sign of the mad gleam of the Qlippah.

Martin's eyes fell on Patrick's dead body tied across from him. He cried out, "Oh my God ... what's happening?"

A ceiling beam split and crashed down toward the floor. Cain barely leapt out of the way in time.

Robin ran to Martin, squeezed his shoulders. "Hold on. *Don't let it back in.*"

The energy whooshed around the room, then blew straight against the table, flipping it, crashing it against the wall. The four of them struggled against the blast, screaming. Patrick's dead body jumped with the force of it. Glass blasted inward as all the windows suddenly burst, showering them with shards of glass. Rain gusted in from the outside; lightning branched in the sky. A guttural, disembodied howl of rage tore through the room. The energy cycloned, shaking the windows, making the fire blaze up, shredding the curtains, spiraling papers and plaster and broken furniture up into a funnel of black wind and rage.

And then it was as if the cyclone had been sucked into space. Suddenly, everything was still.

The silence was deafening, like a ringing in Robin's ears. The four of them looked around them, stunned.

The lounge was wrecked, broken furniture and glass everywhere. Curtains billowed inward as rain blew in from the smashed windows.

Lisa gulped out, her voice tiny. "Is it ... over?"

Cain took a deep breath. "It's gone ... I think ..."

Then Robin felt her heart leap wildly in her chest as Patrick's eyes suddenly opened.

The corpse jerked up to a sitting position, grinning wolfishly. The dead voice grated. "Did ... you ... miss me ... children?" The dead eyes were black, fathomless.

Lisa stared at him, her face white. He waggled his tongue at her and she bolted back.

Patrick's voice was slow and thick, his face distorted, the muscles slack and grotesque as the Qlippah tried to speak through dead vocal cords. "Big ... boy ... wouldn't ... mind ..."

Lisa and Robin backed away, shaking.

Behind them, Martin gasped out, "Burn him."

Cain whipped around, staring at him. Martin looked up at Cain from where he was still tied in the chair. "Fire. We have to drive it out."

Cain's face tightened. "Cut Martin loose, quick." With his good hand, he fumbled his pocketknife out of his pocket.

Robin leapt to take the knife, then sliced through Martin's ropes with the blade. She helped Martin stand shakily and the four faced Patrick.

The corpse jerked spasmodically in the chair, the Qlippah trying to work the dead muscles. It strained against the ropes, bellowing, "NOOO. NOOOOOO ..."

Martin spoke loudly over it. "Burn the body. Drive it out. Fire is pure light."

"*NNNNNNOOOOOO!*"

Patrick's body writhed grotesquely. The chair started to rattle on the floor. Darkness seemed to gather around it.

Beside Robin, Cain gasped in disbelief. "Oh shit."

273

The three of them watched, stupefied, as the chair rose slowly into the air.

Martin shouted, "Burn him! Do it!"

Cain spun and grabbed the Coleman lantern, from where it lay overturned and dark in the debris on the floor. He twisted the lamp open and threw the fuel over Patrick, soaking the corpse's clothes.

Robin spotted the matches on the mantel and grabbed for them, but then she hesitated, looking toward Lisa.

Lisa stepped forward, staring at the writhing corpse above them. Her voice was deadly and sure. "Kill it."

Robin struck a match, ignited the matchbook, and threw it at Patrick.

The Qlippah bellowed. "NOOOO – LIFE – LIFE – NOOOO—"

Flames exploded around Patrick, licked up his clothing, eating at the rope. The corpse shrieked, straining and contorting its chest; the chair bobbled wildly in the air.

Then suddenly, the ropes binding Patrick burst. The chair fell to the floor.

Patrick's corpse lurched grotesquely forward, dead limbs flailing like a puppet with its strings cut. Flames ignited his hair, searing the dead flesh.

All four of the others stood paralyzed, staring in horror and shock. Around them, reality seemed to ripple: What was left of the lounge was suddenly insubstantial, as if there was nothing but darkness around them, swirling forms in the wind. Robin groped for the Star of David in her pocket.

Cain grabbed Robin's arm, shouted, "Everyone *out*—"

Lisa and Martin were already backing for the door. Robin clenched the metal piece in her hand, thinking mindlessly, *Help …*

And at that moment, across the room, she saw him. Just a shade, incorporeal, very still in the swirling chaos of the room, standing at the top point of Cain's chalked pentagram: the pale young man from the yearbook, from her dreams.

As Robin stood, transfixed, Zachary locked his bottomless eyes on hers and raised his fist to his chest: the gesture from the ritual.

Cain pulled violently at her arm, shouted in her ear above the maelstrom. "Robin! *Now!*"

"Zachary—" she gasped out. Cain stared at her, uncomprehending. Martin and Lisa hesitated by the arched doorway, glancing back blankly.

They don't see, Robin realized.

She looked back toward Zachary, who again pressed his fist to his chest. Robin's eyes widened in comprehension. She spun to the others, shouting, "Finish the ritual. The others didn't finish."

At the archway, Martin stopped in his tracks. He grabbed Lisa and spun back, shouting, "Yes."

Robin faced the staggering, burning corpse and raised her arms before her, shouting, "We close the portal of earth!"

She pulled her hands together, shutting the curtain. The burning corpse started to howl.

"LIFE. WARM. BODY. BLOOD. LIFE."

Robin's eyes were streaming. She gagged on the stench of burning flesh, but she spun to Lisa. Terrified, Lisa faced the burning corpse and shouted.

"We close the portal of water!"

She raised her arms, shut her hands together. The corpse staggered jerkily toward her, burning arms raised. As Lisa stumbled back, screaming, Robin and Cain surrounded the corpse on the other side. Martin raised his arms, shouted over the howling, "We close the portal of air!"

The corpse turned away from Lisa, jerked toward Martin spasmodically.

"BREATH LIFE BODY GOD BLOOD DAMN BLOOD."

Cain raised his arms, shouted, "We close the portal of fire!"

The burning corpse flailed horribly, screaming.

"*GOD DAMN DAMN GOD DAMN YOU.*"

Cain and the others all pulled their hands together at once.

And Patrick's screaming body exploded in flame.

The force of the explosion tumbled the four of them backward. Flames ripped through the room, searing the walls and furniture.

Cain, Robin, Martin, and Lisa staggered to their feet, beating sparks off their clothing.

Above them, the roof beams burst into flame. Fire raced over the walls, lapping at the dry old wood of the paneling and furniture.

"*Run.*" Cain shouted.

For a split second, Robin looked toward the specter of Zachary, still standing on the point of the pentagram. Time seemed to stop. Then Zachary raised his hand to Robin – a farewell, or a blessing. Tears pushed at Robin's eyes; then she turned away and shouted to the others against the wind, "*Go.*"

She seized Martin's arm and ran for the door. Cain

276

grabbed Lisa and ran with her.

The four scrambled into the hallway, running full force for the front door. Behind them, there was a whoosh and a crackling roar as the lounge turned into an inferno. Flames billowed into the hall behind them. Robin could feel the heat like breath on her back.

Cain lunged forward for the front door, shot the bolt, and jerked it open.

The four of them burst through the door onto the porch, slamming the door shut behind them, running down the steps, running as hard as they could from the burning building, into the grove, into the night.

Inside the dorm, windows began to burst from the heat, tongues of flame licking out. Firelight glowed and danced from the upper floors.

And inside, one last demonic howl of rage roared, rising to a crescendo, then was sucked away.

Into the Abyss.

Chapter 32

Ash Hill Courier, December 21, 2006:

> *Ash Hill police today attributed the death of Waverly Todd, business student at Baird College, to another troubled student. The student, whose name has not been released, allegedly killed Todd before setting fire to a campus residence hall. The student perished in the blaze.*

Chapter 33

They stood in the copse of oak trees, in front of the memorial bench from 1920, Martin, Robin, and Lisa watching as Cain mounted the new bronze plate onto the marble under the names of Zachary Prince and the four other students.

Lisa placed a bouquet of wildflowers gently down on the bench; then Cain and Robin stepped up and put their arms around her.

Martin hovered apart until Lisa looked at him and reached out a hand.

He stepped to her side and the four of them looked down at the new bronze plaque under the old names:

IN MEMORIAM — PATRICK O'CONNOR
OUR FRIEND

Epilogue

The sun was setting over a Midwestern campus, pouring golden light over gently rolling hills. Students walked the footpaths between modern buildings.

In the lounge of Norton Residence Hall, several students sprawled around the room, watching the old big-screen TV, playing Game Boys, half-studying.

A few of them looked up when an excited voice came from beside the built-in cabinets. A girl pulled a familiar-looking rectangular game box from the shelves, turned to the room.

"Hey, look what I found. Anyone want to play?"

THE END